"Kay?" I plead. "Kay?" Nothing. I slide back to the floor, my head in my hands.

And then, after a few minutes, she's back.

"Sunshine?" She's whispering, but there's something else, a tone in her voice, something I never thought I'd hear. Kay sounds scared.

"Kay! Are you all right? Did you guys get in trouble? How's Baby? How's Rice? How's my mother?"

"Amy, I don't have a lot of time. Gareth hacked me in to the system so I could contact you . . . but I'm being watched closely."

"By Marcus?"

"No time, sunshine. You making it okay out there?"

"I'm handling it."

"Good girl. Listen, I need to tell you something. . . ." She pauses so long, I think she's cut out again.

"Kay, what is it?!" I ask desperately.

"It's . . . Baby."

My stomach turns over as dread seeps into every pore of my body.

"Dr. Reynolds has Baby."

IN THE END

DEMITRIA LUNETTA

HARPER TEEN
An Imprint of HarperCollinsPublishers

HarperTeen is an imprint of HarperCollins Publishers.

In the End
Copyright © 2014 by Demitria Lunetta
All rights reserved. Printed in the United States of America. No part
of this book may be used or reproduced in any manner whatsoever
without written permission except in the case of brief quotations
embodied in critical articles and reviews. For information address
HarperCollins Children's Books, a division of HarperCollins Publishers,
195 Broadway, New York, NY 10007.
www.epicreads.com

Library of Congress Control Number: 2014933034
ISBN 978-0-06-210549-3

Typography by Laura DiSiena
15 16 17 18 19   CG/RRDH   10 9 8 7 6 5 4 3 2 1
❖
First paperback edition, 2015

For Justin, who always listens to what I have to say

IN THE
END

PART
ONE

FORT BLACK

CHAPTER ONE

I long for the comfort of night.

The sun feels warm on my face. Before, sunshine was a good thing. But this is the After, and outside of New Hope, the light means only one thing if you're not armed: death.

It's early spring, but in the place that used to be Texas, it gets oppressively hot early in the year. I stop walking and open my canteen. The water drips from it and sizzles on the asphalt when I take a drink.

My synth-suit shields my otherwise bare feet from the burning ground, though my calluses also offer protection. I always wear my synth-suit in case I come across someone unfriendly—and out here, everyone's unfriendly. In the After, I learned to live without noisy shoes, and continued to run without them while I was in New Hope. I'm grateful I kept up with my running, or I wouldn't have made it out here these last three months. Even a simple supply mission like this could turn deadly.

I close my canteen and scan the area. On the horizon, I see a strip of houses that lies by a dried-up lake. I haven't hit this neighborhood yet for supplies, and as it's a fair way from the main road, I'm hoping no one else has either. As I get closer, I see that at some point this must have been a cozy little community. The walls of the houses are stucco, the roofs red tile, as if designed to look like a Spanish village. An old swing on a backyard jungle gym sways, its metal links creak in the wind. The houses, obviously cheaply made, aren't suitable for shelter anymore. After just over three years, many are missing doors and windows.

Houses like that don't stand a chance against Them.

At about a hundred feet away, I break into a full run. There seem to be more survivors in this area, more than I ever saw in Chicago. They won't be active during the day, but if someone's staking out this place, I don't want to give them time to catch me. There's no sign of anyone, so I flatten myself against the wall of the first house and peek inside. No hint of life, not even a breeze.

As I make my way inside, I let out a sigh. The place is wrecked. It's not the old bloodstained walls that sadden me. Evidence of past Florae attacks have become so commonplace, I barely even register scenes of death anymore. I'm just disappointed that the house has been ransacked already. The cabinets are thrown ajar and empty, the couches overturned. Even the pillows have been ripped open, the stuffing strewn across the floor.

Some people are worse than Them, I sign, then bite my lip to keep the tears back. I'm talking to Baby in our secret language. But she's not here with me anymore.

A quick check of the other houses reveals nothing but a half-empty bottle of vodka. I toss it into my pack. You never know when you need disinfectant or a Molotov cocktail. My time with the Guardians taught me that.

At the last house, I freeze when I see it in the backyard: an orange tree, full of fruit. I haven't seen fresh fruit in a long time, not since New Hope. Hands shaking with anticipation, I pick every one. When I can't fit any more into my pack, I sit on the ground, peeling orange after orange and jamming the sections into my mouth. The sweet taste helps the emptiness for a while. I eat until my stomach feels like it will burst.

I rest in the shade of the tree, satisfied. My contentment is fleeting, though, and soon the emptiness returns, not just a gnawing in the pit of my stomach but a hollowing out of my entire being. It's impossible to avoid the loneliness that has haunted me since leaving New Hope, so I let it wash over me. I nearly give in to it, and sit under the tree, waiting until something hostile finds me. In the end I fight the despair, pushing it down inside where I don't have to deal with it. I stand, determined not to give up.

Time to go, I sign to the empty air.

CHAPTER TWO

On a shady side road, I make my way back toward the place I've made my home. I pick up my pace, anxious to return before nightfall. I used to be afraid of the day, but the sonic emitter that Kay gave me keeps me safe from the Floraes. Night is what worries me now, when I hear the occasional voice nearby or a gunshot in the distance. There are people out here. Not many, but enough. They are alive in the After, which means they were either smart and figured out the Floraes' behavior, or they are just mean enough to survive. I don't want to find out which.

When I reach my new home, I bypass the large plantation house and head to the backyard. Beyond the overgrown tangle of grass is a field. I scan the area for any sign that the yard was breached while I was gone. I'd set traps, pressure-activated alarms that would send the Floraes running. So far, no one has disturbed the yard and my luck seems to be holding; everything looks as I left it. I sprint to the overgrown tree in the far corner and scramble up the trunk, into the tree house.

The tree house, a remnant of Before, has held up well. It barely creaks as I walk across the wooden floor and make my way to my sleeping bag in the corner, careful not to overturn the stack of books next to my makeshift bed. The tree house is large, larger than my room in the Ward, with two giant glass windows, one facing the house, one facing the field. Seems silly to have glass windows in a tree house, but judging from the mansion up front, that family had money to spare. There was a rope ladder that I cut down. I can climb up the tree without it. It's not ideal, there's no running water, but the tree house is sturdy and hard to spot in the mess of leaves and branches. Even without the emitter, I wouldn't have to worry about Floraes up here.

In the three months since I've left New Hope I've had too many close calls. The first couple of nights were sheer terror. I thought about going to Fort Black, since Kay had dropped me so close, but I didn't see the point. If it was as bad as everyone said, I wanted to stay away. I had nowhere else to go, so I wandered aimlessly. At least I didn't have to worry about Floraes. The emitter kept them at bay.

One night, while I was scavenging a house, I heard voices, whispered but deep. I hid in the bushes and waited, knowing what kind of men banded together. The kind who Amber brought to my home in Chicago, the kind who attacked New Hope. Still, I wanted to check them out.

When I looked at them through the leaves, I could see there were no women with them. Not a good sign. After they moved on, I ran in the other direction. I've had a few encounters since then, but I always hide. I was lucky to find this place. Anyone looking to scavenge will head straight to the mansion up front.

This place is only twenty miles from where Kay said Fort Black would be. After I decided not to go there, I started to feel the loneliness. It was small at first, just an itch that I knew I couldn't scratch. But now it's an ever-present sadness. Even if I don't feel safe going to Fort Black, I like at least being *near* other people. In New Hope, I grew used to being in a community, to being part of a family again. As much as I was mistreated there, as much as I don't want to admit it to myself, the horrible truth remains. I miss New Hope.

And now, I am all alone.

I try not to feel sorry for myself, instead passing the time by working out to stay fast, or by reading or scavenging for supplies. But the memories come back. I think of my mother, who loved me, but not enough to save me from Dr. Reynolds. I think of Kay, my real friend.

I think of Amber, who betrayed us all and paid a horrible price. She brought a gang to the doors of New Hope, and they tried to create a panic, kill the leaders, and take everything we had. I forced her to tell the truth, and for a brief moment I thought I'd done something good. I'd saved New Hope. But then I found out all the people in the gang were put to death, without so much as a trial. And Amber, she was unmade, given a lobotomy to keep her placid.

Sometimes I even allow myself to think of Rice, how good and safe it felt to be held by him—then I stop. I can't let myself think of that or I'll go crazy. And I think of Baby, who I love more than anyone, who's safe in New Hope. I wanted to take her with me, but Kay talked me out of it. That she was better, safer, where she was.

Suddenly I freeze, holding my breath, not moving a muscle. Outside something is rustling the long grass in the field near the house. I silently crawl along the floor, peeking up out of the window. A lone Florae shuffles slowly. I stand up behind the window, turning on my flashlight. The monster swivels toward me and immediately begins loping. At one hundred feet away, it will run into the sound waves from the emitter.

With shaking hands, I reach to the emitter at my hip and switch it off. My pulse races and every nerve screams against what I am doing. For a moment I feel truly alive, awash in adrenaline. For a moment I forget my loneliness.

The green monster crosses the hundred-yard line, creeping menacingly, its yellow teeth bared. Looking up, it knows exactly where I am. And I look curiously into its horrible eyes.

You used to be a human.

What are you now?

The creature circles the tree house, and I peer out over the doorway. It tries to climb the tree and makes it up a few feet, surprising me. Startled, I come back to my senses. What am I doing? I fumble with the emitter, pressing it on. The creature falls from the tree and staggers back, unsure of which way to run to escape the sound. It darts toward the house at first, and I fear it will set off one of the alarms, but it changes direction and speeds back to the field, not stopping when it breaks away from the sound radius.

I exhale, realizing I had been holding my breath, and shakily sit down. Was I that desperate to see another person that

I would risk my life . . . or was it something else? Something darker that I don't even want to begin to think about? I shake my head. No. I want to live, even if it's this solitary existence. I sneak a look out the window, searching for the Florae, but it's long gone.

Leaving me alone again in the black, hot night.

I spend the next two days roaming through the surrounding neighborhoods, searching through houses I've missed or skipped before. Supplies are getting dangerously low, and I've combed through the area too thoroughly. If I want to keep living this way, I'll have to start traveling farther out to scavenge. I make it home with nothing more than a dented can of spinach and some shampoo. There's a pond I found a while back that I've been using for water, but I'm sure I can spare a couple of bucketfuls to wash my hair. The synth-suit keeps my skin clean, saps sweat away from my body, but my hair is another story, especially if I don't wear my hood often.

As I settle into my sleeping bag, I hear a familiar crackle. It's my earpiece. Kay remotely turned off the communication ability, so Dr. Reynolds couldn't track me. It has a solar-powered micro-battery, though, good for years, and I've been using it to amplify faraway sounds, keeping it in my ear at all times. It's been so long since I've heard anything, I forgot that someone might actually try to use it to contact me.

"Sunshine? Are you there?"

I sit up in anticipation. It was nothing more than a whisper, but I know who it is. "Kay?"

Just the thought of talking to someone friendly makes my eyes flood. But she doesn't answer.

"Kay?" I plead. "Kay?" Nothing. I slide back to the floor, my head in my hands.

And then, after a few minutes, she's back.

"Sunshine?" She's whispering, but there's something else, a tone in her voice, something I never thought I'd hear. Kay sounds scared.

"Kay! Are you all right? Did you guys get in trouble? How's Baby? How's Rice? How's my mother?"

"Amy, I don't have a lot of time. Gareth hacked me in to the system so I could contact you . . . but I'm being watched closely."

"By Marcus?"

"No time, sunshine. You making it okay out there?"

"I'm handling it."

"Good girl. Listen, I need to tell you something. . . ." She pauses so long, I think she's cut out again.

"Kay, what is it?!" I ask desperately.

"It's . . . Baby."

My stomach turns over as dread seeps into every pore of my body.

"Dr. Reynolds has Baby."

CHAPTER THREE

The world goes black. I blink hard, trying to regain focus on the now spinning room.

Dr. Reynolds has Baby.

"Amy, are you there?"

"Yeah," I say. My voice sounds far away.

"Dr. Reynolds took Baby as soon as you escaped. I thought if I asked about it, it would look suspicious, so I had to wait until I could get to Rice. He told me that Dr. Reynolds just wanted to hold her at first, to use her against you in case you were found. But then he saw the mark on the back of her neck."

I suck in a breath. "No," I whisper. I had found Baby in

an abandoned supermarket, alone. Later I discovered that as a toddler she was a foster child experimented on by the government. Rice has a similar mark, and I can only assume he was also part of the experiment. My mother, as it happens, was the main scientist on the project.

She also was in charge of another project: the creation of a bacteria that turned humans into Floraes. Meaning she is the person responsible for the apocalypse.

But I don't let myself think about that.

The scars on both Baby's and Rice's necks are from the original vaccine my mother was developing so that American soldiers would remain unaffected by the Florae virus. It was never actually proven to work, but when I found Baby, she had a large bite on her leg. She'd been bitten by a Florae and remained human. So it seems, in this case, the vaccine worked just fine.

"They've been testing Baby," Kay went on. "Taking her blood. Trying to replicate the results. The original vaccine doesn't work. . . . Rice told me so. But somehow it did for Baby. They think it has something to do with her blood chemistry. All their attempts to modify the vaccine have failed. They just can't get it right. They make us bring survivors directly to them for experimentation. And we never see them again."

I gnash my teeth at Dr. Reynolds's—and my mother's—cruelty. So they're turning people into Florae to test their vaccine.

"And Baby?" I ask. "Are they hurting her?"

Kay sighs. "They're taking her blood day and night, following up any lead that comes to them. It's blood draw after blood draw, and Rice says Baby's anemic and really weak. She's hanging in for now, but she's not in good shape."

The blood pounds deafeningly in my ears. This can't be happening. My greatest fear.

"You said she'd be safe there!" I hiss. "I could have taken her with me!"

"Amy, she *was* safe. How was I supposed to know Dr. Reynolds would take her?"

"You should have contacted me sooner."

"You don't know what it's like here now. Everything's changed. I'm not even in charge of the Guardians anymore. Marcus is. He could try to kill me at any time."

"I'm coming back. To get her. Now."

"Amy, you can't."

"Why?" There is a pause. "Kay? Are you there?"

"When you escaped, Dr. Reynolds went nuts." I can hear the regret in her voice over telling me. "The doctors in the

Ward, the Guardians, even your mother. Everyone was punished."

"And Rice?" I wince at the concern in my voice, but I can't help it.

"He's fine. He wasn't suspected."

In spite of myself, I'm flooded with relief.

"I've got to get Baby out of there."

"No. You've got to go to Fort Black and find my brother. Ken. That's how you can help Baby."

"Why? What can he do?"

"He's a researcher. For New Hope. But he's in Fort Black working on developing a Florae vaccine."

"Why?"

"New subjects. Also, Dr. Reynolds doesn't want all his researchers in one place. So he's got a lab set up there."

"What does that have to do with Baby? What can Ken do for her?"

"He's ruthless about his research. He'd do anything to get a test subject like Baby for himself, even if it means breaking her out of New Hope. And he could do it. He's been with Reynolds for a long time, since before the Floraes. He has access."

"But he just wants to run tests on her too!"

"Yes, but you could monitor the situation. You could protect her. As long as she's away from Reynolds."

My mind races. She's right. I could never take on New Hope alone. This is the only option.

"But where–"

"Gotta go. Someone's coming. Be–"

"Kay?" For several minutes I yell her name, but she doesn't respond. Kay's gone.

CHAPTER
FOUR

I try to get some sleep, but after a couple of hours I give up. I need to leave, to get to Fort Black. I pack up everything the Guardians outfitted me with when I left: my Guardian gun with spare clips, my water filter, a map. My sonic emitter. I've barely used my gun, so I still have plenty of ammunition. I throw my backpack over my shoulder and pause to look around. The tree house has done me well these past few months, but I won't miss the solitude.

It takes eight hours to reach Fort Black by foot. I could have made it in less, but I didn't want to push myself and arrive exhausted. The journey is surprisingly uneventful. Nothing more than a long, tense walk, my backpack biting into my shoulders. If it weren't for the synth-suit, my skin would be wet with sweat. Even though the suit controls my temperature, I was still pretty hot once the day broke, my face sweating in the early morning sun. I sighted some Florae, but they backed up when I got close, fleeing from the emitter waves. I silently thank Rice for the gift (he gave it to Kay) and Vivian, who invented it.

The bigger danger is other people. I have no idea what things are like at Fort Black, or how often people leave to scavenge. I'm certain there are plenty of people who would kill me without a second thought if they knew what was in my pack.

Once I'm a mile out, I stop to rest on a highway overpass. A few years ago, this road would have been full of speeding cars. People hurrying to work, worried about getting to a meeting on time. Now there are no meetings. No work, other than to stay alive. The only cars now are abandoned, left to rust in the elements. My father used to go on a hippie anti-fossil-fuel rant about how the car-to-person ratio in America was nearly one to one. Now it's a hundred thousand to one . . . give or take a few thousand. Not that a car would be much use to me. Sure, I could have made it the twenty miles very quickly, but I would have had to find a car with keys and plenty of gas. Besides, they make too much noise, and I never learned to drive anyway.

I walk around one of the many abandoned cars to the edge of the highway and peer over the railing. I can see it now, in the distance: Fort Black. It takes me a moment to process what I'm looking at as I study the surrounding area. Then it hits me that Fort Black isn't a fort at all.

Fort Black is a prison.

CHAPTER FIVE

Formerly the Fort Black Correctional Facility, the walls of Fort Black jut up, cutting into and marring the blue-white sky. The sides of the great prison are three hundred feet high, at least, and laced at the top with two rows of barbed wire. There are few windows, and the ones that are visible are covered in thick metal bars. Around the Fort, there's nothing but brown dusty earth.

I pull my canteen from my pack and take a long sip of water, then look back and forth, surveying the area and the sun-scorched ground around the walls. A long ribbon of broken asphalt leads off to my left, linking the jail to the highway, which curves out of sight over the distant hill. I study the road from the top of that hill until it slips beneath me, under the overpass where I now rest, and disappears around the bend to my right. There are no Floraes that I can make out, yet my hand goes automatically to the emitter.

The feel of the small plastic device comforts me. I reach into my pack for my Guardian sunglasses—standard-issue, but better than the best binoculars. I adjust the zoom until I can see Fort Black as if I were standing next to it.

The place is humongous, its gray concrete more formidable than I'd originally thought. Men patrol the high, broad walls, armed with rifles. At each of the guard towers rests an immense crossbow on a thick post. Even from here, I can feel the hum of too many people living in a small space. The noise sets my skin tingling. It's strange to hear it, after all the miles I traveled alone and in silence. Now that I'm so close, I can't bring myself to walk the last stretch. I rummage inside my bag, allowing myself another sip of water and a bite of food. I don't know when I'll get to eat again, or if my food will be confiscated or stolen inside those dark walls.

I stand again, narrowing my eyes at the massive, dark structure. My mission: find Ken. He's the only way to save Baby. I know it won't be easy, but there's a chance, a sliver of hope. And

Kay will help if she can by contacting me on my earpiece. My hand goes to my ear to reassure me it's still there, the one thing that can keep me in touch with Kay. It's small, like one of those micro-hearing aids from Before. There are three buttons: The top one turns the earpiece on and off, the middle one activates the sound amplifier, and the bottom one calls in. When I was a Guardian, the earpiece was set to automatically call all the Guardians, but there's a central hub in New Hope where all the earpieces are programmed. Gareth is a bit of a hacker and has mine deactivated remotely . . . until Kay needs to contact me.

A glint on the scorched landscape catches my eye and I snap my head up. A shape is moving quickly over the road toward the prison. I crouch down and turn on the sound amplifier on my earpiece, then quickly drop my hand to my Guardian glasses and zoom in on the figure.

It's not a Florae. It's a man.

CHAPTER SIX

The man is on a bicycle, pedaling furiously. Something is wrong with his bike, though, and every few seconds it makes a grinding sound, like metal moving against metal. Behind his bike is a hitched trailer, the kind parents used to haul their kids around Before. The trailer is filled to the brim with bundles of cloth and canned goods.

Out of the corner of my eye, I see movement, and then I see Them. Two Floraes have topped the rise on the highway. Their pea-green skin almost fades into the baked landscape, their milky, yellow eyes useless, but their heads move, searching for sound. The man's bike makes that horrible grating noise again, and the Floraes focus their attention, quickly sprinting down the road to the prison, hot on the cyclist's heels.

From the prison wall, an arrow flies through the air, narrowly missing the nearer of the two Floraes. Another arrow hits the second Florae in the shoulder, slowing it down slightly, but doing nothing to lessen its hunger, its craving for the man's flesh. The first Florae is a few feet away from the cyclist. Just when I'm certain the guy doesn't have a chance, the first Florae drops to the ground. Because of its incredible speed, it skids a few feet before stopping completely. The second Florae is taken down just as I hear two loud cracks echo toward me.

I adjust my earpiece as the man stops at the gate and calls up, "Whewy, boys. That was a close one! Think you coulda taken 'em out a *little* sooner? Something on my bike crapped out a while back, and I thought I could make it okay. . . . Should have known better." He gets off the bike, plants his hands on his knees, and pants for a minute. He straightens and shoots a worried glance back the way he came, squinting up at the gate again.

"Don't mean to be ungrateful or anything . . . that was some fine shooting. . . . But what say you fellas let me in now?" When they don't respond, he adds, "I made a couple of really sweet finds out there. . . . You boys get first dibs, of course." That does it. A small door next to the gate opens, and he rushes through, pushing his bike.

I take another sip of water to steel myself. I can't stay out here forever, and those gunshots will bring more Floraes to the gates. My emitter has only a hundred-foot radius, and I should make a move while there's a clear path. I don't want anyone in Fort Black to see Them fleeing from me as I walk down. I'm not prepared to answer their questions.

Hefting my bag to my shoulder, I walk slowly toward the imposing walls of Fort Black and the unknown.

Eager but cautious, I take my time, careful and alert as I make my way to the gate. As I approach, someone calls out, "Halt!" I can't see the man who barks down at me from the top of the wall.

I stop dead and consider raising my hands in the air, but I don't. Maybe I should have moved my Guardian gun to my pack, instead of wearing it at my hip. My heart pounding in my chest, I peer up at the gray concrete wall.

"I would like entrance to Fort Black!" I yell, trying to sound strong. I hear whispers, but I'm afraid if I reach to adjust my amplifier, I'll be shot. I try mimicking the earlier man's tone: "And if you don't mind, I'd really like to be inside before the next batch of Floraes arrive."

There are a few more moments of muttered voices before the door by the gate opens. I stay where I am and peer inside. It's almost dark in there. It's the interior of the wall, I realize, a dank corridor that must surround the prison.

"In or out." I see two figures waiting for me. "Now or never."

I cautiously step inside.

Two men, armed, stand there and as my eyes adjust—the hall is dimly lit with electric lights—I see one of the men grinning as he ogles my clinging synth-suit. The corridor smells sour after weeks of breathing fresh, clean air.

The door closes behind me with a loud bang. With a shudder, I realize *I'm trapped.*

CHAPTER SEVEN

"It's a girl," the grinning one says. He's young, probably still in his teens, with dusty blond hair and dull eyes.

The second man moves closer, into the dim light. "Looks like a *woman* to me." His eyes flick up from my body to my face then back down. He licks his lips as if I'm a tasty treat. He's older, in his thirties at least, and towers over me. Bruises, red and purple, mark his face and arms.

"Who'ja think she belongs to?" the first man asks, as though I can't hear him. "I can't see her arm through her clothes."

I take a step back, but I know I can't leave. If what Kay said was true, every minute is precious.

"I don't belong to anyone," I spit.

They look at me as if I'm insane. Then the second man's eyes light up. I can see now that there is some green to a few of his bruises from fights, new and old. He's so large, I can't imagine anyone wanting to scrap with him.

"You've never been here before?" he asks, a glint of surprise in his eyes.

I shake my head.

He licks his lips again. "Well, cupcake, welcome to Fort Black. Pete, go get Jacks."

"But I saw her first, Tank," Pete whines.

"Go. Get. Jacks," Tank orders through clenched teeth. Pete turns sulkily and leaves through a door behind him, letting bright sunlight momentarily stream into the corridor.

Tank takes a step toward me and almost as a reflex, my gun is out of its holster and trained on his chest in seconds. "Don't."

It's not how I wanted to arrive in Fort Black. I didn't want to pull my gun, but I need to let him know I can protect myself. It's only an intimidation tactic, but it seems to be working.

Tank truly looks at my face for the first time. "Hold on there, cupcake." He hasn't even had time to raise his shotgun at me. "I'm not going to hurt you."

"No. You're not." I keep the gun leveled at him.

"You don't know how it works here, little girl," he tells me. His forehead gleams with oily sweat. I realize the rank smell is actually coming from him. "I can teach you." His eyes gleam.

My skin crawls at the idea of him teaching me anything. I want to back away from him, but I'll look weak. I grip the gun harder to hide my shaking hand. I'm sure I'm faster than he is—most people his size aren't very quick—but I might not get the separation I need to escape.

If he gets to me, the pure bulk of him will overwhelm me. I can't let him any nearer. He needs to believe that I will shoot him. *I* need to believe it. I narrow my eyes at him as he stares at me, smirking.

Tank and I are still deadlocked when Pete returns with another youngish man. He's slight, only a few inches taller than I am. He eyes us warily, me with my gun pointed at Tank.

Is he in charge here? Rice isn't much older than I am either, and he was in charge of my intake in New Hope.

This new guy wears a loose-fitting T-shirt, showing off his arms, which are covered in elaborate tattoos. As he considers us, he pushes his hand through his dark brown hair, flashing a well-developed bicep.

Not so slight after all.

"See, Jacks?" Pete asks him. "Toldja it was a girl."

"You won't need that just now," he says, nodding at my gun. His voice betrays a slight Southern twang.

"I'm not giving it up." My eyes flick to Tank.

"That's fine. You can keep it," Jacks says. "But, you know, maybe just drop the barrel for now?"

I stare at him as he looks at me. There's something in his eyes—warmth and something more, honesty maybe. He watches me with a quiet understanding. His unexpected sincerity makes me listen to him. I hesitate another moment, then slowly lower my weapon but keep it in my hand.

Tank snorts and mutters, "I'll show you a big gun, cupcake."

"Apologize," Jacks says without raising his voice.

Tank still stares at me, but his cruel smile has been replaced with a tight, irritated frown.

Jacks speaks again, in the same calm tone. "I could make you."

Tank grits his teeth. "Sorry, cupcake."

Jacks turns to me again. "Now . . . cupcake, is it?"

Tank snickers.

"Amy. My name is Amy."

"Amy." Jacks smiles. "Yeah, that's better." He shoots a look at Tank. "People call themselves all kinds of stupid names these days." Tank bristles, but Jacks ignores him.

"Pete says you've never been here before. So you'll have to come with me." He motions to Tank and Pete. "These two are staying here. I'm guessing you could probably use some fresh air after hanging with Tank for this long."

Pete barks out a laugh and Tank gives Jacks a black look.

"My gun?" I ask, still debating if I should just run for the door.

"Hold on to it. No one will take it." Jacks begins to walk down the corridor, deeper into the dark of Fort Black.

I hang back, thinking it through. I know it's a risk to go with him, but what are my options? I've come all this way; I can't let myself turn back now. Not with Baby's safety at stake. I'm a trained Guardian and I'm well-armed. I can protect myself.

Pete giggles for no reason, and I'm suddenly aware I'll be alone again with the two of them once Jacks turns the corner, out of sight. Pete is grinning stupidly at me, and Tank's giving me that same, mouth-breathing leer.

I'm moving. Fast.

Tank laughs at my back. "See you around. When you're all checked out, you come find me, you hear?"

Like hell I will. I stop, turn, and stare him down. I've survived the After. I've survived the Ward. I'm not going to let one repulsive man get to me.

But the look that Tank gives me chills me to the core. There is something less than human about the way he stares after me. I back away, then turn again and hurry down the corridor after Jacks.

My adrenaline is up and my heart's pounding, but I put my gun back in its holster and try to cool off.

Jacks waits for me down the hall. "Tank's not exactly the face of Fort Black," he says. "And you caught him just before his shift ends."

"Lucky me," I say, watching Jacks. Although his voice is gruff, his posture isn't threatening.

Jacks shrugs, his face stony. "He has his purpose. We mostly get people returning from supply runs or groups of men making their way across the country. He keeps them in line."

"I bet," I mutter. I think of Marcus, Dr. Reynolds's crony in the Guardians. "Mindless muscle does have its uses."

Jacks shakes his head. "He's not mindless. Don't think that for a second. If you stay in Fort Black, you'll have to watch out for him."

I nod and try to suppress a shudder. As if I needed such a warning.

Jacks leads me down the hall to a door and motions me through. I glance inside and see a middle-aged man sitting at a desk. His gray hair is cut short around his gaunt face, almost as pale as the white lab coat he's wearing. I'm immediately on edge and I suck in a breath.

The smell of disinfectant hits me like a punch in the nose. Scanning the rest of the small room, I spot an examination table.

The Ward.

"Doc needs to have a quick look and take some blood—"

Not again. I can't go back. I won't.

I shake my head and go back into the hall. "No."

Jacks stares at me, puzzled. "It's just a routine examination."

I barely hear him. I'm shaking, panting. "No needles," I hiss between clenched teeth. "No drugs. Never again."

"But, Amy, we're just going to draw some—"

"You will not put me back in the Ward!" I scream as my hand goes to the knife at my thigh. All I see are white walls; Dr. Reynolds's self-satisfied face hovers in my vision.

"Whoa . . . What are you talking about?" Jacks asks, his arms up in surrender. "There's no ward here."

Doc is at my side now. "Just calm down for a moment."

I push Doc away, desperately trying to breathe. My breath

is coming in short, hard gulps now. I can't get any air.

"I'm going . . . outside. . . ."

And then I turn and am running blindly. I know I have to get into this place—it's my only option to break Baby out. But I have to get away from that examination room.

I hear someone follow me as I run, but they're slow and I quickly leave them behind.

The running is good—it soothes my panic, calming me down. Oxygen fills my lungs. Then, whipping around a corner, I hit a wall at full force.

It's not a wall, though. A wall doesn't reek of sweat and filth. A wall doesn't hold on to your arms so you can't escape.

And a wall doesn't talk.

"I didn't think I would see you again *this* soon, cupcake."

CHAPTER EIGHT

Tank wraps me up like a straightjacket, his massive arms squeezing what little breath I have out of my already struggling lungs. *Is this the end?* Will he kill me right now, or after some other horror that I can't even imagine?

Remember your training. I can almost hear Kay's voice telling me what to do.

I go limp so Tank thinks I've given up. He loosens his grip just enough for me to turn slightly sideways, raise my leg, and stomp the top of his foot. He didn't expect it and jerks back in shock, leaving my right arm free. I turn and thrust my hand upward, my palm connecting with his nose.

"Ahhh." He lets out a wounded animal's wail, clutches his face, and staggers back against the wall. "You little bitch!" Blood pours from his nose; the little that is visible of his face is contorted with pain and rage.

By the time he drops his hands to look for me, I have my gun out, trained on him. Earlier I was bluffing when I pulled my gun. But now my fear controls me, and I know that I can take his life, even if I don't want to. In this moment my desire to live trumps all.

I feel a hand on my shoulder. I grab it and duck down and back, twisting it, slamming whoever it is against the wall and then snapping the gun back on Tank before he's taken more than a step toward me.

"Back!" I scream.

"I'm not going to hurt you." It's Jacks, his voice muffled by the wall I have him pinned against.

Then I see Pete just down the corridor, mouth gaping, his shotgun aimed at me.

"Drop the gun!" I yell, my voice high-pitched and strained.

Tank moans and clutches his face again. "I think she broke my nose."

Pete's face shows his uncertainty. I can see he's not used to making decisions.

I keep my voice low and even. "Shoot me, and my gun will go off and kill Tank. Plus, that's a shotgun you're holding. From there, the pattern will take out both me and this guy." I pop my shoulder into Jacks's back. I can't see his face, but I can hear his jagged breathing.

"You'd end up alone in here with three bodies. Unless you miss, and I kill you."

"Pete," Jacks says, "put down the gun and get Tank out of here. Then go back to your post." Pete hesitates, and looks from him to Tank. *"Now."*

Pete sets the shotgun at his feet and grabs a fistful of Tank's sleeve. The two of them shuffle into the darkness, Tank glaring back at me over his shoulder.

"Okay," Jacks says calmly once they're gone. "Now can you let me go?"

"No."

"Look, it's just you and me here. I understand you're scared. Someone must have really screwed you over. . . ." I stare at the back of his head and wonder why he doesn't struggle. He's strong, but he doesn't even try to break my hold.

"I'm not scared." My shaking voice betrays my lie. "I just don't know if I should trust anyone, really . . . especially not doctors."

"All right. I get it. Doctors can be dicks. Believe me, I know." He tries to adjust his position, but I tighten my grip on his arm. "Okay, okay. Listen, I'm not a doctor, I'm a tattoo artist. I just help Doc out."

"I don't understand what a doctor would want with a tattoo artist. That doesn't really make sense."

"Hey, I'm in a lot of pain here. Kind of hard to make my case . . ."

I keep his arm pinned. "I'm looking for someone," I say. "It's important. If I get in, will you help me find him?"

"Release the death grip and I'll think about it."

I can't hold him forever. "Fine." I let him go, stepping back out of his reach in case he lunges at me. I holster my gun, glad to be done with it. If Jacks plans to fight me, I can use my Guardian training to take him. I'm grateful when he doesn't move toward me at all. Instead he turns slowly to face me, then backs up against the wall, rubbing his shoulder. It takes him a moment to regain his composure.

"What now?" I ask.

"That's up to you," he says. "Look. I'm not going to tell you that Fort Black is one-hundred-percent safe and you never have to worry again."

"That's reassuring."

"But," he continues, "I guarantee that you can keep your weapons. Clearly, you can take care of yourself. These walls will keep the Floraes out. For most people that's enough. I can see you're not most people, though. Just remember, if you don't want to be here, you don't have to be here. You can leave. No one will force you to stay."

"And Tank?"

He allows a small smile. "I think you've just proven he can't stop you."

I exhale slowly. "So what do I have to do, exactly, to get into Fort Black?"

"Doc just has to examine you."

"No."

Jacks holds up his right hand and puts the left on his heart. "I can vouch for Doc."

"Yeah? And who will vouch for you?"

He drops his hands and shrugs. "You've got to trust someone at some point."

I want to trust him, but I'm not sure yet. I need more time.

"Why does Doc have to examine me?"

"We've had an outbreak of the Pox."

"The Pox?"

"You haven't seen anyone with the Pox?" he asks, unbelieving.

I shake my head.

"Then you're lucky. You must not have had much contact with other survivors."

He looks at me again, as if he is trying to figure out a puzzle—not calculating, but curious. "We still have to test you to make sure. We also have to check you for bites."

"Florae bites? Why?" Do they know? How could they? Only a few people in New Hope knew the truth.

"To make sure you're not infected."

"Infected?" I say densely.

Jacks cocks his head at me like he doesn't know why I'm confused. But when he speaks his voice is kind. "We need to make sure that you're not going to turn into a Florae."

"And how," I ask, my voice a little too high, "could I possibly turn into a Florae?"

I know I sound hysterical, but I can't believe they know. It's not possible, not after all I went through in New Hope to discover the truth myself. Not after all I was put through by Dr. Reynolds to make sure it remained buried.

"Amy, you've been out there a long time," Jacks says slowly.

"You must know what happens when a person is bitten by a Florae?"

My limbs feel heavy, all my adrenaline gone. "So you know that the Floraes are people?"

"Of course." He frowns, looks at me, and shakes his head. "It's not like it's a secret."

CHAPTER NINE

We walk back down the corridor to Doc's office. Jacks motions me inside, pointing to the exam table. I sit on the edge and try to force myself to relax, but I can't stop shifting.

"He's just going to take some blood," Jacks says from the doorway.

The sting of Tank's attack is still fresh. How many people here are just like him?

My training will get me through a lot, but part of besting Tank had been him not expecting me to know how to fight. In his eyes I was just a girl, fresh meat. But now he knows what I can do. He seems like a dumb brute to me, but Jacks clearly thinks he's dangerous.

Before I can ask Jacks more about Tank, Doc steps up and stands there in front of me with a small, tired smile. His face is lined and weathered, his salt-and-pepper hair cut military short. "Let's just take your blood pressure for now." He puts his hand on my wrist. "How old are you, Amy?"

"Seventeen."

"And how long have you been on your own?"

"I don't know. . . . I was hiding in a house. Why are you asking me?" I move to pull my arm away, but Doc holds my wrist firmly.

"Where did you come from?" he asks. "How have you survived this long alone?"

"What's with the twenty questions, Doc?" Jacks asks from the doorway.

Doc drops my wrist, turning to glare at his assistant. "I was just trying to find out a little more about our mystery survivor," he says in a measured voice. "Maybe she's seen other colonies." He turns back to me. "Have you? Been to any other survivors' colonies?"

"No." The lie is on my lips before I even knew why I'm saying it. My skin crawls at the thought of New Hope. "Are we almost done here?"

"I'll just take a blood sample to test and give you a few shots to boost your immune system." Doc looks at my arm, still sheathed in my synth-suit. "You'll have to remove your clothing for the examination, anyway."

I shake my head. "No." I don't like Doc. There is something about him that makes me uneasy, and I don't want him touching me again.

"I'm afraid the blood test is nonnegotiable. You could carry any number of communicable diseases. You might even carry the Black Pox. If you don't let me take a blood sample, you'll have to leave."

"No."

"You're not going to find your friend out there," Jacks says, nodding at the outside. "Unless he's a Florae."

I pause, thinking, looking at Doc and Jacks. I know Jacks is right; there's nothing left to do. "Fine," I relent, pulling the superstretchy material of the synth-suit down over my shoulder and freeing my arm from it. "But this is it. No examination, no shots."

As he takes my blood, the doctor keeps pressing. "I have to check you for bites or gashes that can be caused by a Florae—"

"Just test my blood," I tell him. "I'm not infected."

Doc frowns. "You don't seem to understand." He sighs,

as though having to deal with me is making him very tired. "The bacteria lies dormant in the bloodstream until just a few moments before the infected begins to change. It can take up to twenty-four hours before the person shows the first signs of infection."

"Then I'll wait it out here."

Doc opens his mouth to protest, but Jacks cuts him off. "I'll watch her," Jack says from the doorway. "I'm off work soon, and I'll keep an eye on her till my next shift. If she doesn't change within the next day, she's not going to."

Doc considers, softening as he looks at Jacks. Maybe my initial instincts were wrong about Doc.

"Okay. But if she starts to change, you have to give her the injection. . . . No hesitation."

Jacks's eyes flick to me before returning to Doc. "I'll watch her," he says. "You have my word."

Doc has left us to have my blood tested, giving me one last, hard look before leaving the room.

"What's in the injection?" I ask after a few minutes of silence. I scan the room for the syringe and find it resting on a metal tray on the counter across from me.

"Potassium chloride." He pulls over a chair and sits between me and the syringe, but not too close to either. "If you start to change, I'll have to give it to you," he says. "It'll stop your heart."

I grin darkly. "Why don't you just ask Tank to take care of it?"

"I wouldn't want to give him the satisfaction."

"So what's his deal anyway?" I ask. "Are there a lot of guys like him in Fort Black?"

"Tank is . . . complicated." Jacks looks away. "He may seem dumb, but he's really good at manipulating people into doing what he wants."

"Like his buddy Pete?" I ask.

"Exactly. Last year, a fourteen-year-old girl went missing. A rumor spread that she ran off, but then another girl vanished a few months later."

"You think Tank . . . ?"

Jacks nods. "People die here, people leave, but we all try to keep track of the women." He avoids catching my eye. "There aren't a lot of you left."

"I see."

"After the third girl went missing, some of the men got together and led a lynch mob against Tank. Tank somehow got one of his cronies to take the blame."

"Was there any proof?"

He shook his head. "There wasn't any proof, no witnesses, but I'm sure Tank let that man pay for his crime. With one of the girls, Tank was stalking her for a while, showing up everywhere she went. She complained about it all the time, but her father couldn't protect her. Then she just disappeared."

"No one found her body? She could have just run away."

He shakes his head. "She wasn't the type. Tank got to her and hid the body. I don't know how connected he was to the two other girls, but he eventually moved on to someone new. Became obsessed with her. If that's not proof enough, he has a . . . prior record of abducting teen girls." His voice sounds hollow and sad. "It's why he was in prison."

"What happened to the new girl he was bothering?"

"She died, but not by his hands. I know he would have tried eventually. There's something not right with him."

My stomach drops. "And now he's taken a liking to me?"

"That's why you need to be careful." He sees the look on my face and quickly adds, "Hey, do you really want to be talking about this stuff right now?"

I swallow my dread and shrug. "What better way to kill time while you wait for me to change into a Florae?"

Suddenly there's a commotion outside. A man pops his head in the door. "Jacks, we need you."

Jacks looks at me uncertainly.

"Don't worry, I won't go all Florae on you."

"Stay here. If you don't, I won't be able to help you if you run into someone like Tank."

I nod as he rushes out. I hear more shouting. Footsteps running down the hall. Then nothing.

I sit up and slip off the exam table. Moving quietly to the door, I open it a crack. Doc's voice is echoing down the hall. I inch the door open farther and look both ways, checking for Tank or any other guard. There's no one around, the hall quiet except for the hum of the lights and the far-off commotion Jacks is dealing with. I close my eyes and try to make out what Doc is saying.

"...blood pressure normal...CBC normal..." Doc's voice carries up the hall. "Now, which inoculation are we on?" he asks, then answers his own question: "F1T13." He continues chatting away to himself. "Patient refused examination and all immunizations."

He's talking about me.

"I will try to convince her of the importance of having an up-to-date shot, then release her into Fort Black." Doc continues to talk to himself, rattling off names of people who are due for an updated flu shot. Nothing sinister there, just a slightly loopy doctor going over his charts with himself.

I open the door wider and glance around the hallway. It looks clear, both ways, and I don't hear anyone but Doc nearby. I step into the hall, closing the door with a barely audible click. Ken could be here, in these very rooms. This might be my last chance to explore unsupervised.

I make my way down the hall and try the first door I reach, but it's another examination room. So are the second and the third. When I come to a set of stairs, I pause. Last time I did something like this was back in the lab in New Hope. My mother came to my rescue then, making sure I wasn't discovered. Now there's no one to rescue me.

I grab one of my knives from its sheath and hold it in front of me as I walk quickly up the stairs, my body pressed against the wall. The second-floor layout is the same as the first. I try the first door and see that it's a file room, the musty air thick with dust. I slip inside and the lights snap on automatically, motion-activated. The sudden brightness makes me jump. After a quick scan, it's clear there are only cabinets, a table, and some chairs strewn with files. I close the door quickly, hoping no one can see the light from outside.

I make my way to the first drawer and pull it open. The

folders are alphabetized by last name, and when I look at the drawer I see it is marked *A*. With shaking hands, I yank open the *O* drawer, but his folder isn't there. As I check more drawers and more folders, I realize these are files on the prisoners. I close the drawer and turn to leave, accidentally knocking into a chair piled high with papers.

My eyes immediately snap to the door and I hurry to hide under the table, waiting for someone to investigate the noise. I'm breathing too fast, my body tense.

After a few minutes my breathing slows as I realize no one is coming. I crawl out from under the table and am about to stand when I look down at the paper my hand is resting on. It's a mug shot, and I recognize the face—Tank's crony Pete. *Keller, Peter M.* was doing eight years for armed robbery. A handwritten note is scrawled across the top: *Highly malleable personality. Recommend for guard duty w. Lawson, Ellis H., a.k.a. Tank.*

When I think of Tank, I clench the paper so tight, it crumples. I debate whether to take the time to look for his file. Maybe if I knew something about him, I could protect myself better in the future. I look quickly through folders on the floor. When I can't find what I'm looking for, I move on to the folders on the chair and quickly shuffle through them, then move to the *L* file in the cabinet. His file isn't there, either.

I hate that I'm spending time on this and am about to leave the room to continue my search for more clues on Ken when I hear a loud whistling coming toward me from the hallway. I shrink against the wall, but the whistler soon passes. I can hear his heavy footsteps head down the stairs.

Curious, I slip out of the room and follow him. I make my way to the top of the stairs and catch a glimpse of the man as he trudges down the steps. He's tall, dressed in a suit, but wearing a Stetson hat and cowboy boots. When he hits the ground floor, the whistling stops and he disappears around the corner. I follow, slowly, keeping a distance between us. He vanishes into the room where Doc's voice was coming from earlier. The door closes. I make a dash for my examination room, freezing when I hear my name spoken in a gruff, authoritative voice, then Doc's slightly exhausted tone.

"That's what she said. . . . I checked in for today and already gave my general report."

"Did you sound the alert?"

"No. I wanted to tell you first. Should we detain her?"

"Let her in," the gruff voice responds.

"You know I can't do that. What about . . . ?" I don't hear what Doc says because a noise behind me takes me by surprise.

I turn to find Jacks motioning to me from the hall outside the door to my holding room. He opens his mouth in shock, then wider, as if to shout an alarm.

CHAPTER TEN

"What the hell are you doing?" he asks in a loud whisper, waving me to the door. "Get in here before they find you."

I pause for just a second before I hurry back to the room. Jacks shuts the door, his face scrunched. "You're covered in dust. Where did you go? You were supposed to stay here."

He looks at the knife I've been clutching the whole time.

"I'm not going to tell on you. Put that away."

I hesitate, then sheath it. I've got no choice now but to trust this guy.

"Quick, clean up before Doc comes in here."

He motions to the sink, where I quickly wash my face, the

dark material of my synth-suit hiding the rest of the dust.

"Where were you?" he asks.

"I told you. I'm looking for someone. I thought I could just take a quick look around to see if I could find him."

"And?"

"I found a disorganized file room. . . . Tried to look up Tank's file so I could find out what he did exactly, but it wasn't there."

"You could have just asked me."

"You were being pretty vague. . . ."

"I don't like to talk about it." Jacks looks down at the floor. "I have his file. If you promise not to wander off again, I'll let you read it."

"Why would you take Tank's file?" I ask. He looks at his feet but doesn't answer. "Can't you just tell me what's in it?"

He pauses. "He likes to hurt girls," he says, his face full of pain. Jacks takes a deep breath—and it feels as if he is sucking all the air out of the room.

"So, where'd you go, anyway?" I ask, trying to forget about Tank for a minute.

"A couple of guys were anxious for entry. It happens."

The lights flicker and I glance at the ceiling. "What's up with the electricity?" I ask.

"The electricity is powered by a diesel generator and only used for the perimeter wall . . . and the Warden's suite. The rest of Fort Black is dark."

"And you allow weapons inside?"

"Yeah . . . it's not like there are rules, really. People have to defend themselves."

He sits in a chair and stretches, allowing me to see that one wiry-muscled arm is patterned in tribal symbols surrounding a tree on his bicep, its roots hanging down his arm, reaching toward his hand. The other has a bright scene that is too cluttered to make out from where I sit, but I spot a bright gold ribbon that winds from his wrist and up his arm, disappearing under his sleeve and showing up again on his neck, peeking out of his collar.

I'm still trying to make out the tattoo, when I realize he's been speaking to me. My eyes snap up to his face. "Sorry, what?"

"How did you make it here?"

"I ran."

He crosses his arms. "Come on. You owe me. I could have had your ass out the door just then."

"That's true. Thanks."

"So?"

I think for a moment. How did I make it here? Because the Guardians taught me how to survive. But I can't talk about New Hope. For one thing, I don't know what would happen to me if I did.

I shrug. "Luck, I guess. Plus I'm fast. And smart."

Jacks laughs. "Are you sure you haven't been here before? You definitely talk the talk."

"Well, like you said. I've made it this far."

Jacks stands and goes to the counter. I tense, remembering the potassium chloride. I get ready to spring up and run for it, but Jacks just grabs a cup from the cabinet. He fills it with water from the tap and brings it to me.

"Uh, thanks," I say warily, but I'm starting to trust Jacks. When I had him pinned, he never tried to fight back. Instead he stayed cool and talked me down. He doesn't want to harm me. If he did, he could have told Pete to shoot me or let Tank have another crack at me.

"Well water. You get used to it."

I take a sip and wince at the rusty, metallic taste. As I force it down, the door bursts opens and Doc and the man in the Stetson hat walk into the room. The wannabe cowboy is in his midforties, and has dark hair and a well-kempt beard. His bushy eyebrows nearly meet the hat pulled low on his forehead.

"Hello again, Amy." Doc smiles thinly. "This is the Warden. He's come to welcome you to Fort Black."

"Hiya, Amy," the man says with a heavy Texan accent. "I hope my nephew has been taking good care of ya."

My eyes flick to Jacks in shock.

Jacks is the Warden's *nephew*?

Jacks's voice cuts through. "I have. As you can see, she's still human. There's no need to worry."

"Not yet . . . but it hasn't been the full twenty-four hours. It is important we take precautions," Doc says, not meeting my gaze.

The Warden, on the other hand, looks me up and down. "Well, Jacks has given his word to watch her for any change, and Doc says she's free of the Black Plague." He smiles, and for a moment I see his resemblance to Jacks. "If you have any trouble, you just let me know," he tells me. "We'll find you a place to stay if you want."

"I'm fine," I say quietly.

The Warden ignores my statement and looks over my shoulder to Jacks. "Jackson, you take care of this little girl, ya hear?"

I stifle an incredulous snort.

"Bye now." The Warden dips his hat to me and leaves, followed by Doc.

Once the door closes, I turn to Jacks, who's awkwardly avoiding my gaze. "Your uncle's the *Warden*?"

He shrugs and nods, looking down as if embarrassed.

I study him. He didn't tell Doc or the Warden about my disappearing act. He seems sincere, not guarded the way Rice always was when he was trying not to tell me the truth about New Hope and the Floraes.

"Look, if you're this hooked up, you must know how to get to this guy I'm looking for."

"I know some things," Jacks says. I look into his eyes. The intensity of the stare he gives me back makes me blush and look away. I can still feel his dark eyes on me.

"Well, maybe you know him. Ken Oh?"

He shrugs. "I've run across a couple of guys named Ken, I guess. Ken O, though? Like the initial *O*?"

I shake my head. "No, that's his last name, *O, h*. He's Japanese-American and might be working as a doctor or in a medical job."

He thinks for a minute, then shakes his head. "I don't know any Asian guys named Ken . . . and Doc's the only doctor I know of, and I'm his only help."

Frustration wells up. Suddenly an image of Baby strapped to a table flashes through my mind.

"Then I've got to look myself. Am I clear to go inside?"

"Almost." He stands and shakes his arms out. "Have a seat." I sit back down on the examination table. He opens a drawer and pulls something out, plugging it into the wall. I realize it's a tattoo gun. "I just have to mark you clean."

I think of the scar that Rice and Baby share on the back of their necks. They were marked as part of an experiment. I swallow. "I don't want a tattoo."

"Sorry, but if you want to come into Fort Black, you need the mark. It lets everyone else know you've been tested and you don't have the Pox."

"And what is that, exactly?"

"It's like the chicken pox, but you break out in black bumps. It's extremely contagious. You don't want to touch the victim at all, especially not any of their sores. They either die or get better. Only about half make it."

"Sounds fun," I mumble. "So this tattoo . . . Will it hurt?" I wince at my weakness. After all that's happened to me, why would a silly tattoo bother me so much?

Because it's not my choice. It's Fort Black's.

"It's not too bad, but you're going to have to take off those gloves."

I look at my hands. They aren't gloves. They're part of the synth-suit. I stretch down the fabric of my suit, the same as I did when Doc wanted to take my blood, freeing my arm through the neck hole. The material bounces back to my body, making it look like an off-the-shoulder spandex top.

I sigh and hold out my hand. "I suppose I must just screw my courage to the sticking place."

Jacks looks at me blankly. "What?"

"It's Shakespeare." Rice would have known Lady Macbeth's famous quote. "It just means I have to stay strong. My father loved to read Shakespeare. . . . I used to read a lot of his plays, for fun."

"Sounds like a laugh riot," he mumbles. "Here"–he holds my wrist gently–"it sort of feels like your skin is being scraped with a really dull knife. It only hurts a little."

Right. A little. I force a smile over the pain.

"What other tats do you do in here?"

"A lot. People like to look tough. And the women get tattoos once they're claimed. . . . They get their man's name on their arms to show they're under someone's protection."

"You're joking."

"Nope . . . There aren't a lot of women here. This used to be a men's prison, and last year a lot of the women died from some superflu that Doc couldn't cure. He came up with an immune booster and injected them all, but most of them died anyway. It's easiest for a woman to find a protector and keep safe."

"What about the Warden? Isn't he in charge? Shouldn't he protect people?"

"My uncle . . . He's just out for himself, really." Jack's tone changes yet again, and he shakes his head. "He keeps the walls guarded and has Doc keep track of the diseased, but he doesn't do anything to keep things peaceful. I think he likes people scared. It keeps them from realizing what the real problems are, like him. Only murderers get punished. Everything else is allowed to sort itself out. He doesn't protect anyone unless he sees an advantage to it."

"Charming." I'm seeing the Warden in a new light.

"All done!" Jacks removes the needle from the tattoo gun, throwing it away before placing the gun back in the drawer. I study my wrist: there's just a small black square. It didn't hurt that much. I place my arm back into the synth-suit, the material forming back against me like a second skin.

Jacks looks me over. "Hey, do you have any other clothes?

That skintight catsuit thing you have on now will get you a lot of unwanted attention."

I shake my head, crossing my arms over my chest. I know the suit leaves little to the imagination; I left the clothes I was forced to wear in the Ward where Kay dropped me, and my pack didn't have room for anything else.

"Well, walking around here with that on will make you a target." Jacks peels off his shirt, revealing more tattoos over a well-muscled chest and stomach. My face reddens when he catches me staring.

"Here, put this on for now."

Jacks hands me his shirt, which I pull over my head. It smells pleasantly worn. It's too large, but I tie it off at my waist, so I can still easily reach my gun and the knives sheathed on either thigh.

"I can lend you some sweatpants later if you want," Jacks offers, and I nod. I could always wear my synth-suit under my clothes. Part of the perks is that it seeps the sweat away from your body, keeps you dry and cool, and doesn't need to be washed. It was designed for long-term wear. Also, I'll feel safer with it on, in case I have to leave Fort Black in a hurry, or if I'm ever alone with Tank again.

"Are you going to keep those gloves on? It's pretty hot out-side."

I smile and hold up my hand and wiggle my black-clad fingers. "Not gloves . . . They're attached. . . . Or why wouldn't I have just taken them off when you tattooed my wrist?"

"I don't know. . . ." His face reddens. "I wasn't going to ask. . . ."

I can feel my own face heat up and wonder what's got-ten into me. "Here, look"—I pull up my hood and cover my face—"it's all one piece. The hood attaches to the neck with a Velcro-type fastener . . . except it's quiet." I don't know why I feel the need to babble.

He's staring at me with an amused look on his face. I pull my hood back down and stare at the floor. "Why don't we just go?" I say awkwardly.

Jacks nods and leads me down the corridor, opposite the stairs, back to where I first met Tank and Pete. Two different men are standing guard. I get the same leering reaction from them I got from Tank and Pete, though. So much for the cam-ouflaging magic of Jacks's shirt.

"This the fresh meat?" one calls to Jacks.

The other chimes in. "You'd better claim her fast, Jackson," he says, as if I'm not even there. "She looks sweet as pie."

I shudder and look at Jacks, who ignores them and opens the inner door for me. I hurry through, only to be brought up short by the bright sunlight. I shield my eyes as Jacks stops next to me. He turns and smiles grimly.

"Welcome to Fort Black."

CHAPTER ELEVEN

The first thing that hits me is the smell. The stench of unwashed bodies, of too many people and not enough space. Gagging, I put my hand over my nose and mouth.

"You'll get used to it," Jacks tells me. He grabs my hand.

"What are you doing?" I ask, pulling away from his grip.

"Trust me," he says, taking my hand again. "You don't want to look unclaimed."

I look at him for a moment, then let my hand relax in his as he leads me through the open yard, crowded by a maze of shacks made of plywood and cardboard, with a few tents mixed in. People live so closely here that even the fact that they're out in the open doesn't get rid of the stink—or maybe it's just the walls that keep the air oppressive and unmoving.

I try to place my feet on what little concrete is visible around the hovels, but there's barely any room to walk. I drop my hand from my face and force myself to start getting used to the smell.

"This was the exercise yard," Jacks explains. "It's where the people with no skills live, and the children with no parents."

"That's awful."

"No argument from me," he says grimly. We keep walking.

"Where do *you* live?"

"In the cells. That's what being the Warden's nephew gets you. That and my cushy job as Doc's assistant."

"But you don't know anything about medicine?"

"I've got the basics, enough to help Doc with his examinations. Mostly I take notes for him. Make sure he doesn't get hurt."

"So you're his bodyguard, too, then."

He shrugs. "Bodyguard, secretary, gofer," he says. "Pretty much whatever he needs."

A gunshot sounds from above and I flinch, involuntarily squeezing Jacks's hand tighter. "Probably a Florae outside," he says. "They try to shoot them before they reach the walls."

"The gunshots only bring more."

"This isn't exactly a quiet place," Jacks says. "They'll come anyway. But the walls keep them out." He's right. Fort Black must attract any Florae within a ten-mile radius. I start to ask why they don't use the crossbows, then answer the question myself, remembering how ineffective they'd been against the Floraes chasing the cyclist.

As I look around at the flimsy structures these people call home, I see a man shoot up out of a cardboard box. He collides with me. I barely feel the impact against my shoulder, but it knocks a *humph* from him and sends him staggering. He nearly goes down before scuttling away without a word or glance back at me. He's painfully thin—obviously malnourished—and the sharp stench he leaves behind him has me gagging again.

I shake my head, taking a look at the people around me. They're not all as bad off as that man, though, and some of them do turn their eyes to me as I pass—wide, frightened, desperate eyes.

They're just people, trying to survive. They don't want to create a perfect society or further the human race. They want protection from the Floraes, and given all that I know, maybe that's better than anything New Hope has to offer.

Jacks continues to pull me along, and I follow, clinging to

his hand. I need to find Ken, and Jacks can help me with that. Maybe I don't need to find out what else there is to know about this awful place. Jacks holds my arm as I leap over a pool of sewage. A man pushes by Jacks and stops dead in his tracks when he sees me. He's all sinew, gleaming black eyes and rotten teeth.

"Well, hi there," he says with a leer.

Jacks knifes between us. "She's mine," he says quietly, nose-to-nose with the man. Jacks's face has hardened into a mask. It's the same expression he wore when he spoke to Tank and Pete. The man with bad teeth doesn't argue and gives me one final glance before moving on.

"Yours?" I ask as we resume our trek through the chaos of the exercise yard, as if nothing had just happened.

"Listen, it's just how it works. I told you. Do you want a bunch of ex-cons fighting over who gets to own you?"

I shake my head. Subservience—even fake—doesn't come easy, but if it means my safety, I'll let people think that I "belong" to Jacks.

A child scurries by me, and I feel his small fingers brush over my hip and rest on my pack. I grab his arm and he looks at me, wide-eyed and innocent. He can't be much older than Baby, and my heart softens. I take a protein bar from my pack and give it to him. He scowls and runs away without a word.

Jacks watches this interaction with a strange expression I can't quite place. Does he approve, or is he thinking I'm weak?

"You have food?" he asks.

"Some . . . and a few other things."

"You're better off than a lot of these people. They have nothing to barter."

We continue to make our way through the pathetic shantytown. Emaciated children eye us warily through the holes in their boxes. Because of the crowds, progress is slow.

"What do they eat?"

"They grow mushrooms and edible flowers if they can find a few bare inches that get sun. A few—the brave ones, or the desperate ones—go outside the walls to gather berries and any other free-growing food they can find. Some catch rabbits and squirrels."

Despite myself, I cringe. I thought I was done eating squirrel.

"How big is Fort Black?" I ask, remembering when I asked Rice that same question about New Hope, and was shocked to learn almost four thousand people lived there.

"About two thousand people, all crammed into the space of six football fields. It's crowded, but it's better than being outside." He motions around him. "These walls are thick on both sides of us—they keep the Floraes out."

"So it's like a double wall?"

"Yeah, exactly. Here." He pulls me toward the side and up a flight of wooden stairs to the top of the wall. It's comparably empty here. A man stands with a rifle, surveying the empty expanse that is the world outside Fort Black. He glances at us and offers Jacks a curt nod. On the wall, Jacks leads me to the front so I can look out over the prison. As we walk, he explains that the corridor in between the two walls used to let the guards get from one end of the prison to another without going into the prison itself. It runs around the whole facility, three floors high. Most of the rooms in the wall, former offices, serve as guard quarters, handy for Florae control, just a flight of steps or two from the top of the wall.

Jacks stops suddenly and turns, motioning for me to look. I gasp. The entire prison is laid out before me. The front half is the exercise yard, which Jacks says people just call the Yard. It's about the length of a football field, a hundred yards or so, but squared, taking up the front half of the prison. From this vantage point, it's even more disturbing than it was walking through it. Desperate bodies everywhere. People are packed in so tight that even from up here it's hard to spot pavement.

Beyond the Yard are three large gray concrete buildings. "Cellblocks A, B, and C," he tells me, pointing each out in turn. "I live in the middle one there: Cellblock B."

"What's that?" I ask, pointing to a relatively empty area to the left of Cellblock A.

"That's the Arena. . . . You should avoid the Arena." He points to the opposite area on the other side, next to Cellblock C. Instead of an open area, it's occupied by another tall building, but this one is black. "And that used to be the cafeteria, library, and visiting center. . . . See how it's connected to the side wall? In the back is the parking garage, and visitors would check in, be escorted through the wall, and taken to the top floor. Prisoners would have to go through the bottom and three security checks before being brought to the visitor area."

I take it all in. "And what's in the back, past the buildings?"

"The Backyard . . . don't laugh. And don't go there, either. The corridor at the back and the rooms above it are blocked off now, used to quarantine people recovering from the Pox, and as a morgue. Doc took over almost all the offices in the front wall to keep track of who came and went, and to monitor their condition, trying to stop infections before they spread."

A man with a rifle walks past us, searching the horizon for Floraes. "And the guards will let me leave if I want to?

Anytime?" Once I get to Ken, we'll need to go straight to New Hope.

"Yup. Anytime. But you'd really choose hungry, flesh-eating creatures over a protected, walled complex?" He's looking at me as if I'm crazy. "I'd take a prison full of criminals over the Floraes any day."

"Yeah, well, you don't have a three-hundred-pound socio-path named Tank sweet on you," I say. Why would anyone stay here? But then, I have my sonic emitter, synth-suit, and Guardian gun, and I've been to trained to fight the Floraes. Any normal person would just want a place to escape Them. They would gladly trade the Floraes for a place with high walls, regardless of the people inside.

"What about you?" I ask. "Did you make your way here after all this started?"

"Actually, I was here when the infection broke out." He looks at me, but I remain motionless. "I had this great shop in downtown Amarillo—you should have seen it. At first I just loved that I could practice my art, but after a while I got sick of the local crowd. A lot of people don't understand that tattoos are more than just a thing people get when they're drunk or want to look like a rebel. They can tell a story. It's more than ink on skin; it's a window into a person's past. It's an art."

"So tattoos were your passion."

"They still are. At the time I wanted to study everything I could about the art. Different techniques and practices. I had the start to an amazing portfolio. I was supposed to study tattoo practices in the Pacific Islands. I had my plane ticket and everything. Then my uncle suggested I start by studying some prison tats and their meanings."

"Interesting form of research."

"I almost brushed him off and said I'd do it after my trip. But my uncle can be very convincing. He said I should come here first, talk to some of the prisoners. It was only an hour's drive, so I thought, why the hell not? I could visit him before I left the country and do some research. Kill two birds with one stone. I didn't know being here would save my life. It's like my uncle somehow knew what would happen. He was desperate to get me out here."

"Were you scared?"

"No . . . My uncle helped me out. Also everyone liked that I was a professional tattoo artist. Anyone with tattoos wants to show them off, especially if they let everyone know what a badass you are." He smiles. "I'm not going to say it wasn't tough at first, though. Everyone was scared of what was going on. Some guards went to go find their families. The Warden decided to let the prisoners out. He said anyone who wanted to leave could go. A lot ran."

"But they're dangerous criminals. . . ."

"Amy, it was the end of the world. The Warden said that the criminals weren't any more dangerous than the Floraes. And with everyone dead, who was left for them to hurt?"

"I was left out there. There are others. . . . Not many, but–"

"Look, my uncle isn't exactly a stand-up guy. . . . He knew the prison wasn't going to be getting any new food shipments. He thought he could get rid of some people. The problem was a lot of the worst criminals stayed. The ones who left were mostly in for petty crimes."

"Did they know the danger?"

"Some didn't want to believe it. People were saying aliens, others said zombies. Some of the prisoners thought it was bullshit, or maybe they just wanted out and thought they were bad enough or strong enough to survive. I went up the stairs and walked the top of the wall. I saw for myself. One by one the Floraes killed them.

"Except no one was calling them Floraes yet, just creatures. The monsters were everywhere. The guards tried to help, shooting to clear a way for people to escape, but it was no use. That's when we found out people could change if they were bitten. One guy started turning into a Florae while he was being fed on." He lowers his voice. "Some tried to get back in, but we couldn't let them. We were all so scared of the Floraes getting inside. It would have been a bloodbath. I haven't left the prison since I came here." He shrugged. "There's nothing for me out there anymore."

"The rest of your family?"

Jacks shakes his head, his face darkening. "My parents got divorced when I was little. My dad . . . He wasn't really around at the best of times. I mean, he'd send us money and call on our birthdays, but we never really saw him. My mom died just before the infection broke out. Cancer. My dad offered to take my sister, Layla, but I was eighteen, and wanted her to stay in the same house and school. So I became her legal guardian. . . . We got along really well. She was so excited for our trip. Thought it would be the best summer vacation ever. She thought she would come back and go into school the coolest ninth-grader because I agreed to let her get one tattoo."

"So she's here? Your sister?"

He shakes his head and looks down, his jaw tight. "She didn't survive Fort Black."

We're quiet for a moment, and I try not to imagine what it would be like to lose Baby forever.

"I'm so sorry. You have your uncle, though. Here."

"Yeah. Right." Jacks snaps back to the present and motions around us. "If you ever need to get out of the Yard fast, come up here to the wall. . . . There are stairs all along the perimeter now. They're new. Built a few years ago. That's why they're wood and not stone." I nod and continue to look down at the human chaos below.

My heart pounds against my chest as I look out at the crowd. It's so different from New Hope. So much more . . . free, unplanned. And frightening.

"So now I know the layout. . . . Tell me about the setup here. Prisoners, guards, and random survivors—all mixed together?" How would the guards cope with living side by side with men they were once in charge of?

Jacks nods. "Anyone good with a rifle becomes a guard now and gets to shoot Floraes all day."

"You said helping Doc was one of your jobs. Does that mean you also shoot Floraes?"

"No. I'd suck at that. My second job is still tattoo artist. Tattoos are in high demand," he tells me, perking up. "People trade food and clothes for them."

He points out a group of men below. They jump another man and run off with his half-eaten can of food.

"Survival of the fittest," he says.

"Well, I can protect myself," I say with a confidence I don't feel.

He studies me. "So where are you going to stay, after our twenty-four hours are up?"

"I'll figure it out."

"I've got space," he offers, not looking at me.

"I don't think so. Besides, I'm not staying. I'm just here to find–"

Suddenly I see a flash of white in the yard. A lab coat. The man wearing it has dark black hair. . . . It can't be Doc.

"That's him." I turn to Jacks. "That's Ken. Hey . . . *Ken*!" I yell.

"Amy–"

"It's got to be him. I'm going down there."

I can hear Jacks shouting behind me, but I've already broken into a run and am flying down the stairs.

Yet once I'm in the yard, I can't see anything. It's so

crowded, I can barely put my hand in front of my face. The noise of voices is deafening.

"Have you seen a guy in a white coat?" I ask. But no one will talk to me. Even the kids turn away.

And suddenly I feel hands on me and my arms are pinned behind me. Then everything goes black.

CHAPTER TWELVE

"Jacks!" My head is covered in a musty cloth. Several hands hold my arms. My legs go out from under me as I'm dragged. My legs bump against the hard ground as I'm pulled against the concrete. I scream at the top of my lungs, but no one does anything.

I'm shoved into something soft, a rotting cardboard box by the smell of it.

"Well, what have we here? Aren't *you* a tasty snack?" a voice rasps.

"I found her in the Yard. She's gotta be a newbie," responds the person holding my wrists in a death grip. "And a full pack, too? What goodies could be in here?"

"Let me go!" I yell, trying to wrench free. Someone pushes me down and puts their knee into my back. My mouth is full of dirty cloth, muffling my screams. Even with all my training, this is going to be tough to get out of.

I wrench my right shoulder up, trying to surprise my captives and break free. The man holding me falls to the side, and I roll around to my back, trying desperately to get to my feet. I'm not fast enough, and another pair of hands forces me back down, grabs my face, and presses it firmly into the hard ground.

I try to think beyond my fear. I lift my head to free my mouth. "Jacks has claimed me!" I spit, my mouth barely able to form the words. "I belong to Jacks!"

I can hear everyone go quiet. "Well, he's not here now, is he?" the raspy voice says at last.

"Let. Her. Go." It's Jacks. I've never been so glad to hear a voice in my life.

Immediately the vise-grip hands release from my arms, and I pull the makeshift hood from my head. Three dingy men surround me, their attention at the opening of their cardboard hovel.

"Sorry, man," one of them says. "She was by herself. Didn't see her tat that says your name. . . . Her arms are all covered up."

"I *said* I belonged to Jacks," I hiss, pushing myself up and scrambling toward him. I take his hand, squeezing it gratefully.

"Jacks, man, don't tell the Warden I messed with your girl. He'd toss me out."

Jacks pulls me toward him and embraces me in a half hug. Then he turns to them. "Stay away from her," he says, growling. "Don't let me catch you near her again."

He grabs my pack and we head back into the Yard. "What the hell is wrong here? Why didn't anyone help me?"

"Those people are too weak to help anyone. And the last thing they need is some guy with a grudge against them who'll remember them later. So everyone minds their own business."

"So people really are on their own," I whisper.

"Yeah. Which brings me to my point. You can't just take off like that. If you're looking for this guy, you need to be careful. Or else you'll end up dead." Jacks stares at me for a minute, his soft brown eyes studying my face. The look reminds me so much of the way Rice would gaze at me sometimes. There's concern in his face, and a warmth that makes me feel at ease. Then Jacks leans in and for an anxious moment, I don't know what to expect. But he wipes some of my attackers' filth off my face and smiles.

"Also, if you start turning into a Florae, I need to be here to kill you."

I exhale. "It's nice that you care," I reply with a smirk.

Jacks grins. "Seriously, I can help you. I can even protect you—as long as you don't do anything idiotic, like run into the Yard alone."

I nod. "Okay. That's a deal. But I do think I just saw the guy I'm looking for. Can you come with me to look?"

"If . . . and that's a huge if, that was him, he's long gone. Why don't you rest a little and think of a plan?"

"At your place?"

"Well. We can kick one of those kids out of their cardboard boxes, if you want."

I look out into the Yard. Someone at the end of the row yowls.

"Fine. I'll sleep on your floor for tonight."

"Oh, I've got an extra bunk. We're talking luxury."

With no other choices, I put my hand out for Jacks to take. If I want to find Ken, there's nothing to do but play the game.

Jack looks down with a faint smile as he takes my hand, and we make our way back through the crowds, I assume in the direction of his cell. Again, I'm horrified by the desperation in the eyes of the hungry.

"Can't anyone help these people?"

"Sometimes the Warden makes a show of giving them food," Jacks says. "He'll have the Scrappers throw them a dented can or two. They're all expired, but mostly they're still good."

I nod. "What's a Scrapper?"

"Someone who travels far outside the walls to find food and supplies." He steps over a rusty can, pointing it out to me.

"Thanks," I say, although I'm in no danger. A sharp can won't tear my synth-suit if a Florae's claws can't. But Jacks doesn't know that.

We're most of the way across the yard when another gunshot stops me in my tracks.

"Feels like the Wild West in here, doesn't it?" Jacks says, pulling me back into motion. "People are just left to sort things out for themselves."

"Yeah, or not sort them out."

"Right," he says. "Well, it makes things exciting. It's weird, but I sort of like it. I always wanted to be a cowboy when I was young. . . . It's a Texas thing, I guess." He chuckles at his childish admission.

We come to a heavy, open door in the center of a massive

gray building, the middle of three that rise past the shantytown of the exercise yard. The structure is built of cinder block and stone. The walls drip with condensation.

"This is our cellblock–B. It's the middle one. . . . Don't forget," Jacks says, pointing out the large *B* on the door as we walk through an entryway and into a sort of multileveled atrium surrounded on all sides by jail cells. Walkways soar above us, and the walls echo with voices. Garbage litters the floor: empty cans and broken pieces of plastic and debris. Most of the cells are open; the ones that are closed are secured with thick chains and padlocks.

Jacks points at the second floor. "I'm level two, number sixteen."

I follow him up the metal stairs to the second floor and down the walkway between the cells and the railing, stepping over shattered glass and around a discarded broken chair. I'm glad to see the cells are at least separated by solid walls instead of just bars. There will be that much privacy, anyway.

I'm passing the second cell down when a man with an ear-to-ear grin leans out like he's been waiting for me. "My, my," he says. "You anyone's yet, sweetheart?"

I lurch away against the side railing. I can see on his wrist, in large block letters, the word POX.

Again Jacks steps between us and stares the man down. Without Jacks having to say a word, the man steps back and fades away into his cell.

Jacks takes my hand and leads me quickly past more cells. His aggression unsettles me, but when he looks back at me, I see he's grinning. "Does it help if I don't actually say the words 'She's mine'?"

"Sort of." I offer him a small smile, but I don't feel any better. "Does he have the Pox?" I ask. "Why is he out here with everyone?"

"He had it and recovered. Now he's only contagious if he . . . well, exchanges bodily fluids with you. His tattoo lets everyone know so he doesn't accidentally infect someone."

I grimace as we reach Jacks's cell, the door held closed with a bike lock. He pulls a key out of his pocket. "I know this seems like a total suck-fest, but it'll be okay. One day at a time. And I have a feeling you'll find this Ken guy soon."

"Especially with your help," I say.

Jacks undoes the bike lock and pulls open the cell door. "Home sweet home," he says bleakly.

I walk into the dimly lit box. It's tiny, crowded even with its sparse contents—a set of bunk beds, a single chair, and a small table strewn with notebooks and sketch paper. The walls are covered with artwork, life drawings, and vibrant tattoo ideas. In one corner a sheet hangs from the ceiling. Jacks pulls it aside, revealing a small metal toilet and sink.

"You can wash up," he tells me, trying to place his art supplies into more organized piles. "There's no electricity in this building, not like in the wall, but at least the plumbing works." He hurries to the bunk beds and begins to clear papers off the top bunk.

"I'm okay for now," I tell him, though the fact is, I could definitely make use of the toilet, and I know I could stand to clean up. Maybe I'll get over my shyness later—I'd better—but for now, I'd rather wait until I'm alone in the cell.

There's barely room to walk, the cell is so crowded. Not knowing what else to do, I study his artwork. It's amazing—the colors in his intricate tattoo designs practically light the room, and the people he's sketched look as if they could step down from the walls . . . *Not* a good thing in one case.

"You drew Tank?" I ask, pointing to a sketch near the tiny window. He studies it with a pained look, then shrugs and almost snarls, "I draw what's around."

"You captured his look perfectly." Tank's eyes stare back at me from the drawing, a predator after his prey. I shudder.

"Maybe we can take that one down for now?"

"Sure." Jacks rips it from the wall and throws it on a stack of papers. "Sorry about the mess. I wasn't expecting to get a roommate."

"That's okay." I pick some more papers off the floor and put them on the table, trying to be of use. Shoved under the table are boxes of paints and paintbrushes.

"Where do you get all this?" I ask.

"From the Scrappers, in exchange for tattoo work," he tells me, breaking down an easel from the middle of the room. Just putting that aside makes me feel like I have room to breathe.

I turn back to the table and shuffle through the drawings. Jacks must have sketched half of the people at Fort Black, each one of them so lifelike, I almost expect them to blink at me. I can't stop looking at them. My eyes are drawn to maybe the hundredth sketch. The man's face looks familiar. His features are delicate, almost pretty for a guy. Other than a heart-shaped mole on his left cheek, he seems like someone I should know. I pick up the drawing.

And then I realize why I recognize him. He looks familiar because he looks like Kay.

CHAPTER THIRTEEN

I twirl around. "Who is this?"

Jacks takes the sketch. "I'm not sure. . . . This is a pretty old drawing."

"I think that's Ken."

"You think?" he asks, confused. "You mean you don't know what Ken *looks* like?"

"No, his sister told me to find him, and this guy's practically her twin."

"Oh," he says. "I thought this Ken guy was your man or something."

I feel myself blush. "No, nothing like that." I've only told him I want to find Ken—not why. And I'm not ready to do that yet. "My friend Kay thought he could help me with something." I reach for the drawing and Jacks gives it back to me. "Maybe I can show this to people?"

"Well, you saw how eager everyone in this place is to help."

"But I can try."

Jacks leans against the bars and crosses his arms. "This really means a lot to you? Why?"

"It's my sister. She's—" I stop myself. I can't let on about my connection to New Hope. "She's in trouble and Ken can help."

"You have a sister?" he asks, surprised. "Who is alive?"

"Yes," I say quickly. "Not biological, though. I found her after everyone else died. She was a toddler, wandering around in a supermarket. But we're very close. We may as well be sisters."

Jacks is quiet for a moment. I can't read the look on his face.

"So you let yourself get attached to someone weak," he says, his attitude suddenly fierce. "And you let her get hurt. Not exactly smart."

"Excuse me?" I'm surprised by his dramatic change in demeanor. "I protected her for years," I snap defensively. "And I'll save her again. Like you saved me today, when you rescued me from that guy in the yard." I look away. "Why are you looking after me, anyway?"

"It's my job to make sure you don't turn into a Florae, remember? I've got potassium chloride duty."

"You didn't have to offer to watch out for me."

"Maybe you remind me of someone. Someone who needed protection and didn't make it." The tone in his voice tells me not to ask any further questions, but it didn't need saying. He's talking about his sister, Layla.

Jacks crosses the cell and clears off the top bunk, then throws up a pillow and an old sheet. "I need to get some sleep."

"I could sleep some too," I say. Like, for a week. I'm exhausted.

I also have to use the bathroom. Jacks catches me eyeing the toilet.

"Okay," he tells me, moving to the cell door and stepping outside. He turns and shuts it, then locks the bike lock. I feel a flash of panic before he tosses a key to me through the bars in the door. "I'll give you some privacy," he says. "Should, um, fifteen minutes do it?" he asks.

I nod, relieved I'll get some alone time. I look around the hastily rearranged room, packed to the brim with art supplies. I should probably look for something that would tell me more about Jacks, but he has so much stuff, I wouldn't know where to begin. I clean up in the bathroom area, then sit on the bed and think about how I can find Ken. How much can I trust Jacks?

When he comes back, I'm waiting in my bed, and I unlock the bike lock for him, then climb back up in my bunk. He shuts the door and relocks it, then hands me the key.

"This is my spare. You can keep it, just in case," he tells me with a shrug, then starts getting ready for bed.

I stare at the ceiling as Jacks settles in on the bottom bunk. Nice as he's been to me, I take my knife and hold it again with the hilt to my chest. Like Jacks said: *Just in case.*

I feel like I've barely closed my eyes when I awaken to a series of gunshots. I fly off the top bunk, crouching low on the floor, knife held in front of me.

"Holy shit!" It's dark in the cell, but there's just enough murky light to see Jacks staring at me, wide-eyed, from his bunk. "Amy, what the hell?"

"I heard gunshots."

"Oh. It's just the guards." He rolls over and puts the pillow over his head. "Look out the window," his muffled voice instructs.

I go to the window. I must have been asleep longer than I thought; it's already nighttime. The darkness is cut by bright beams of light streaking across the sky. More gunshots ring out.

"What are they doing?"

"Fishing," he says again. When I look back at him, I find him peeking out from under his pillow. "They do it once a week to help out the Scrappers." He sits up and rubs his face. "They bait all the Floraes to the prison and shoot them, leaving the surrounding area clear."

I look back down to the exercise yard, which is filled with a warm glow. "What's that light? I thought there was no electricity in most of the prison."

"Candles."

I think of all that cardboard and plywood. "Isn't that a fire hazard?"

"Yeah, there was a fire last year." Then, almost in a whisper: "A lot of people died."

"And what was done so it won't happen again?"

"Nothing," he says after a long time. He lies down again. "I'm going back to sleep."

I climb back up to the top bunk.

"Does the knife make you feel better?" he asks through the mattress between us.

"A little bit," I admit.

"Just don't kill me in my sleep."

"I'll try not to," I say. "No promises."

He lets out a small huff of a laugh, and I can't help but smile.

I try to go back to sleep, but just when I think they've finally stopped, gunshots crack the night again. How does anyone sleep here? Eventually I sheathe my knife and remove my gun holster, trying to get more comfortable. I make sure the safety is on and place my gun under my pillow, for easy access.

It can't protect me from my memories, though: When I do drop off again, I dream of the Ward.

Dr. Reynolds's face hovers over me. He licks his lips, his eyes lit by pure evil joy. "Let's begin," he says.

The pain blasts through me like a lightning bolt, and my entire body seizes. Every nerve, every synapse is on fire. I am burning from the inside out. I bite down on the piece of leather in my mouth, wishing I were dead, that the excruciating agony would stop. I wait to lose consciousness, but the pain continues, burning my nerves and melting my skin.

At last I wake in a cold sweat, clutching my gun desperately. I can hear Jacks's steady breathing below me. I roll onto my back and close my eyes.

I am not in the Ward. I am not in New Hope. I'm in a

prison, but I'm not trapped.

Or am I?

I think about Rice. His piercing blue eyes filled with kindness but often covered with his shaggy blond hair. What would he think of Fort Black, of Jacks? Not much, probably. Rice is so smart and Jacks is . . . well, Jacks is Jacks. Hard but still kind. At least they'd have that in common. Rice just wanted to protect me. And, what's more, he promised to watch over Baby.

My heart aches as I think of my sister. Kay's words echo hauntingly in my mind.

Dr. Reynolds has Baby.

I shouldn't even be sleeping—I don't have the time. Yet I can barely move. As I drift off, I make Baby a promise:

Tomorrow I'll find Ken. And we'll get you out of there.

CHAPTER FOURTEEN

Someone shakes me awake and I dart up, my legs dangling off the side of the top bunk. Jacks is looking up at me, his arm resting on the bed, not quite touching my leg. Light streams in through the tiny window.

"Is it morning?" I ask.

"Afternoon. It's been almost two days."

"What?" I rub my hands over my face. "Two days?" How could I have let myself sleep for so long?

I move to get down from the bed, but my muscles ache from disuse. I didn't know I was this exhausted, but it makes sense. I hadn't slept for days before setting out on my twenty-mile trek to Fort Black. How often had I even stopped to rest?

Jacks tilts his head. I can see the tattoo of the snake, where it peeks out from under his collar and winds around his neck. "You were having nightmares. Whimpering in your sleep. I was almost afraid to leave you when I went to work yesterday, but Doc said that your body needed rest. That's why you shut down." He hands me a fork and a can of baked beans. "I thought you should eat."

"Thanks."

I'm ravenous. I pull the can tab, my mouth watering at the sweet, tangy smell, and begin to shovel the beans into my mouth. Every bite is delicious.

Jacks takes a step back and sits at the small table. The room looks a little less messy today. Although the walls are still covered with sketches, the floor has been cleared up.

I pause midbite. "Where's my pack?"

"Here." He retrieves it from under the bed and tosses it up to me. "I didn't look in it or anything."

I put down the can and quickly check. Nothing missing. The emitter is safe. Its battery is dead, so I switch it off and quickly close the bag. I'll have to remember to charge it. It's solar-powered, so I'll just need to place it in the window during the day.

I go back to my beans and begin to eat, more slowly this time. "Sorry," I say. "I didn't mean to accuse you or anything. I see you've cleaned up."

"Yeah, it's good you slept so long. It took me awhile."

I think of Baby again, my stomach turning. I hate myself for wasting so much time.

"Well," I say, "I've got to get out there. Ken's not coming to me."

"Wait." His tone surprises me—almost nervous. I glance up, and we lock eyes for a moment. "I got you something."

Jacks picks up a large book from the table and hands it to me.

I touch the smooth, worn cover. "*The Complete Works of William Shakespeare*," I mumble. I open it and thumb through the pages, stopping at one of my father's favorite plays, *The Tempest*. My eyes catch a line that gives me chills. *"Hell is empty and all the devils are here."*

I close the book and stare at the cover, desperately trying not to cry.

"Thanks," I manage, shaken by my conflicting emotions of happiness and fear. Love and heartache. "Where did you find this?"

"The prison library. Well, it's not the library anymore—

people live in there—but all the books are just stacked against the wall. You sounded really sad when you told me that line. I didn't know it, so I asked the old dude who used to be the librarian. He showed me the book and which pages to read."

"You read *Macbeth*?"

"Well, I do know how to *read*," he tells me with a hint of a smirk. I look over, thinking I might have hurt his feelings, but he's impossible to decipher. "Anyway, I thought it would remind you of your dad. I know"—he pauses and looks out the window—"it's good to have reminders. That's all."

I stare at the cover again. "I love it. Thank you."

"No problem. I should probably admit that I read that part about courage, but then I gave up. It's kind of hard to understand."

I nod. I'm anxious to go start looking for Ken, but I know that I owe Jacks. "It really isn't that difficult if you concentrate. I'll show you."

His eyes slide toward me and I think he's going to say something light. But then he gets up and climbs next to me on the bed. He's so close to me that for a moment I'm paralyzed. After being alone for so long, it's nice to have someone close to me, someone who isn't trying to hurt me. I'd forgotten how good that can feel. His arm brushes mine and my skin burns under my synth-suit. After a few long seconds I adjust my position and move away. If there's one thing I can't afford right now, it's to get close to someone else.

I start to read aloud, and for a tiny moment I forget where I am. I forget New Hope and the Ward. I forget about finding Ken and being in Fort Black. I allow myself to forget everything . . . everything but Baby.

I could never forget Baby.

After a few minutes I stop and Jacks gets off the bed.

"We should continue this later," he says. "I need to go to work and you should rest some more."

I've been sleeping for two days. What I need now is a plan of action. "No more resting. I'm going to look for Ken."

"Sorry, you'll need to stay here, in the cell," Jacks says apologetically. "Just for a while. I can't take you with me to work and if I don't do my hours, I lose this palace you've been lounging in . . . no matter whose nephew I am."

I stare at him. "I'm not actually a prisoner. I can leave if I want."

"It's not safe for you to walk around without me. Not until word gets out that you're with me."

I nod. I understand, but I hate that he's locking me up again, even if I have a key. I know I can't go out in Fort Black without him. I don't even want to risk it. He clanks the door shut apologetically and disappears.

Before he leaves, he pauses in the entryway. "I left something for you . . . on the table," he tells me, staring at the floor. "You should know what you're up against."

I rush to the table, thinking he has info on Baby or Ken, but the file is about one person: Ellis Lawson. Tank. Deflated, I open it and look at the first page; there's no mistaking that hard face staring back at me from his mug shot with a creepy, crooked smirk.

I skim through the pages, then start back at the beginning and read through each page one by one.

The second page is an information sheet on his crimes. Sentenced to sixty years to life for the disappearances of two teenaged girls, one seventeen, one fifteen, both of whose bodies were never found.

Next is a court transcript. Testimonial, Daniel Nahon, ten years old:

I threw the Frisbee far, past the trees, and Cordy went to grab it. She was taking a long time, so I followed and saw a big man pulling her by the neck into a green car. I ran at them and shouted, but the man just looked at me. He put his hand to his neck and pulled it across, like he was going to cut off my head if I didn't shut up. But he had Cordy, so I yelled louder and ran after the car as he drove away. Then I found a policeman in the park and told him what had happened.

I close my eyes, sickened. What a thing for a little boy to witness. A kid just a few years older than Baby. The girl just a few years younger than myself. What happened to her? The body wasn't found. No coroner's report to read.

Then there's a newspaper article in with the papers, dated the year I started high school.

Ellis Lawson was convicted today of the murders of Cordelia Embry and Jasmine Norman. Though their bodies were not found, there was eyewitness testimony, and DNA evidence was found in Lawson's house. Lawson is suspected of abducting three other girls, but the district attorney did not have sufficient evidence to charge Lawson with those crimes. The families of the girls have pleaded with Lawson to reveal the location of the bodies, but Lawson asserts his innocence. There will be a memorial service for Cordelia Embry at Harrison's Funeral Home on Tuesday at two p.m.

So Tank was caught, seen snatching one girl, and convicted of murdering her and another, but he was smart enough to hide the bodies. How many other missing girls was he responsible for, ones that the cops didn't know about? Tank isn't just a dumb brute; he's a serial killer.

A bit of handwritten ink catches my eye. *Lacking almost any moral fiber, can be used for a vast array of tasks.* I fold up the papers with a shudder and shove them under my pillow.

In the After, even a serial killer can get a job.

I pace the cell, anxious for Jacks to get back. Even though I know why I should stay here, I just can't. I grab the drawing of the man I believe is Ken, pull out my key, and head toward the door.

Just as I'm about to open the lock and let myself out, I hear a voice. "Hey!" I look up to find a petite, slim woman staring at me through the cell door. "Do you know when Jacks will be back?"

"Soon, hopefully. He's at work."

"Oh." She reaches for a crossbar and leans against the cell door, revealing a tattoo running up her forearm that reads MAD MIKE's in purple graffiti letters. "I wanted to talk to him about getting my man another tat, as a present."

I step closer. She's in her early forties, at least, her

shoulder-length hair a mixture of black and gray. "I can let him know you stopped by."

"Sure. Mike and I are right next door." She motions with her head to the cell to the left. "I'm Pam." She holds her hand through the cell bars and I shake it gingerly. My hands aren't massive, but hers feel like a child's. "To be honest, I've been dying to find out about you. . . . Word got out pretty quickly that Jacks claimed a girl full of hellfire."

She grins at me.

"Um, thanks."

"Jacks is a good man. You've got quite a catch there."

I laugh uncomfortably. The idea of me "belonging" to a man is weird enough, but me "catching" one is just ridiculous. The only other guy I've ever had feelings for is Rice. Of course, with him, things were tricky. He lied to me, for one thing. Even if it was for my own protection.

And then there was that kiss.

". . . Jacks," Pam is saying.

"I'm sorry, what?"

"I was just saying you're lucky to have Jacks."

"And what makes him such a good protector?" I ask.

"Well, the boy can fight like the devil. But really, he's got the connections. Everyone knows Jacks. The Warden takes care of him. Doc takes care of him." She laughs lightly.

"Also, people don't want to mess with the only tattoo artist in all of Fort Black. If anyone got into it with Jacks, he'd have half of the population of Fort Black on them. Everyone here loves their tats."

"What they lack in common decency, they make up for with a love of tattoos," I say, meaning for it to be a joke but sounding cold. Pam's face drops. "Sorry," I say. "Except for Jacks, people haven't been exactly welcoming."

"It's okay. It's hard here. I heard you just found Fort Black. You were out there for so long, poor thing." She backs away. "Just tell Jacks to find me. I'm going to deliver some sewing now, but I'll be back soon."

"Hey, can I come with you?" I feel I'll be safe with this woman. She seems like a veteran. Besides, if I befriend her, I can find out more about Fort Black.

"Sure." She nods. "I'd like that."

I grab my Guardian gun from under my pillow and place it in its holster, then check that my knives are in place—one on each thigh. I throw on one of Jacks's T-shirts and a pair of his shorts. I'm sure I look strange, like I'm wearing black gloves and tights under my clothes, but I don't care. I need all the protection I can get in this place.

I unlock the cell door with the key Jacks gave me and step out into the hall. Pam walks to her cell and grabs a basket of clothing, locking her door with a giant padlock.

"Is that how you make a living?" I ask, locking my door and walking toward the stairs, past the other cells. "Sewing?"

"Yeah, Mike is a guard. A Florae sniper, mainly, up on the wall. That gets us our accommodation. The sewing just brings in a bit extra."

"Was he a guard here Before?"

"Nope, a convict. Armed robbery." She tells me this casually. "I was his defense attorney."

"And you got together . . . how?" I ask, trying not to sound shocked.

She smiles. "Oh, he was always flirting with me. He swore up and down that he wasn't guilty, told me I was beautiful and amazing and was sure to get him out. It didn't go anywhere, of course. How could it? It was a different world then and I was his attorney, not to mention married. Plus I knew enough to be wary of cons. *All* of them are innocent, I reminded myself, and every one of them thinks any woman they see in here is beautiful and amazing. If they're lucky enough to see any at all!" She laughs boisterously at her own joke, the lively sound bouncing through the cellblock.

The loudness makes me uncomfortable. I glance back down the walkway and spot a figure lingering by my cell door. It's not big enough to be Tank, but a surge of alarm runs through me. Could it be Ken? Maybe Kay was able to contact him and tell him I was here. I take a step back toward the cell, but Pam puts her hand on my arm to stop me.

The figure approaches us and I shrink at the man's leer. He's not Ken. He's just another creepy man. He's so dirty, I can't tell the color of his skin. He brushes past us a little too closely. Pam steps aside, pushing me against the railing. My skin tingles as he sweeps by, my muscles tensed and ready. He doesn't do anything but look, though, and is soon gone.

Pam leans in. "Sometimes it's better just to get out of their way," she tells me. "Some men are just plain mean." She takes in my apprehension and adds, "But not all. Not my Mike. Not Jacks. You'll learn how it is here." She resumes her walk and motions for me to follow.

"You've been here the whole time," I ask, catching up.

"I was here when the infection broke out," she says, "meeting another client. The prison went on lockdown and by the time the guards told me I could leave, the news was so grim. I couldn't get ahold of my husband, so it was obvious that he—well. So I decided to stay." She shifts her load onto her other hip.

"When they let the prisoners out, Mike came and found me. He protected me from a lot of bad things that could have happened." She looks at me, a soft expression on her face. "I love him for that."

"So . . . was he innocent?"

She laughs. "Hell no. Even when I was his attorney, I knew he'd done it. I guess holding up a liquor store doesn't automatically make you a bad person."

I smile. "I guess not."

I like how talkative Pam is being. I'm sure I can get a lot of information out of her if I just let her ramble on. She's paused in her story. I see my opportunity to ask her what I really want to know.

"Do you ever do sewing for a man named Ken?"

"Ken Gibbons?" Pam asks. "Big Hispanic guy who goes by Yaya?"

"Um, no . . . this Ken is Asian."

"There's an Asian family who lives in the Yard. Actually, I don't know if they're a family. There are five guys who share a tent. . . . They're all Filipino, and they have complicated foreign names, but one might use Ken for short."

Ken isn't Filipino, and I doubt he'd be living in a tent in the exercise yard.

"I have a picture." I yank the sketch out, holding it up.

Pam looks for a moment, then shakes her head. "You sure he's alive?"

"No," I admit. "But if he is alive, I really need to find him."

"I can keep my eye out. But people die here like that." She snaps her fingers. "I came close last year. Mike saved me." We walk up the stairs toward the third floor as Pam continues. "Doc was telling some BS story about how the women needed an extra shot, a vitamin shot or something. I told Mike that I'd seen enough people perjure themselves to tell when something was fishy. Mike stood up for me when I refused, made sure Doc didn't give me a hard time. I'm one of the few women who made it through."

"What do you mean? I thought the shot was an inoculation."

She looks me over. "Now, you don't look like the kind of girl who believes everything you're told. Did you let Doc give you a shot?"

I shake my head and she nods in approval. "It will be hard to stay away from Doc, Jacks being who he is and all, but you should try. I don't trust him."

"You think Doc had something to do with the women dying?"

"I can't say for sure," Pam tells me, stopping on the stairs, "but there's something off about him. Mike told me he makes the Scrappers give him almost all the drugs that they find. A lot of them have a second stash they keep hidden to bring in for the rest of us."

"Um . . . he *is* a doctor," I say. "Doesn't he need those drugs?"

"Well . . ." She shuffles around, muttering. "I think he self-medicates."

I nod. Everyone has to deal with the After in their own way.

"I see him sometimes," Pam continues, "talking to himself like there's someone else there."

"I've heard him do that too," I admit. "When I first got here, I heard him rattling off about who needed flu shots, like he was talking to someone. But a lot of people talk to themselves. He didn't seem sinister to me, just a little strange." Although he did give me the creeps when I first met him. I try to fight off my paranoia. Doc doesn't have to be evil—he could just be incompetent.

"Well, I wouldn't be surprised if he loses it one day."

Pam pauses at the railing, looking down at the rows of

cells. "There's another thing," she whispers. "My friend Anna, who used to live on the first floor, told me that after the birth of her child, he tried to convince her to leave Fort Black, go to some place up north. Some kind of colony."

"What?" I grip the railing in surprise. *New Hope?*

"Did she go?"

Pam shakes her head. "She didn't get the chance. The next week Anna and her child were both dead."

"I'm sorry," I tell her.

"It's okay," Pam says, starting up the stairs again. "You learn to live with loss." I pause before joining her, wondering. *What is going on here? Is Doc working with Dr. Reynolds?*

I turn and quickly follow Pam through the door onto the third floor, where she stops at a darkened cell and softly calls in, "Sewing!"

Inside are two sets of bunk beds with barely room to walk between them. A figure rests in each bed. A young man in one of the bottom bunks sits up.

"Hey, Pam," he calls, getting sleepily out of bed and shuffling to the door. Pam hands him a small, neatly folded pile of shirts. The young man takes them, staring at me. I wait, uncomfortably.

Finally Pam speaks up. "So we agreed on a can of corn and

two cans of peas . . . ," she gently reminds him.

"Right." He goes to the foot of his bed and grabs a back-pack. He puts the laundry inside and takes out the cans, returns to the doorway, and hands them to Pam, who puts them in her basket. "Who's your friend?" he asks, staring intently at my face. His eyes flit to my arm, covered by my synth-suit.

"She belongs to Jacks."

"Oh," he says, his face falling. Then a scared look comes over his face. "I–I didn't know."

"It's okay. I won't tell him." Without another glance in my direction, he heads back to his bed and flops down.

When we've moved on, I ask, "Is he that scared of Jacks?"

"Yes and no. He's more scared of Jacks's connections." I'm starting to wonder if people will think I belong to Jacks, or to the Warden. "Poor kid," Pam is saying. "There aren't enough women to go around, and he's one of the nice guys. He and his roommates are the ones who remove garbage from Fort Black and dump it outside."

"So there are four people living in that one room?" A cell seems hardly big enough for one person, much less four.

She shakes her head. "Not four, twelve. They sleep in eight-hour shifts."

"And Jacks has his room all to himself, all the time?" I

hadn't realized how well off Jacks was due to his relation to the Warden.

"Like I said, he's a catch." Pam winks at me.

Our footsteps rattle on the iron-grid walkway. Our next stop is a cell down the hall, a man with two older boys. One sits in the corner, playing with a deck of cards. The other lies in bed, a wet washcloth across his eyes. I stay in the doorway while Pam steps inside.

"Do you know what it is?" Pam asks the man.

The man shakes his head sadly. "Doc said it could be some new form of pink eye. He might not be able to see again."

Pam hands him a bundle of clothes. "On the house," Pam tells him.

The man steps over to her and hugs her. "Thanks, Pammy."

"They've had some hard times," Pam tells me when we resume walking down the hall. "He was a prison pencil pusher. That man managed to leave Fort Black, get his boys, and make it back without a scratch on either of them. . . . His wife wasn't so lucky."

We next stop at a cell with a red curtain covering the bars, blocking our view of inside. A handbell is attached to the door with a wire, and Pam rings it. A woman appears, sweeping the curtain aside dramatically. She wears a pink bathrobe and way too much eye shadow.

"How's business?" Pam asks her with a smile.

"Slow." The woman yawns. "It'll pick up after first shift."

Pam hands her a bundle. On top is a lacy black bra. She takes her clothes and gives Pam a small package. "There's Vicodin there, for your man's back. I asked the Scrappers specifically to look out for more and make sure Doc doesn't snatch it all up."

"Thanks." Pam puts the medication in her basket. As we walk away, Pam tells me, "She's always bringing me ripped clothes."

"So she's a . . ."

"Yep. She practices the oldest profession."

I shake my head at how Pam just tosses this off. "How can you be so comfortable here? It's remarkable. You seem to be thriving, not stuck pining for your life as an attorney Before. Doesn't it bother you to throw aside all your training and experience?"

She shrugs. "I used to be a lawyer and now I mend clothing for a prostitute. I know it sounds so weird. And I have lost a lot that I'm sad about. But here, well, at least I'm alive," she tells me with a smile. "My grandma taught me to sew and I always thought it was so pointless, since I could just buy anything new I needed. Now there isn't a day that goes by I'm not grateful she took the time to teach–" She stops dead in her tracks, her face full of fear. "Let's go," she tells me, wheeling around and heading back the way we came.

"Why?" I have to trot to keep up with her. "What's wrong?"

She motions back to a black sheet hanging on the door of a cell. "Black Pox. That's a new infection. We don't want to get too close."

"Could we catch it from out here?"

"Probably not, but I don't want to take any chances." We're most of the way back down the hall. "There are people who already have had the Pox who deal with the infected. Someone will come later and remove them to the back wall."

"What about until then?" I ask. "Are they getting food and water?"

"Don't worry about it," she tells me. "They'll get better or they won't. We can't do anything."

We walk back to Jacks's cell in silence. I wonder how Pam can be so kind to that man with the sick son and so cold to someone else, alone and dying. But by now, I know the answer: People do what they have to in order to survive.

Before we say good-bye, Pam leans in and whispers, "Maybe don't mention to Jacks what I told you about Doc. It's a touchy subject for him."

"Sure. But why?" I ask, uncertain. Is he so attached to his boss?

"You know"—she widens her eyes—"because Doc is Jacks's father and all. Jacks is really sensitive about Doc's addiction."

"Oh!" I nod, stunned. Suddenly it all clicks into place. Jacks isn't just connected through his uncle, the Warden, but through Doc as well. That must be why he's Doc's assistant, even though he has no medical background.

"It's not exactly common knowledge," Pam continues. "I think Jacks wants to keep it hush-hush . . . but, you know, I hear things. It's not like these bars are exactly soundproof. Jacks used to talk to his sister about it . . . about forgiving Doc for whatever wrong he had done to them way back when."

"You knew Jacks's sister? What was she like?"

Pam's face falls. "She was a sweet girl. Too good for this place. Me, I can adapt. I learned to lose my educated facade." Her voice becomes louder, more coarse. "And act like I ain't never lernt nuthin' from no books." She smiles, slipping back into her normal voice. "But that girl was never going to make it here. Jacks did what he could, and of course she had the

Warden and Doc looking out for her, but you can't expect to make someone like that happy in a cage."

She looks me up and down. "I don't think you'll be happy in a cage either. . . . But you won't let it come to that, will you? You won't lock yourself up in that cell and refuse to face the world. No, I think you'll do just fine here. Let Jacks take care of you, and make sure to take care of yourself."

"I will," I tell her, unlocking the bike lock and stepping inside. "Bye."

I pace the room, opening and closing my fists with impatience. I need to talk to Jacks. Why wouldn't he just tell me that Doc is his father? Unless Doc really is working for Dr. Reynolds and Jacks is in on it too, charged with keeping an eye on me. I don't want to believe it, but I can't force the dark thoughts from my mind.

How much can I really trust Jacks? Here I am, stuck in a horrible place with no end in sight. Another day is almost gone, and I'm no closer to getting back to Baby. I gaze out over the exercise yard, the mess of crude shelters littered across the muddy concrete. People mill in and out of the shacks, trading for food, fighting, and surviving.

This is their home—probably the only one they'll ever know now. But where is mine? I thought I'd found one in New Hope with my mother, but instead I almost ended up dead. The fact is, I have no home. Not until I can get Baby and take her to a safe place . . . wherever that may be.

"Hey, you." A voice cuts through the cell.

I turn to find the man I saw lingering earlier, the one covered in dirt who brushed past me and Pam on the walkway.

"What do you want?" I ask, my heart racing, glad for the bars that separate us.

"I heard you asking Pam about Ken." He leans in, his grimy face pushing through the bars. "I can take you to him."

I take a step back before I remember there's a locked door between him and me. I try to make my voice sound strong. "Why should I trust you?"

"Jacks sent me. He said you was to come right away or Ken would be gone."

I try not to let my desperation decide for me. What if he is lying? Why wouldn't Jacks come himself? I look at the man again. He's small and thin. I could easily take him in a fight. I take a deep breath. I can't let my fear get in the way of finding Ken.

"Back up," I tell the man. He steps away from the bars and I unlock the bike lock. As I pull open the bars, he rushes forward. But I am ready for something like this.

I step aside and trip him. He falls forward into the room but gets to his feet surprisingly fast. He turns and lunges at me, leading with his shoulder, trying to take me out with brute strength. I move out of his way, but in the small room, space is tight. I hit the bunk bed at full force, my hip crashing into the hard metal frame. The man pulls me to the floor, yanking at my synth-suit, leaving my arms free. I grab one of my knives and hold it up to his throat.

His hands go still. "I didn't mean nuthin' by it." He grins at me, as though he hadn't just attacked me. I push up on the knife, forcing him to lean back, then scramble out from under him. He tries to flee, but I grab his filthy hair and once again hold the knife to his neck.

"Some people was saying that you really ain't Jacks's. That you was looking for a man. That you was fair game."

I push the knife into his skin, and a small trickle of blood runs down his grubby neck to stain his collar. "You tell people that it doesn't matter if I belong to Jacks. I don't need him or the Warden to protect me. I can take care of myself."

I kick him out the cell door into the walkway. He scurries to his feet and down the hall. I take a deep, shaky breath and sheathe my knife. I turn and sit on the bottom bunk, resting my head in my hands. It was a long shot, but I'd hoped the man was telling the truth and could take me to Ken. I let out a sharp bark of a laugh at my foolishness and rub my face. I stay like this for a good long while, until I hear a voice at the door.

"Amy. You're awake."

My head jerks up as Jacks steps into the cell, clicking the bike lock shut after him. "You really should keep this door locked."

"Sorry," I say, breathing hard. I make a quick decision not to tell him what just happened. Even though I took care of it myself, I don't want him to think he needs to protect me all the time. "I was just walking around with Pam."

"Without me?" He looks upset.

"We survived. She wants you to do a tattoo for Mike."

"Still, you should have waited. After what happened before . . ."

I bristle at the memory. I shouldn't have needed Jacks to come save me. I didn't need him just now. I know I can take care of myself.

"I don't have time to wait," I snap. His possessiveness annoys me. "Anyway." I stand to confront him. "Pam doesn't know Ken, but she told me something, about Doc." I study him.

"What about Doc?" he asks carefully.

I don't answer but instead stare him down. He holds my

gaze for a moment but then drops his.

"Is it true? Doc's your father?"

"Yes." He takes a seat in a chair and motions to me to sit again. "And I'm sorry I didn't tell you. . . . I don't really talk about it, though. Doc wasn't ever really a father to me. My mom and he got divorced when I was just a little kid. I didn't know why then, but my father had issues with chemical dependency. He got fired for stealing drugs from the hospital where he worked. He couldn't find a job after that, till my uncle gave him one working here. That was part of the reason my uncle was so crazy about getting me and Layla to come out here before our trip. . . . He wanted us to make up with our dad. Do you know how long it's been since I actually called him Dad? Years. Layla was still a baby."

"Does he still use?" I ask, my earlier suspicion waning.

He shrugs. "He started off strong here. Even after the world ended, he had his brother, he had me and Layla. He always said he was blessed to be with his family. He asked me to be his assistant and taught me so much. He thought there was hope for us all. It took the end of the world to bring our family together. But last year a lot of women here got ill. Most didn't make it. Doc blamed himself. He started taking pills to be able to sleep. Then after Layla died . . . Now it's like he's given up.

He takes more and more. . . ." Jacks shakes his head. "I guess he *is* still an addict. I won't make excuses for him."

I stand and place my hand on his shoulder. He leans his head in to my side unexpectedly. After a moment, I move away.

He looks up at me. "I'm sorry I didn't tell you, but I didn't lie either. You have your secrets too, Amy."

I nod. "I understand, I just . . . I didn't know."

He stands and reaches toward me, his hand resting on my upper arm, warming my skin. "We're still good, right?" His breath teases the top of my head, and I'm afraid of what will happen if I look up.

"Yes, of course." I pull roughly away from him and step toward the door. I'm all mixed up, Jacks bringing strange feelings to the surface. I push down my confusion and try to recover my wits. "So, are you ready to go out now, to look for Ken? I've got a lot of ground to cover," I say, changing the subject.

"Now's not a good time," Jacks says.

"Why?" I've had enough false starts, enough dead ends. I'm also not sure I want to be in such a confined space with Jacks at the moment, not feeling the way I do, flushed and tight, like my skin is too small for my body.

When I hear shouts from outside, I welcome the distraction and hurry to the window. A crowd is gathering, pushing its way through the exercise yard.

"What's going on?"

Jacks won't look at me. "A trial," he says grimly.

"A trial? What for?" Below me, the crowd is swelling, pushing toward the front wall.

"Murder."

"Murder?" I turn around and look at Jacks. Doesn't that happen here all the time? "And how does the trial work? Is there a judge or a jury or something?"

"There's no judge or jury."

"Does the Warden decide the verdict?"

He shakes his head.

"Then how will it be decided if the person is innocent or guilty?"

"Amy," he tells me with a sigh, "they're *always* found guilty."

CHAPTER FIFTEEN

Despite Jacks's protests, I drag him to the trial. If this is a main event at Fort Black, and if Ken's in the prison at all, he might be there.

When we leave Cellblock B, I don't think I'll ever be able to find Ken, let alone see the trial. There are too many people pushing to the walls across the Yard. In fact, it looks as if the wooden stairs might collapse against the weight of so many people. Jacks grabs my hand, and we head away from the crowd, past Cellblock C and the black building that used to be the cafeteria and visitor center. On that side of the wall, we pop through a door and circle around within the corridors of the wall to the opposite end of the exercise yard, then climb up so we're standing on top of the outer front wall of the prison.

If it were empty, we could see for miles outside of the prison, but the area is packed with spectators pressing for a view. Jacks slices through them and I run along behind him until, somehow, we're at the front railing. The still-swelling crowd pins me against the iron, cutting off my breath. I can feel the three crossbars that make up the railing shifting under the pressure, and the top bar digs into my rib cage.

As the pressure gets harder, I concentrate on breathing and pressing back, so I don't get cut in half. Then Jacks wedges himself behind me, reaching around either side of my waist and grabbing on to the railing in order to relieve the strain.

"Better?" he asks from behind me, his breath in my ear.

"Yes, thanks. But I don't know how I'm going to find anyone in this crowd."

All at once they begin to chant in unison. I can't make out what they're saying at first, but then it becomes clear.

Guilty. Guilty. Guilty.

"There," Jacks says, his voice strained.

On the corner of the wall, in the guard tower, the Warden stands.

"People of Fort Black," the Warden's voice booms over the

loudspeakers throughout the compound. "We have a good thing going here. The monsters are outside and we're safe in here." He says *thing* like *thang*, laying on his Texas drawl.

The crowd buzzes excitedly, and the Warden gives them a moment to calm down before starting again. "But we have to have some rules. We have to have some order. We're not animals," he spits. "A man has taken another man's life. . . . And for what? To settle an argument? Well, the good book says an eye for an eye, and I say a life for a life!" The crowd goes wild at that, and Jacks lets out a sigh, his breath hot on my neck.

"Let this be a lesson to y'all," the Warden yells. "I don't hold none with murderers!"

Everyone is screaming and I'm not sure what is happening until I look down. A man has been released out of the prison through a side door below us. He takes a few steps away from the wall, stunned, then runs back, trying to get inside.

"The people's calls will bring the Floraes," Jacks says.

"*This* is his trial?" I shout.

"This is Fort Black justice."

The man is still at the door, banging desperately. His mouth is moving, and I reach up to my ear to turn on the sound amplifier.

"Please," the man begs. "Please let me back in. I'll do

anything." He falls to his knees, sobbing.

A Florae appears on the rise across from us, pausing at the same housing development I rested at before approaching Fort Black. I don't have my Guardian glasses, so it's just a speck, but I know what it is by how quickly it moves as it jumps from the edge of the development down to and across the highway. More people have spotted it, and the chanting becomes more frenzied. Closer it speeds, and still the man blubbers next to the door.

"Run!" I scream, my voice lost in the crowd. But of course it's too late. The Florae hits him so hard, the man slams into the wall and bounces off it. He tries to push the Florae away, but it's already feeding on his flesh. Its claws secure in his sides, its face in his stomach.

Before I can turn off my amplifier, I hear gurgling as blood spills from the man's mouth. Then a gunshot sounds and the Florae lies still, its head blown open into the mess of the man's stomach. Another gunshot, and the man's body twitches, blood pooling around what is left of his head.

Some people stick around to watch the guards pick off the other Floraes attracted by the noise and blood, but, with the spectacle over, most of the crowd slips back into the prison.

"That was barbaric," I say at last.

Jacks doesn't answer, but drops his arms, allowing me some space.

There is another volley of shots—more Floraes, probably—but I don't look for them. I continue to stare at the remains of the man below us.

"In the place I was before," I say, "they would banish people sometimes, but they wouldn't watch gleefully while the person was devoured."

After a moment Jacks asks, "And does that make it better, not watching?"

I turn to face him.

"No. I guess not."

He nods. "Shutting your eyes doesn't make you a better person. It just makes you a coward. You'll notice my uncle didn't watch the man he sentenced to death actually die. He turned away."

I close my eyes and think of Dr. Reynolds. He had the same depravity as the crowd, the same delight in doling out punishment for transgressions, real and imagined. I open my eyes again, looking at Jacks. I'm so tired of running. I so desperately want to trust him, to have a real friend.

"I shouldn't have brought ya here," he says, his tone filled with concern, his accent more pronounced.

"No. I . . . was thinking about the Ward."

"You talked about the Ward before, then you freaked the hell out. Over a hospital?"

I shake my head. "No, it only looked like a hospital."

He doesn't say anything, just waits for me to go on.

"I . . ." I'm trembling, but I want to tell him. I have to. "I was placed in the Ward, a sort of institution . . . because I questioned the rules of the society I was living in. But when I was in the Ward"—I pause for a moment—"there was a girl I knew . . . I didn't even like her, but she didn't deserve what they did to her. They damaged her beyond repair."

I picture Amber's lobotomy scar. The dead look in her eyes.

"What happened to her?"

"They didn't kill her, but they destroyed everything that she was. They . . . unmade her." I stare down at my shaking hands. I grasp them behind my back, trying to hide them.

"Were they going to do the same to you?"

I swallow hard and nod. "I'd rather let a Florae kill me than let that happen." Jacks is lost behind a wavering screen of tears. I blink him back into view.

Jacks puts his hands on my shoulders and looks me in the face. "Amy, you have every right to be scared. Look at this screwed-up world. Everyone is afraid, and if they say they're not, then they're lying . . . or really, really stupid." He wipes a tear from my cheek. "You just have to keep going. I know, it sucks. But you have to be strong."

I nod, unable to speak. Rice told me the same thing.

"Maybe we should head back, let you get some rest."

"No! I can't rest. I need to find Ken."

"Okay, then let's go."

I have to pull it together. I wipe my face on my sleeve and shake out my arms. The truth is, I won't ever be okay with everything that has happened to me. But I need to stay strong for the only family I have left.

We head down the metal stairs to the Yard. The crowd has subsided, so we cross the Yard instead of circling it on the wall. Still, we keep to the edge. Then we come to the area Jacks called the Arena, separated from the exercise yard by a chain-link fence. To one side of it is exercise equipment, muscular men using weights, and other machines used for strength training. I recognize some of the equipment; we had it in the gym in the Rumble Room in New Hope. On the other side are two sets of bleachers facing each other across a concrete square. In the center of the square is painted a red circle about twenty feet across.

"What's this exactly?" I ask.

"People call it the Arena. Another blood sport. Right now the fighters are training, but once a week the Warden puts on fights to entertain the masses."

"Boxing?"

"More like UFC–"

"Get off me!" someone shrieks.

I spin around. A boy with a shaved head stands at the entrance to the Arena. Two men have him by his arms as another, smaller man punches him in the stomach. They all look strangely similar, muscular, their heads shaved like the boy's. Without thinking, I run toward them.

Before I can get there, the boy jerks his legs up, supported by the men trying to hold him, and kicks the smaller man in the chest. Using that momentum, he breaks their hold.

When I reach them, the men have circled back around him, joined by two other skinheads. I pull out my gun, but Jacks runs up next to me and pushes the barrel down.

"That'll only make it worse," he says, then sprints forward between two of the men.

I put my gun away and follow Jacks to stand next to the boy, who I can now see is a girl. I mistook her because of her shaved head and muscular build. The men still outnumber us, each one clearly fit, but none of them are nearly the beast that Tank is. I sparred with men as big as these in Guardian training. Nobody around us moves to help, just like when those men grabbed me when I ran into the Yard alone. Everyone is struggling to survive; no one wants to get involved in someone else's problems.

Suddenly, as if by silent agreement, the men come at us as one. I focus on fighting off the two nearest to me and hope Jacks and the girl will do okay.

One man grabs for a handful of my hair. It's grown out a bit since Baby cut it into a Mohawk, but it's still short enough for me to whip it out of the way, slap his hand, and snap a punch to his jaw. The other man lunges at my middle, getting his shoulder into my ribs. I elbow him twice in the back of the neck, but he doesn't let me go and ends up driving me toward the wall. Before he gets my back to it, I twist and run hard up against the surface, crashing him into it as I flip to my feet.

As I watch him crumple to the floor by the wall, the first man comes at me again. I drop down and sweep his legs out from under him with a leg whip. He careens into the other man just as he's struggled to his feet, and the two of them slam, grunting, into the wall and go down in a tangle of arms and legs.

Looking around wildly, I see all assailants either down or

bleeding. One of the men at my feet grabs my ankle weakly.

"Do you really want to keep going?" I ask.

The man shakes his head. Slowly, the group gets up and limps away into the Yard.

I walk to Jacks, adrenaline pumping through my veins, and smile. *Be strong*, Jacks told me.

I don't have to *be* strong. I *am* strong.

"Hey, Jacks," the girl says, "thanks for the assist. Although I'm sure I could've handled it on my own."

"There were five of them, Brenna," he points out.

"Yeah, and you only helped out with one. Your girlfriend at least took on two." She gives him a wicked grin and turns to me. "I'm Brenna."

"Amy." I offer her my hand, and she shakes it as though it's a test of strength.

"That little one"–she points to the guy still on the ground, moaning in pain–"he thought he'd jump me because I beat him in the Arena last week. It's not my fault he's a whiny little bitch!" she shouts toward him.

"You fight in the Arena?"

"Yep, it's better than being some guy's property." She looks me up and down, trying to figure me out.

"So you aren't anyone's?" I ask.

"Brenna isn't a huge fan of men," Jacks says with a smirk. "I don't think there's a man alive who can handle her."

Brenna makes a disgusted face. "I can't imagine belonging to a man. . . . Having them touch you." She feigns throwing up. "Why would anyone want that?" She looks at me again. "No offense, I mean, if anyone's claimed you. It can get rough here."

"I've noticed," I say, wincing. My hip still aches from my earlier altercation.

"Well, you can fight, that's for sure," Brenna tells me appraisingly. "But it's an easier life to be protected."

"Actually," Jacks says, "Amy is mine."

Brenna looks at Jacks, eyebrows raised skeptically, before barking out a laugh. "Really Jacks? *You* claimed someone." She looks at my arm, covered by my synth-suit. "Did you tattoo your name under her ninja getup?"

"You know I didn't," he tells her between clenched teeth. "But she's still mine, and you should let everyone know."

Brenna grins. "Jacks may seem all big and tough, but he's really the sensitive type. He tries to hide it, but I know he wouldn't want anyone to feel like his property," she tells me. "Well, you should keep on pretending, because life is hard here for girls. Keep your arms covered, and as long as people say you're Jacks's, you should be fine." She looks away toward the weight training area. "Shit, I lost my place on the shoulder press machine. I'll catch you guys later."

She turns to run, and I notice a tattoo on the back of her neck, a spinal column that disappears into her shirt. That must be how she knows Jacks: his tattoo work. Watching her go, I ask, "You think she'll be okay?"

"Yeah. Brenna will be just fine."

I watch Brenna get into an argument with the man on the machine she wanted. After a few seconds he moves away, shaking his head, and Brenna takes over the machine. Beyond her I see another man lifting dumbbells, and the back of my neck goes cold.

It's Tank.

He's a machine, lifting a weight in each arm marked 50 LBS. Jacks catches me staring and follows my gaze.

"He's a monster," I say.

"No." Jacks steps in front of me, blocking my line of vision. "He's just a very, very sick man. And he's not going to get to you. I'll make sure of it."

I nod and follow him, but I can't help looking back at Tank. Man or monster, he's terrifying.

The next day, Jacks insists that I stay in the cell while he's at work, even though I've proven I can take care of myself. He seems to be scared of something–but won't tell me.

"But you *saw* me," I cry, seething with frustration. "I know how to take care of myself."

"Just trust me." He glances at me, then away. "Please. I'll try to get back soon."

He slinks the gate shut. I kick the bars. I pace for a few minutes, waiting for him to leave the cellblock, then open the gate back up and call for Pam.

"Yeah?" she says, poking her head out. "Oh, hey there, Amy."

"You want company today on your sewing rounds?"

"Sure I do. Just got to finish up a few things. I'll come get you when I'm ready."

I sit on the bed, and before I can again begin to feel the frustration take over, there is the sound of metal on metal at the door. . . . A knock? I look up to find the Warden staring at me through the bars. In his grasp is a handgun, the butt of which he used as a door knocker.

"Well, hello, little lady."

"Um. Hi," I say, confused. "Jacks isn't here."

"I know. Can I come in and have a little talk with ya?"

I stand, uncertain. The last time I opened the door to a man who wasn't Jacks, I was attacked. And that man wasn't brandishing a gun like it was a fashion accessory. The Warden catches me eyeing his gun and holsters it.

"I ain't gonna hurt you, Amy." He takes a key out of his pocket. "Here's my spare anyway." He unlocks the door and lets himself in. "I just want to have a little talk about Jacks."

"All right," I say, backing away. Distrust is nagging at me, but I try to quiet it. He is Jacks's uncle, after all. He was nothing but kind the first day we met. The Warden comes in and sits down on the chair, putting his cowboy-boot-clad feet on the table. I stifle my unease and sit on the bed, eyeing him warily.

"J. J. seems quite taken with you," he says finally.

"J. J.?"

"Jackson Junior. He didn't tell you? The man that everyone just calls Doc is my brother, his father." He tells me the information as if it should be a shock, and if Pam hadn't already outed him, it would be.

"Oh, yeah. Jacks told me," I say. The Warden looks disappointed by this fact. His face drops slightly.

"Well, I just have his best interests in mind." He kicks his feet off the table and sits up, adjusting his Stetson hat. "I wouldn't want him to find out certain things about you. . . . Things that might hurt him in the end."

"What things?" I ask carefully, studying his face. He stands suddenly and hovers over me.

"Now, Amy, you and I both know you ain't what you seem." His hand reaches up and grabs a strand of my short hair. He tugs on it. "I wouldn't want you doing anything to hurt Jacks."

"I wouldn't," I say, swallowing hard. The Warden is too close, and I have no idea what to do. I want to lash out, to fight, but what will happen then? And he isn't actually hurting me, just being vaguely threatening. I decide to go against my impulse and do nothing. I stand still, though every nerve in my body screams to push him away.

"I *will* protect him," he tells me.

"Like you protected Layla?" I ask. I don't know why. It just slips out.

The Warden's grasp on my hair tightens, pulling my head closer. "A girl can die really easily in here. Especially a sweet little thang like you. Watch your step. Do you understand?" He gives my hair another tug, and it feels as if he may pull the roots from my scalp.

"Yes," I say, gasping.

"Yes, Warden," he tells me.

"Yes, Warden," I repeat.

"Amy." He backs away, his anger gone, replaced with a teasing smile. "You're practically family. Call me Johnny."

I nod, uncertain of what has just happened but grateful he's stepped away from me.

The Warden smiles. "See ya later, Amy." He dips his hat and saunters out.

I lock the bike lock behind him and walk to the sink, putting cool water on my flushed face. My hands shake, and I clench them into fists. Did the Warden pay me a visit just to intimidate me? I think of everything Jacks has told me about him: his corruption, his greed for power. Was he just trying to get the upper hand? Or was he trying to insert himself between me and Jacks, make me rethink asking Jacks's help? I sit on the bed, confused. And what does he really know about me? Was he bluffing or does he know about New Hope?

After a few moments Pam's voice carries across the cell. "What was *that* about?"

I shrug, unable to answer.

"Are you shaken, honey? Do you still want to come along with me?"

"Oh, yes. Please. I need to get out of this room."

"Well, come on then."

I spring out of the cell and grab her basket of clothes.

"I'm making deliveries to the next cellblock over—Block C," she explains as we walk down the stairs to the first floor.

"Did you hear the whole thing?" I ask Pam, and she gives me a nod. "What do you think the Warden came for?"

"Oh, you mean Johnny?" she asks with a half smirk that makes me feel better. "I think he just wanted to show you who's the big boss. Maybe he thinks Jacks is getting too attached to you. Have you asked him to miss work or do anything the Warden might think of as going against him?"

"No . . . I . . ." I did ask him to help me find Ken. He told me at first he didn't want to, but I pushed him. That can't be it, can it?

We step out of Cellblock B and into the shantytown that was originally the exercise yard. I know Pam makes the trip all the time by herself, so I quiet my unease.

As we leave Cellblock B, a greasy-looking man stares at us, eyes narrowed. Pam flashes her tattooed arm at him. He backs away.

"That's all you need to do?" I ask. Did that filthy man yesterday really think I was fair game just because I don't have a tattoo?

"Yep. All you have to do is show off your tat. . . . It works, especially when your man's well known for his skills with a rifle"–she eyes me–"or when you belong to the Warden's nephew. You should show off your tat of Jacks's name. . . . It would save you some time explaining to everyone. You do have a tattoo, don't you?"

"Oh, yeah." I don't meet her eyes as we walk the thirty or so feet to the entrance of Cellblock C. "Of course."

"He must have done something special for his girl. Can I see it?" She asks me with a half smirk. She knows I'm lying. I stop and turn to her.

"Um . . . look, Pam, I don't really have a tattoo. I . . . I'm afraid of needles. You should have seen how much trouble I had with the one on my wrist. I almost fainted," I lie. "Jacks didn't want to put me through the trauma. Maybe you could tell everyone you've seen it, though?"

She appraises me with a penetrating gaze, and for the first time I see how she must have been as an attorney. After a second the calculating look drops from her face, and she smiles kindly. "All right. I don't know exactly what's going on with you two, but you're entitled to your safety. I'll talk it up for you. I'll just say it looks a lot like mine."

"Thanks, Pam," I say, relieved. Pam turns to enter Cellblock C, and I move to follow.

And then I see him outside, down a ways from where we are.

A slight man with dark hair.

I shuffle around Pam to get a better look. The man turns to glance to the side, then back, over his left shoulder. He has a large heart-shaped mole on his cheek. My mouth drops. Could it be? He looks like Kay, like the sketch Jacks had. He looks like . . . Ken.

"Gotta go," I say to Pam, shoving the basket of clothes at her. "I'll see you later."

Pam shuffles the basket to her hip and grabs my arm. "Hon, you sure you want to be running around here alone?"

I shake her off. "It's important. Don't worry. I'll be fine."

I run through the alley between Blocks B and C, trying to catch up to the man, but there are children underfoot and men who press too closely when they pass, slowing me down. I see him skirt the corner of Cellblock C and head through the Backyard. I rush after him, my heart beating wildly when I lose him for a moment, but then I see him disappear through a door in the back wall. I rush to follow him, but an armed guard suddenly appears and blocks my way.

"No entry."

"I've got to get in there," I plead.

"There are people infected with the Black Pox in there."
He shows me his wrist: POX is tattooed in block letters. "Unless
you've already survived the Pox, you'll want to steer clear."

"I just saw a man go through that door. I really need to talk
to him."

He looks at me curiously. "I didn't see anyone go in here."

"I know what I saw." I know it was Ken. I'm sure of it.

He looks me up and down. "You need a man, honey?"

"No. . . ." My mind spins wildly. "I–uh . . . have a man.
Jacks, who helps Doc . . . the Warden's nephew," I stress. Even
if Jacks's relationship with Doc isn't well known, his relation to
the Warden seems to be common knowledge. It might get me
the access I need. "I have business back there."

"Look, Jacks ain't allowed back here neither. You go fetch
Doc, then we can talk." He hefts his gun to his other arm and
gives me an amused look.

I step forward, thinking of pushing past him, but he drops
his gun, all amusement gone. "I got one job, honey, and it's a
good one. You ain't coming in here."

If the gun were aimed at my chest and not my head, I would
have a chance to push my way through. The bullet would hit
my synth-suit and hurt like hell, but it wouldn't kill me. As it is
now, my head is unprotected. If I reach back to pull down my

hood, will he think I'm reaching for a weapon and shoot me?

Frustrated, I decide to retreat. He's eyeing me, but I can always come again later and watch for Ken. Leaning against the back wall of Cellblock B, I look who comes and goes. Mostly it's coughing men, covered in sores. They make my skin crawl, but Jacks said I'd have to actually touch someone with the Pox to contract it. I rub my synth-suit-clad arms, glad for its thin layer of protection from the world.

Ken doesn't reappear. When it starts to get dark, I give up and head back to my block. I don't want to be caught out in the dark, alone.

As I walk back, I wonder if maybe I wanted to see Ken so badly that I imagined him being there. I shake my head. No! I wasn't crazy in the Ward, and I'm not crazy now.

When I finally get back to our cell, Jacks is there, sitting on his bunk. He jumps up when he sees me.

"Amy, where the hell have you been?"

"I was out with Pam to take sewing to Cellblock C, but right when we got there, I thought I saw this guy. . . . He looked exactly like your sketch," I tell him, still irritated that I let Ken get away. "I followed him to the back wall, but I wasn't allowed in. I waited for him, but he didn't come out again. Maybe I should go back and wait some more. Maybe Ken lives there."

"No one *lives* back there," Jacks tells me sharply. "Not by choice, and not for long, anyway. It's full of people infected with Pox who are about to die. They keep them there until the bodies can be removed."

I look at his dark, scowling face. "What's wrong with you? Why are you angry?"

"Amy, I have every right to be pissed. I didn't know where you were. I've been waiting for hours. You shouldn't wander off by yourself," he scolds.

"I'm not a child." My voice is just as sharp as his is. "Contrary to what you've been telling everyone, you don't *actually* own me. You've done a lot for me, but I'm not yours. Maybe you should remember that."

His face softens slightly. "You're right. I was just worried. I thought . . ." He looks at the floor. "I thought something had happened. Or maybe . . ." His voice trails off. "Or that maybe you decided to leave Fort Black. I thought you . . . just left me."

In the silence that follows I wonder what it took for Jacks to admit that I'd hurt him. Already his face has begun to harden again.

"I'm sorry," I tell him before it sets in stone again. "I promise, I won't leave Fort Black without telling you."

There's another long silence, but this time I hold his gaze, neither of us daring to look away. "Jacks, your uncle came to see me today. He kind of threatened me I think."

"Threatened you how?" he asks.

"He just . . . got really close to me." As I say it, it sounds ridiculous, but it's hard to explain how it made me feel. Helpless. "He told me that a girl can die really easily here and to watch my step."

Jacks nods. "I'm sorry if he scared you, but that's how he is. He tries to intimidate everyone. It's my fault. I was stupid and asked him about Ken. He told me he didn't know who that was. . . . But, Amy, he must know something, or he wouldn't have come to talk to you. He doesn't like that I'm helping you."

Almost in a whisper, I ask, "Why *are* you helping me?" My heart beats faster as I utter the question. I'm not sure how I want him to respond.

"At first I thought you needed protecting, a messed-up girl on her own. You remind me a lot of my sister. Although Layla wasn't half as aggressive as you are," he says, shaking his head. "I wasn't able to keep her safe, so I thought maybe I could help you."

"And now?"

He shifts from one foot to the other, looking almost nervous. "You're just . . . not like a lot of people here, Amy. You stood up to Tank. You question things. You're not a sheep. You're fearless." He breaks my gaze. "And I'm scared all the time," Jacks admits quietly. "Those Floraes—they scare me shitless. I don't think I can ever leave the prison, not with them out there. But you . . . You were outside these walls for years. I can't even imagine leaving for a few seconds. That's all it takes for the creatures to kill you, you know, a few seconds. But it doesn't even bother you. I was wrong before, on the wall after the trial. You're not afraid of anything."

"No, you're wrong now," I say. "I *wish* I were fearless. But I'm scared of so many things." Of facing Dr. Reynolds, of never seeing Baby. I'm frightened of the ways that Kay and Gareth are being punished for my escape. I'm afraid that I'll never find a place to belong. That I'll be stuck wandering the After for the rest of my life.

"Just try to make it work here, Amy," Jacks says. "If you shoot half as good as you fight, you could be a guard."

"And work with Tank?" I ask with a tight laugh to hide my terror.

"Or you could be a Scrapper," he tells me quickly. "You're fine with going outside the walls. You'd just have to bring back things people want to trade for. . . . Or you could help Pam with her sewing. You could make a life here."

"I can't do that. Not while my sister's in trouble."

"So bring her to Fort Black."

I recoil at the thought of bringing Baby here. The truth is, I haven't thought about my plan after I break her out. I guess I could find a place nearby. We would live safe from the Floraes, protected by the sonic emitter. We could visit Fort Black; I could visit Jacks.

It worries me a little to realize I don't want to leave him.

"It's not as easy as you make it sound," I say at last.

"Because of that other place. The one you were at before you came here?"

I nod. He's watching me patiently. I take a deep breath. "It's been . . . hard. . . ." And then I start to tell him about my years in the After with Baby. My voice cracks when I talk about her, and when I start to talk about New Hope, I falter again. "When we were taken to the other colony, a place called New Hope, I thought we were finally truly safe, but it was worse than living with the Floraes."

He's listening intently, waiting for me to continue.

"I was tortured by doctors because I found out about the Floraes, what they really are . . . the result of an experiment." I leave out the part about my mother creating the bacteria that turned people into Floraes. "My sister was part of the original test group. So was my . . ."

Rice. What is Rice to me?

"My friend was also a part of it."

I swallow hard. I hadn't meant to tell him so much. "I'm here to find Ken because he can help me get my sister out of New Hope."

"Amy, why didn't you tell me sooner? I . . . I would have done anything to be able to save my sister."

It's my turn to ask. "What happened?"

For a moment I think he won't be able to talk about it, but then he tells me in a strained voice, "I tried so hard to protect her." He shakes his head angrily. "Tank took a liking to her too, you know. He'd follow her around, stare at her. I made sure to put a stop to that shit right away, though. That's why I took his file, way back then. I wanted to see what I was up against. As soon as I read it, I told my father. He said not to worry, so I told my uncle, and he made sure Tank knew she was hands-off.

"Still, she was scared of him. She used to be so vibrant, even in those first days when the infection broke out. She tried to tell me it was all going to be okay. She said it was important to remember that we still had each other, so things weren't all bad. But once Tank started stalking her, she hardly ever left the cell, not even when I was with her.

"The night of the fire, the one I told you burned up the Yard, I tried to keep her safe. I was afraid it would spread to us here, so I made her leave. Everyone was scrambling. I lost her in the crowd." His eyes burn with the memory. "She died in the flames. It's my fault."

I look up, startled at this admission. But the look on his face tells me not to say any more.

The silence stretches out between us, but after a while he speaks up again. "So you think Ken can help you get your sister back?"

"He's the only hope I have. That's why," I say quietly, "I can't promise that I'll stay here. But I can promise that I won't abandon you. If I leave, I'll tell you first."

"I get it." He nods, but he doesn't look happy. He stares at me, as if wanting more, but that's all I have to give.

PART
TWO

NEW SORROW

CHAPTER SIXTEEN

For three days straight I return to the same place and watch the door for Ken, but I don't spot him again. There's always someone guarding the area. Jacks comes with me at first, but eventually he has to go to work, which I tell him he can't skip, especially with the Warden on to us. He relents when he realizes there is no way to convince me to go back to the cell to wait.

"If anyone bothers me, I'll just tell them I'm yours," I say.

Eventually he begrudgingly leaves. With the masses of people walking around, the guard either doesn't see me from where I sit quietly against the wall, or he's choosing to ignore me.

I've begun sneaking back at night, my synth-suit hood pulled down so I blend into the darkness. It's useless; I can't be there all the time. I have to sleep. There are hours when Ken can pass in and out without detection.

When I slink back to the cell for the fifth day in a row of no luck spotting my target, I announce, "I think I need a bike."

"Why?" Jacks says, not looking up from his sketch.

"When I do find Ken, I'll need to get to New Hope." If I need to get to New Hope in a hurry, I could probably snag a car, but again, I'd have to find one that has keys and gas and figure out how to drive the thing. And then, if it breaks down, I'd be completely screwed. It will be good to have a bike as backup.

"Amy." Jack's tone is serious. He puts down his pad and places his elbows on his knees. "I think you have to face the possibility that you're not going to find Ken."

I look at him. "What are you saying?" I ask, trying to hide the edge in my voice.

"I'm saying that no one seems to know this guy. Not me, not Pam, no one. And Fort Black ain't *that* big of a place. For the number of people I've asked, it's just odd that we can't find him."

"But I *saw* him."

"Are you sure?" he asks softly. "Maybe you saw what you wanted to see."

"Yes." Tears fill my eyes. I reach for the bottom bunk for support and sit down hard. "*Yes.* I'm sure. I don't care if everyone thinks I'm crazy. Right now Baby is probably being strapped to a table, undergoing who knows what. I won't give up hope. I can't."

His brow furrows as he looks at me, the tears running down my cheeks. "Okay, okay. We'll get you a bike."

Gruffly, he pats my shoulder, then, realizing his roughness, takes more care when he awkwardly sits next to me on the bunk. "It's gonna be okay," he says, looking at me for a moment before gently pulling me to him.

I sink into him, immediately feeling comforted by his warmth. Despite the fact that we've spent a week together non-stop, I haven't been this close to him. His arms and chest are solid muscle; the material of his shirt is soft and clean. I know I should pull away–but it feels so safe here. I take a deep breath and exhale.

He holds me closer, burying his face in my hair.

"Amy . . ." I feel him move away and angle his head toward my face. Our lips are so close now. I pause, wanting to give in, but then quickly pull away.

"We've got to go," I mumble, shaking my head. I begin to ready my pack. I don't look at Jacks, but I can feel his frustration. His disappointment. The silence is thick.

"Look," I say finally. "I just don't know what's going to happen, and my main priority is—"

He shakes his head. "You don't need to explain," Jacks says coldly, standing to retrieve his keys from the table. "It's fine. Let's just help you find this Ken guy so that I can get my space back."

I stare at him as he steps out of the cell. I follow, my face burning. I barely register that Brenna is standing in the hall until she calls out loudly.

"Hey, lovebirds," she yells, a wicked gleam in her eye. "I was just coming to find you, Jacks. Got some details on my tat I need working out."

"Can't right now. We're going to get her a bike," he says, nodding toward me. "So she can leave."

"Oh." She gives us a strange look. "Well, hate to step in, but seems like you two could use a break from each other." She turns to me and grins. "I'll take you to get that bike."

"I don't think that's a good idea—" Jacks starts.

Brenna cuts him off. "We ain't exactly helpless."

I smile, despite myself.

"Whatcha got to pay him with, though?" Brenna asks, and turns to me.

"I've got enough to trade," I tell her, patting my bag. Jacks already told me that I could trade the batteries and charger for a good bike. I also have that half bottle of vodka I scavenged. . . . Alcohol is another commodity that is in high demand in Fort Black. I start out the door.

Jacks grabs my arm. "I'm sorry," he says.

"I get it." I shrug him off. "Close quarters."

He nods and steps back. "Be safe."

"I'll take care of her, Jacks," Brenna tells him, and we start off. "Geez, you'd think he didn't know you can take care of yourself. I mean . . . we saw you kick ass. Jacks is such an old woman!"

"I heard that!" Jacks shouts after us.

Brenna just laughs loudly. "I call it like I see it!" she yells back over her shoulder.

We walk down the stairs in silence, but as soon as the door to Cellblock B closes behind us, Brenna says, "Seems like I walked in on the middle of something."

"No, it was nothing." We skirt the edge of the yard and head to the Arena. I look around for any sign of Tank, but I don't see him. I can't help feeling that I'm being watched, and I try to shake off my paranoia.

"Jacks is a good guy. And there ain't a lot of good guys around this place." After a pause, she says, "Let's find you a getaway vehicle."

We walk past Cellblock A over to the Arena, where Brenna calls to a tall black man hovering just inside the fence. "Dwayne!"

"Brenna!" He walks over to us and smiles easily. He's trim but not emaciated like some of the people who live in the exercise yard shantytown. "I should be mad at you. You made me lose a package of batteries last week on your fight."

"You should know better than to bet against me," she tells him with a grin. "You know I can't be beat." She pulls me closer. "This is Amy. She wants a bike."

He looks me over, taking in the ill-fitting sweats that Jacks lent me.

"She got something to trade?" he asks doubtfully.

"This is Jacks's girl. Of course she has something to trade."

He nods and flashes a toothy smile. "All right then, follow me." He cuts toward the back of the prison, past the cellblocks to the backyard. We walk between the back building and back wall. Out of habit, my eyes scan it, searching for Ken, but as usual, he's not there. Just a scattering of people leaning against the far corner and a single guard escorting them one by one through a door.

All are covered in black boils. One coughs uncontrollably, while another doesn't move at all.

"Pox," Brenna says. "Don't get too close."

I nod as we walk to the far back corner, where Dwayne and Brenna slip through another door, one I haven't seen before. My heart skips a beat. Is this a different entrance? Maybe I can get to Ken from here.

"Are you sure it's not restricted?"

"It's just a hall that leads to the garage in the back," Brenna explains. "The Pox victims are quarantined to that section of the wall we passed. You won't meet up with them here." She's mistaken my excitement for concern.

We head down the corridor out to the bottom floor of a parking garage. Instead of cars, it's filled with bikes and storage containers. Dwayne walks to a nearby container, pulls out a key, and opens it. He steps inside and wheels out a light-blue bike.

"This is what I got."

I step up and inspect it. It seems to be in good shape. I

take the handlebars and wheel the bike forward. "The creatures don't mind the noise of the bike wheels on pavement," he assures me. "Unless there's something wrong with the chain or something and it makes a messed-up sound."

"Oh, okay." Like the man's bike I saw when I first arrived at Fort Black. "What about a trailer?" That other man's bike had one, and it definitely would come in handy on the road.

Dwayne nods and brings one out, hooking it up to the bike and making a show of demonstrating as he hops on and does a lap around the garage. When he reaches us again, he stops and looks at me expectantly.

"Come on, girlie. I showed you mine. Now show me yours."

I freeze until Brenna elbows me. "What did you bring to trade?"

"Oh." I grab the bottle of vodka from my bag. Dwayne raises his eyebrows and holds out his hand. I glance at Brenna, who nods, so I hand the bottle over. Dwayne takes a swig and grins. "This ain't the watered-down stuff. . . . Where'd you find this, girl?"

I shrug. "We got a deal?"

He considers. "It's good, but not a bike's worth of good."

I take batteries and the charger from my bag and hold

them up to Dwayne. "That's a solar charger. I can give you eight double-A batteries for the bike and trailer."

Dwayne stares at the batteries, considering. "Sixteen for both."

I try not to panic. I have only the eight batteries. That's all the charger holds. "Eight and the bottle of vodka for both, and that's my last offer." When he hesitates, I make a show of putting them back in my bag.

"Okay, okay, you got a deal. I'll even throw in a bike lock."

I make the trade, and Dwayne pulls out a bucket of black paint and a small brush.

"How should I mark it?" he asks.

"Mark it?" I look at him blankly.

Brenna answers for me. "Put Jacks's name on it. That way everyone will think twice before trying to steal it."

I look at her in horror. "Does that make the bike his, then?"

"It's his, anyway. . . . If you're his, which you are"—she eyes Dwayne—"then all your stuff is actually his."

"Fan," I mumble, shaking my head.

Brenna shows me where I can leave the bike, in a line of a handful of other bikes, all marked with writing. Only the Scrappers really need bikes, and I don't think to ask when Brenna yells, "Here's mine!" and points out a light-pink bike with the words *Touch this and die* scrawled across the seat.

When we head back inside, Dwayne is long gone. I thank Brenna, but she just shrugs and says, "No problem." Her attention seems to be on a man walking with a teenage girl who has striking red hair. The girl glances back, her eyes stopping on Brenna, and gives her a small, barely perceivable nod.

"Who's that?" I ask as the girl turns away.

"No one." Brenna blushes. "Look, I have shit to do. Can you make it back by yourself?"

"Uh, sure." I adjust my pack on my shoulders, automatically checking that my gun and knives are where they should be. "I think I can make it the hundred feet back to Cellblock B."

"Smartass," Brenna says, giving me a friendly punch on the shoulder with more than a little force behind it. "See ya around."

I turn to start back when I begin to get that feeling again, like I'm being watched. I hurry forward but hear heavy breathing behind me. I whirl around to find Tank a few feet away, staring at me.

"Hello again," he tells me, his eyes flicking from side to side, seeing who else is around.

My breath catches and I back away quickly.

"Why are you following me?" I think back to those papers and what Jacks told me about his sister. Adrenaline begins to flood my system, making my heart beat wildly.

"Fort Black ain't that big," Tank tells me, stepping forward. His eyes rest firmly on me now, roaming up and down my body.

"And it ain't that small, either," someone says from behind me. I turn to find the Warden walking toward us. "Don't you have somewhere you need to be?" he asks Tank.

"Yes, boss." Tank's heated gaze has cooled, his tone sunken to a dull submission.

"Well, get, then," the Warden tells him. Tank turns and goes through the door that leads to the parking garage.

When I look at the Warden, he's scowling, but not after Tank. "Causing trouble, Amy?"

"No. I was just getting a bike."

"You shouldn't be out here on your own." The Warden reaches out and grabs my elbow firmly. "Let's return you to Jacks." His fingers dig into my skin.

My face burns at how powerless I feel as the Warden steers me back toward the cell. Everyone gets out of our way and most call greetings to the Warden, who smiles and tips his hat.

When we reach Jacks's cell, the Warden gives me a little shove inside. "You missing something?"

Jacks looks up from his sketch and sees us. He jumps to his feet, concerned.

"No, sir. Amy just went to see about getting a bike."

The Warden beckons Jacks closer. When Jacks is near, he says in a low tone, "You can't let your woman just wander off like that. She could get hurt. You have to take care of your property. I thought you'd be more careful, especially after what happened to Layla."

Jacks's face darkens, and he looks as if he's about to defend himself, but instead he drops his head. "Yes, sir," he mumbles.

I glare at the Warden, but he keeps speaking to Jacks in the same disappointed tone.

"It broke my heart when you let that little girl die, and it just about killed your father."

Jacks's jaw tightens. "I know. I'll be more careful."

He gives Jacks one last stern look, then turns to me. "All right now, see ya, little lady." He smiles at me as if I'm a child, and walks away.

"What the hell happened to Brenna?" he asks, deflated.

"She had to go," I snap. "She's not my keeper. And why the

hell did your uncle treat me like that?"

"Like what?"

"Like I'm your dog. Does he really believe in this 'women as property' crap?"

"Well, obviously," Jacks grumbles.

"That's sick. And you just let him talk to you like what happened to your sister was your fault."

"I can't help who my uncle is," Jacks says. "Look, he's an asshole. He's always been a self-centered prick. What happened to Layla can't possibly be his fault, even though he's the big man here and should have protected her. So he blames me. He's just scared, like everyone else."

"Well, why don't you say something to put a stop to it?"

"You don't get it, do you?" Jacks says, seething. "My uncle is in charge. He's like a king. If you don't do what he says, you aren't welcome in Fort Black."

"And you're too scared to risk that," I say bitterly.

Jacks stares at me; then, in a fit of frustration, he kicks the wall.

"I don't have any power, Amy," he says. "You think I like how things work here? I don't. But I don't want to die."

"Neither do I," I say. "But–"

"But what? I get that you fought for what was right at that

other place you were at. And what happened? You ended up out there." He gestures out the window. "And what's more, you're stuck here, while your sister might be dead."

"She's *not* dead!" I scream.

"Face facts. She probably is. It happens to everyone we love. That's the world now." His voice lacks any emotion.

"Screw you, Jacks!" Without a pause, I tear the door open and sprint down the corridor. My footsteps rattle the iron walkway in loud, bullet-like bursts.

I can hear him running after me.

"Amy!" he yells.

"What? Afraid your uncle will find out I'm not under your *control*?"

There's a whoop from the cells below me, followed by catcalls. People are starting to gather in their doorways to watch.

"Get your woman, Jacks!" someone yells.

"Bitch can run!" another screams.

I fly down a stairwell, then another. I don't even know where I'm going—I just need to run. Now I'm out of B and have shot into Cellblock A. Which is when two pairs of hands grab my arms. I look to either side of me and see shaved heads. It's the fighters.

"Hey, I remember you," one says, shoving me up against a

wall. I deliver a swift kick to one of their shins, but the other one's got me pinned.

"Guys," the first one says, backing away. "That's Jacks's girl. You don't want to mess with that."

I can see the hesitation on their faces. I'm about to make another escape attempt when suddenly, from behind me, I hear a voice. Brenna.

"Leave her alone, you bastards."

The men look up. When the one to my left loosens his grip, I wrench free, then throw my elbow in the other man's ribs.

"We was just having a little fun," the larger of the two says, snarling. "We was just going to scare her a little . . . you ugly cow," he adds under his breath.

Brenna just laughs. "You think I care what you say, you stupid monkey? You're not worth my time, not now and not the ten seconds it takes me to kick your ass in the Arena." She glares at them until they back off.

"Come on," she says to me. I move away until we're safely around the corner. She puts her hand in mine.

"You're fine," Brenna says. "You would've had 'em."

"Maybe."

"Listen, I heard you and Jacks fighting. The whole damned place did. Not that smart, you know."

"What?" I look at her, hurt. "I thought you of all people would understand that I hate the concept of being 'owned.'"

"Yeah, I get it. You're not really into playing the game. I'm not either." She pauses. "But if you wanted to win, you could."

"What do you mean?"

"I've heard you're looking for some dude. Pam told me. Someone we've never heard of. Well, you ain't gonna find him by being a pain in the ass to the only guy here who really cares about you."

"But Jacks—"

"Has a crush on you? Who cares? We all do what we can to get by in this place."

I can feel my face go crimson.

"Anyway. Let's go back. I gotta rest up for the fight tomorrow."

"Thanks, Brenna," I say as we approach Jacks's cell. "Seriously. For everything."

"Forget it," she says before we're within earshot of Jacks. "Just remember: If you're gonna break his heart, make sure it's worth it."

"I don't plan on doing that," I say carefully. "But I do have to see this through. I won't be here forever, Brenna."

"All the more reason to play the game and be careful," she

tells me. "It won't help anyone if you're dead."

I nod and make my way back to the cell. Jacks looks up, and I offer a small smile. "Sorry I ran off. Again."

He smiles back. "Sorry I said those things. It's hard to have hope, especially in here."

"My sister is alive. And I'm going to save her," I say with a certainty I don't feel.

His eyes meet mine, and he nods. It doesn't exactly inspire confidence, but it's a start.

CHAPTER SEVENTEEN

After two days filled with long stretches of silences and awkwardly trying to avoid each other in our tiny cell, I decide to win Jacks over by requesting a tattoo of my own. I pick one of his sketches: a small golden sun, round and bright. I like the idea of having the sun with me always, even in the dark. Next to it is a small moon with BABY written in silver flowing letters. Baby will like it when she sees it.

He looks up from the sketch he's working on and catches me staring at it again in the mirror, my synth-suit pulled off my shoulder, my head craning to look.

He grins. "How's the shoulder?"

"Fine." I shrug. I don't want him to think that I'm weak, but it still hurts. "Maybe next time I'll get a full sleeve, like yours."

He holds out his arms to look at them, flexing them slightly. "I don't know, Amy, that's pretty hardcore. You sure you don't want a cute little butterfly on your ankle or something first?"

I shake my head. Maybe at one point, if the world had stayed normal. If I had gone to college and gotten a tattoo to be a rebel. "Do I look like a butterfly kind of girl? I want a unicorn . . . or maybe those Chinese letters that people think mean *serenity* or *peace*, but really say *sweet and sour chicken*."

Jacks laughs at that, deep and unexpected. "It used to happen a lot. People would come into my tattoo shop with letters in a different language, and I always tried to talk them out of it but . . ." He pauses, lost in thought. "Layla wanted a butterfly tattoo. She was that kind of girl. Until we got here." He goes back to working on his sketch.

There seems to be more noise than usual coming from outside, so I walk to the window and look out. The Yard looks deserted.

"What's going on?" I ask.

"Just the fights," Jacks says. "I'm not interested in watching."

A voice booms across the cell, making me jump. "Well, you'd better get interested real quick." I turn to find the Warden staring at us, his presence making my skin crawl.

"What do you want?" Jacks asks, his voice cold.

The Warden stares him down. "I've got all of Fort Black at the fights. How do you think it will look if you and your girl aren't there?"

Jacks takes a deep breath. "I've seen enough blood. . . ."

"It ain't about the blood," the Warden says loudly, talking over him. "It's about the release. It's about people getting a little entertainment."

"It's about you keeping them distracted so they don't see how shitty their lives are," Jacks shoots back.

The Warden just chuckles. "A little. Come on now. I need you there."

Jacks looks to me, and the Warden whistles. "Sorry, didn't know you needed permission from the missus."

Jacks stands and comes to me. "Amy," he whispers, "do you mind coming? It's easier just to do what he wants."

I look at him. He's torn between standing up to his uncle and keeping the long-standing peace between them. There's something else in his expression: shame. He doesn't want me to think he's a coward.

"I'll go with you," I say, then add, "if that's what you want."

Jacks nods, and we follow the Warden down the stairs and

out to the Yard, turning right past Cellblock A to reach the Arena.

The fights haven't started yet, but nearly all the seats in both sets of bleachers are filled with cheering fans. I see Dwayne up at the top with a few seats next to him and wave to him. "Here, let's sit in the back," I tell Jacks, pointing to the empty seats. "Unless you have to be up front?"

"No, the back is fine." We climb the bleachers to the top row.

"Hey, Amy." Dwayne grins at us. "Jacks, you're lucky to have a girl like this."

"I know." Jacks smiles back half-heartedly, and I grimace. I'm not in the mood to watch people fight. But I take advantage of the crowds and feverishly scan for anyone who could be Ken.

"Want some?" Dwayne offers me a flask. "It's not anything like that vodka you gave me, just some nasty toilet hooch, but it gets the job done."

"Um . . . no, thanks." I shake my head.

"Suit yourself," he tells me with a shrug, and takes a long sip.

The crowd has spilled down around the fighters' circle. Jacks explains that only the fighters are allowed in the red circle, and usually the crowd is pretty good about giving them space.

The Warden appears in the middle of the circle and raises his arms to quiet the crowd, whose shouts turn to hushed whispers remarkably fast.

"Fort Black!" the Warden yells. "It's been a long two weeks since the last fight, but what a show! Kid Gorilla is still recuperating, and y'all know Pretty Parker ain't so pretty anymore!" The crowd goes wild, and the Warden takes off his hat and waves it in the air. He lets them scream a bit before raising his arms again. "Are y'all ready?" The crowd goes crazy again, and I give Jacks a glance. He gives me an apologetic look and grabs my hand. For a moment I wish I weren't wearing my synth-suit so I could truly feel his hand in mine.

"I hate this shit," Jacks whispers. "My uncle keeps everyone happy with blood and fear. They don't even care. All they want is a little relief from their crappy lives."

The Warden's voice carries across the Arena. "All right, let's get the first two fighters: Georgie and Young Dan . . . you're up!"

Two large men with shaved heads appear from the crowd. I remember that when we helped Brenna, the man I was fighting automatically tried to grab a handful of my hair. Brenna's shaved head makes sense now. She wouldn't want to give away any advantage.

Both men showboat for a while, trying to work up the crowd. One flexes, while the other shouts obscenities at his opponent. The Warden takes out his gun and fires a shot into the air. The men rush each other immediately.

At first it looks like they're boxing without gloves, dancing around each other, trading jabs and punches. Then one of the men backs up and kicks the other's legs. The man doesn't fall, but he stumbles into the wall of the crowd, which pushes him back into the center of the circle only to be kicked again. He goes down and cowers into the fetal position. The man still standing kicks him a few more times until the man on the ground shouts, "Forfeit!" The crowd erupts in cheers.

"Is it over?" I ask.

"Yeah. Someone has to give up or be knocked unconscious."

The winner leaves the circle, pushing his way through the crowd, while someone helps the loser to his feet. Two more fighters emerge from the crowd and take their places in the red circle.

"Look, it's Brenna," I say. I'm excited, despite myself. She also has on baggy shorts, along with a sports bra. She jumps up and down, punching the air. She looks tough, a real threat. Her spinal column tattoo only heightens the effect, running from her neck down her back and disappearing into her shorts.

It makes her look like a total badass.

"Want to make a bet?" Jacks asks, who seems to have perked up.

"Bet against Brenna? You're crazy." I look over at Dwayne. "He knows better."

"That's right. I learned my lesson last time." Dwayne's eyes are glued on the Arena.

The Warden again stands in the circle. "And now we have a crowd favorite . . . Beautiful Brenna!" Half the crowd cheers while the other half boos, but Brenna puts her pointer finger in the air to show she's number one. "And Beautiful Brenna will be fighting . . . Charlie Boy Brandt!" The man she's fighting is taller than her by a good six inches, but Brenna is at least as muscular.

After a few more minutes of riling up the crowd, the Warden shoots his gun and backs away. At first the fighters circle around the ring. Brenna goes in for the first punch and is knocked down. I stand, concerned, but she gets up quickly, bouncing back into a boxing stance.

I sit and look at Jacks. "She'll be fine," he assures me.

Brenna moves in again, this time more carefully. The man has a longer wingspan and hits her twice in the face. I hold my breath, but when the man, cocky now, steps in for another blow, Brenna drops low and drives a punch into his crotch. He folds over and she springs up, connecting her knee with his face. He crumples to the ground.

"Anything goes," I whisper, shaking my head as Brenna raises her arms in victory.

"I love that girl!" Dwayne jumps up to cheer for Brenna.

I stand up to cheer for her too, amazed at how desensitized to violence I've become. Maybe because the fights in the Arena are very much like the fights I had to participate in during Guardian training. I see Brenna make her way through the crowd, pausing at the girl with red hair for just a moment before moving on.

"Let's go down to congratulate–" I begin to say, until I see who has just stepped into the circle.

Tank places a hand on one side of his head and cracks his neck, then repeats it on the other side.

"We don't have to watch this," Jacks tells me, starting to get up.

"No, I want to." I need to see what Tank can do.

This time when the Warden makes an announcement, a hush falls over the crowd. I missed the first fighter's name, but I hear what the Warden says next, loud and clear: "The undefeated, Tank Laaaaaawson!"

When the Warden fires his gun, Tank charges across the circle in two blurred steps and backhands his opponent across the face. Now he dances around, grinning like an evil little kid who's misbehaved. The man roars and rushes Tank, who spins him easily into a headlock and goes to work on his face with his free fist.

Tank's fight lasts longer than Brenna's only because he toys with his opponent, methodically hammering away at his face under his massive arm, then freeing him to stagger back a step or two before reeling him in for more. Finally Tank grows bored of toying with the man and lets him drop, giving him a long look as he sprawls there coughing up blood. He spits on him before leaving the circle.

I try to swallow, but my mouth has gone dry. The first two fights were at least even. Tank demolished that man.

I elbow Jacks. "Can we go now?"

"Yeah, I've been seen. We can leave." We make our way down the bleachers to the gate that leads to the Yard.

"You okay?" Jacks asks.

"Yeah." I try to get through the gateway, but someone blocks my path.

"Hey there, cupcake." Tank. Of course—he picked me out of the crowd. Was he waiting for me to come this way, or is it just bad luck? "Come to see me win?"

Tank is drenched in sweat, and he hasn't even bothered to wipe the blood from his hands. I take some satisfaction that his face is still bruised from where I hit his nose, even if the swelling has gone down.

Jacks begins to put his arm around me protectively, but I shake him off. I make myself stare into Tank's cold, dark eyes. "Get out of the way," I tell him, keeping my voice steady. "Or I will hurt you *again*," I stress.

"Sure, no problem," he says, bowing. "Here, princess, step this way."

I walk past him, careful not to come within arm's reach. I'm grateful that Jacks walks at my side, between me and Tank. Jacks mutters, "Douchebag," loud enough for Tank to hear.

We get ten feet into the exercise yard when I hear a woman's voice in my ear. "Amy!" It's so loud that I think whoever said it is right behind me. I whirl around but can't find whoever called for me. I hear my name again, but it's much farther away, Brenna screaming after us from the chain-link fence of the Arena. Maybe my sound amplifier is malfunctioning?

I wave to Brenna and she calls, "Did you see me kick that guy's ass?" I nod and give her a thumbs-up.

"Amy!" Again the voice is in my ear, but it's not Brenna

who says it. "Are you there? Get somewhere you can talk."

My heart seizes in my chest. It's Kay. *Kay.* I look up at Jacks. "I need to go back to our cell. Now."

"What? Why? Listen, don't let Tank freak you out."

"No, that's not . . . yes. Yeah, I just need to rest." Jacks nods and takes my hand, leading me toward the cellblock. When we get there I stop and release his hand. "Look, I think I just want to be by myself for a little while."

He looks at me, as though deciding if I should be left alone, then says, "Okay. I'll go check in with Doc. He might need me to take care of a few things, but I'll be back soon."

I run up the stairs and rush to our cell. The cells on either side of me are empty—everyone's gone to the fights.

I hop up on the top bunk and whisper, "Kay . . . are you there?"

After ten minutes, she still hasn't responded. I know I heard Kay's voice. She tried to contact me. I wonder when she'll try again and if I'll have enough time before anyone comes back.

"Sunshine?" Kay's voice is again in my ear. After being called "sweetheart," "cupcake," "princess," and a bunch of other non-flattering things, Kay's nickname for me lights me up.

"Yes," I say excitedly, then remember to keep my voice low. "I'm here. I can talk."

"I'm sorry I couldn't contact you again sooner," she tells me hurriedly. "Gareth is on lookout, watching for spies, but you never know who's listening."

"Tell me—" I stop myself from blurting out questions about Baby and force myself to let Kay talk.

"Are you okay, Amy?" Kay whispers. "Are you surviving that place? Did you talk to Ken?"

"I'm fine," I say hurriedly. "But I haven't found Ken yet. I thought I saw him a couple of times, but he disappeared into a part of the prison I couldn't follow him into." I rip Jacks's sketch out of my pack. "Does he have a mole on his left cheek, just below his eye?"

"Looks like a heart?"

"Yeah."

"That's him. Funny. I used to tease him about it. It's good to know he's alive. I've been out of contact with him for months, since before we broke you out. I was worried—about both of you." She sighs. "All I know is that he was sent to Fort Black to work on his research. But it was good that you didn't follow him into a restricted area. I don't want either of you getting into trouble. Dr. Reynolds has spies everywhere."

At the mention of Dr. Reynolds, my chest goes cold. "Is Dr. Reynolds in charge of Fort Black, too?"

"No, but they're connected. I don't know it all—I'm not a researcher. I don't have the clearance to view medical records. Wait..." Kay cuts out, only to return a few seconds later. "False alarm." She pauses again. "Look, thing are getting worse with Baby. They've moved her from the dorm to the lab. Rice says they're taking too much blood, and she's developed a heart arrhythmia. He's really afraid for her life. Rice fears her heart may give out . . . and even if she holds out, she could suffer long-term brain damage."

Fear, cold as ice, runs through every nerve and vein. "But she's important to their research," I protest. "They won't kill her, will they?"

"Not on purpose. But Rice is concerned. . . . There are so many complications from blood loss—"

"I'll come back," I cut her off. "I'll leave right now."

"Amy, don't be stupid. You'll never get in, and you'll wind up dead. What good will you be to Baby then?"

"But—"

"No. Just find Ken. He has clearance I don't. He has access to New Hope research, to New Hope test subjects. I've already told you: If you want to get Baby out, Ken can do that. He's really the only way. You just have to convince him to take Baby as his own subject."

"Are you sure?"

There's a long pause. "No. Like I said, I haven't been able to contact him. Gareth has been hacking the system so I can briefly speak with you. . . . But the researchers are on a different circuit. It's too risky for me to try."

I know Kay wants me to search out her brother, but I can't put all my hope in a man I can't find.

"Maybe Rice can get Baby," I try. "He would have the right clearance, and Dr. Reynolds's trust."

"I've talked to him. A couple of times. The longest conversation lasted about thirty seconds. He used his earpiece to relay information to me when he knew neither of us was being monitored, just like I'm doing for you. Do you know the risk he was taking? I don't know when we'll be able to speak again. He's scared too, Amy. He wanted me to tell you to be strong and patient."

Be strong and patient. Just like when I was in the Ward. I'm filled with something recently unfamiliar—reassurance. Rice came through for me once. I have to believe he can do it again.

"Find Ken," Kay says. "He'll have access to information I don't. He can give you a better idea of how Baby is, of how to get her out. Do you understand?"

I want to *go*. I want to be *doing* something. But she's right. This is my only option.

"Okay."

"Just be careful."

"I will," I promise.

"If . . . When you find him, he may not trust you. Tell him that you're my friend. And then tell him this. Tell him 'Ted doesn't need you.' He'll know what it means. He'll know I sent you."

My earpiece goes dead. "Kay?" I whisper. "Kay . . . are you still there?"

After a few long seconds her voice cuts back in. "Gareth is telling me I have to go."

"Wait . . . what about my mother? What about Adam? Are they safe?"

There's a long pause, and I thinks she's cut out, but I hear a sigh and before she's gone for good, she responds.

"Sunshine, no one is safe."

CHAPTER EIGHTEEN

I try to wait for Jacks to return, but after a few minutes of pacing I decide to go find him. I double-check my weapons and am about to leave when Jacks appears.

"Hey, I just came to see if you needed anything." He looks me over. "Are you okay?"

I cross my arms and try to rub the cold from them. "No."

He doesn't say anything, just waits for me to go on.

"Baby . . . uh, my sister. She's really in trouble."

"How could you know that?"

"I . . ." I close my eyes, trying to think. "I didn't tell you everything. I wanted to, but I wasn't sure I could trust you."

Jacks puts his arms on my shoulders and makes me sit on the bottom bunk. I think he's going to sit next to me, but instead he pulls up a chair.

"Tell me."

And so I tell him everything. About Dr. Reynolds and my mother. About how I found out about the Floraes and how New Hope doesn't want anyone to know they were the ones who created them. How I was put in the Ward, and Kay helped me escape. I tell him about my earpiece and what Kay told me. I tell him about Ken and how he worked for Hutsen-Prime. How he might be able to access information about Baby–

"Wait. Hutsen-Prime?" Jacks cuts in.

"Yeah. Why?"

"Amy, Doc has Hutsen-Prime boxes in his office. I thought they were a chemical company or something. It's where the flu shots come from."

It takes a minute for it to sink in. "They have to be from New Hope. And if Doc is working with New Hope, he's probably working with Dr. Reynolds. . . . But that also means he'll know where Ken is." I look up at Jacks. "We have to go see Doc."

"You think Doc is . . . what, like a spy or something?" He looks incredulous.

"I don't know what Doc is, but if he's injecting people with something from New Hope, I doubt it's a flu shot. If Ken is working on a vaccine, maybe Doc is testing it." I look down and see I'm clenching and unclenching my fists. Anger, fear, hope, love—all tossing around inside of me. I try to calm myself. Doc isn't Dr. Reynolds, but my rage flares when I think of all the damage Dr. Reynolds has done. If Doc is helping him, he's just as guilty. "I need to find out what Doc knows."

"How?" Jacks asks, his voice heavy with concern. "How are you going to find that out?"

I stand, my hand going to the Guardian gun at my hip. "Any way I have to."

"Whoa, Amy. Let's take this down a notch. I'm sure Doc will tell us if we just ask him. You need a second to calm down."

"Jacks, every second could count."

"I get that. Just"—he takes a breath—"just don't hurt Doc."

I stare at him for a moment, remembering that Doc is Jacks's father. "Fine," I say, nodding once.

I spring into action, and we're out of the cell, Jacks hurrying to catch up with me. But as we rush down the stairs and out of the cellblock, something's bothering me.

"Your father really didn't tell you anything about New

Hope or Hutsen-Prime?" I whisper.

He shakes his head as we enter the exercise yard and make our way through the makeshift shelters. "Amy, as far as I know, my father was a second-rate doctor who blew his career and his marriage because he couldn't stop popping pills. The only one who would give him a job was my uncle."

We're at the front wall now. Jacks grabs my arm and looks into my eyes. "He's a loser, Amy. He can barely keep his shit together. I doubt he's part of some crazy conspiracy."

I think about my mother, her part in New Hope and creating the bacteria that caused the Florae infection. I think about Rice, all his secrets, many I still didn't know. "You can't know someone completely," I say. "Not truly."

He takes a deep breath, steeling himself, then leads me through a side door and straight to Doc's office.

Doc's sitting at his desk, looking over papers while chewing on a pen. When he hears us, he looks up.

"Jacks," he says, pleased. His eyes flick to me, and his expression changes from genuine happiness to feigned delight. "Amy. Hi there. Have you changed your mind about the flu shot?"

That's all it takes. His phony smile, his false upbeat voice. For a second I see Dr. Reynolds, not Doc, sitting in his chair.

I walk over to him, spin his chair around, and pull out my knife.

"I know you're working with New Hope." I push the blade to his neck. "And you are going to tell me everything that I want to know."

CHAPTER NINETEEN

"Amy!" Jacks screams, his hand gripping my shoulder. "Amy. Let me ask him," he says firmly.

"Jacks, I have to know."

"Okay. But you need to calm down."

I back off slowly, dropping my knife to my side, and step away.

"Wh-what is this about?" Doc asks Jacks quietly, his face white.

"Amy has been telling me some things," Jacks says, his voice even. "Things about you and a place called New Hope." Doc glances over at me and he looks nervous. "I hear those flu shots might actually be something else."

Even though we have no proof, just my assumptions, Jacks sounds confident, as if he's completely sure of what he's saying. The power in his voice is impressive. As Jacks talks, Doc tries to look unaffected, but he begins to shift nervously in his chair.

"You have no idea what you're talking about," he says with a tight, pinched face.

"Doc." Jacks leans in. *"Dad."* The word is strained coming from Jacks's mouth, but it has the desired effect. Doc studies Jacks's face, his expression conflicted. Jacks continues in his soothing voice, "There's no reason to keep secrets from me."

My fingers twitch around the hilt of my knife, and Doc's eyes flick to it. "Tell us," I snap, unable control my tone.

"Well . . ." He shrugs, unable to meet Jacks's gaze. "You seem to already know most of it anyway. New Hope sends me the vaccine, and I give it to the people here, tell them it's a flu shot. Then we see if it works."

He says all this so nonchalantly, as if the fact that Dr. Reynolds is using Fort Black as his personal laboratory is nothing at all. I'd thought Ken was sent to study the people here, but it's far worse—they're using them as lab rats.

I push aside my horror. "How do you know if it works?" I manage to ask. "Most people stay behind the walls."

"Most, but not all. Sometimes we'll get a Scrapper who's been bitten or one of the men who clean up the Florae bodies or someone on garbage duty." Another little shrug. "Sometimes I have to create situations in which to test the effectiveness."

Before I can ask what he means, he moves to stand up. My knife rises with him, and then his hands come up too. "I just want to show you," he says. He goes to the cabinet and retrieves a paper. "Here, look." He shoves the paper at me. I glance at it. At the top is typed FIT13. Under that are a lot of chemical names I don't understand, followed by instructions to remove the site of infection if a patient becomes exposed to a Florae's bodily fluid.

"Harmless," he says, as if the meaning of what I'm looking at should be obvious to me. "Jacks, you yourself kept records for me."

Jacks glances at me. "Amy, I swear I didn't know." He looks back to Doc, with a look of realization on his face. "I was injected with that F1T13 thing . . . and a bunch of shots before that. What about side effects? And all those women who died last year?"

"That was . . . regrettable."

After an empty moment, I repeat the word. *"Regrettable?"*

Doc sits back down. No shrug this time, at least. He plays with his ear nervously. "New Hope sent me a fertility drug to test on the women. I was unprepared for the strength of the adverse reaction. So many died. . . . I had no way of knowing that a side effect would be a high risk of hypertension. As soon as I saw the increase in deaths caused by heart attack and stroke, I discontinued the study."

"You wouldn't do something like this. . . ." Jacks's face betrays his horror. I know what he's feeling. I felt that way when I found out what my mother had done, what she had created. Jacks backs away, reaching behind him for something to steady himself on.

I reach out and take Jacks's hand. "You're responsible for their deaths," I say to Doc.

"No. No," Doc protests. "I'm just the observer, the middleman. I get the medicine and instructions. Give this batch to women, give this batch to children. Give the potential Florae vaccine to everyone."

"You gave that shit to me," Jacks says, unbelieving.

"Yes, but the Florae vaccine's only side effect seems to be an increased tendency toward violence."

He says this as if it's somehow a good thing. I'm so angry,

I have to concentrate on keeping my breathing even. These people are making Fort Black even more dangerous. As if it needed the help. And I can't even think about the women they so "regrettably" killed.

"What . . . ," Jacks asks quietly. "What about the Black Pox? Was that you, too?"

"No. That's just an unfortunate mutation of the chicken pox virus. We had nothing to do with that. I'm not responsible for every disease that manifests. Where there are people, there is sickness. There always has been and always will be."

"It makes your job easier," I say with venom in my voice. "When people die by your hand, you can blame some random virus."

Doc looks down and doesn't respond.

I give Jacks's hand a squeeze before releasing it. From my baggy shorts I pull out the sketch of Ken. I hold it up for him to see.

"Do you know this man?"

"No," he answers quickly.

"He's lying," Jacks tells me. I wish Jacks knew sign language. I wish I could take his hand again and have him sign to me, like Rice could. I'd ask him if he really knew Doc was lying or if he was just bluffing again.

"You lied to us for years, *Dad*," he spits out the last word. "About the drugs, about your downward spiral of a career."

"I haven't lied to you about any of this, Jacks. I just didn't tell you. I thought it would be better for you if you didn't know."

It stings, knowing Jacks used this exact excuse for not telling me Doc was his father. Like father, like son. Jacks just shakes his head though, and I realize it's not really the same at all.

"That's the bullshit you used to give Mom. *I didn't tell you because I didn't want you to worry*. No, it's better to have reality come crashing down all at once. It's better to find out from a random nurse that Mom ran into in the grocery store that your father lost his medical license for stealing drugs. It's better to find out that we have no money when the car is being repossessed and the house is being foreclosed on. It's better to find out that your father has been playing mad scientist with people's lives, years after the fact."

Doc considers this for a moment, then looks past Jacks at me. "Amy, are you sure you want to dig any deeper?" he pleads. "You have many valuable skills. You could make a good life for yourself in Fort Black."

"You're insane," I whisper.

But he goes on. "Don't you want to just go back home with Jacks and forget all this? I was going to contact New Hope when you first arrived; I had been told to look out for you. But I saw you two together, and I talked it over with my brother. We knew you and Jacks would get along. We thought it would be better for you both."

"My uncle . . . he knows about all this?" Jacks asks. He shakes his head. "Of course he does."

Doc nods, his jaw tight. "The testing has been going on for a long time," he continues. "My brother sold Fort Black out long before the infection broke. Hutsen-Prime had been using the prisoners as test subjects and paying the Warden a fair price."

"When he hired you, I actually thought he was trying to help you," Jacks says. "He even convinced me and Layla to come here to talk to you. To forgive you. That's why we were here when the infection broke out. I thought he wanted to help us patch things up."

"Don't act so naive, Jacks. You know what kind of man your uncle is. But we're looking out for you." Doc turns to me. "I was told if you came here to report it immediately to New Hope and we didn't. If you back down now, you can live here. You'll be safe with Jacks. Why get involved?"

"I'm already involved," I tell him. Even if I wanted to forget

New Hope, I couldn't. Not with all I left behind there. I hold up the sketch. "Do. You. Know. Him?"

Doc doesn't look at it again. Instead he looks at me, his eyes cold. "You're talking about Ken Oh. He's a researcher for New Hope. He works on the vaccines and brings them to me when they're modified."

I let out a long breath. Finally I'm getting somewhere. "And where can I find him?"

"I've already let him know that you're looking for him." He taps his ear with a sad smile.

"How . . . ?" I start, but then I realize. He contacted Ken the same way Kay contacted me. Through an earpiece. I can just see it glinting in his ear.

"Ken's been listening in the whole time," he says. "He says he doesn't know what you want with him, but if you're this determined, he'll send for you when he has a free moment." Doc's eyes narrow as he listens. He looks back up at me. "Go to Jacks's cell and wait for him."

I just stare at him, my head spinning. *I've gotten to Ken? Finally?*

"Amy, let's go," Jacks says, glaring at Doc. "We got what we came for."

I turn to Jacks. "How do we know he's telling the truth?

He's lied to you for years—"

"I didn't lie. I just kept information from you that was best withheld," Doc tells Jacks. "Calling the vaccine a flu shot made things simpler."

I whirl around, my voice shaking with rage. "Do you think people are too stupid to decide for themselves if they want to be tested on, or do you just not care?"

"Amy, relax." Jacks pulls me from the room and hurries me down the hall.

"Relax?" I ask, my voice a thin screech.

"Don't be stupid," he says through clenched teeth. He looks at me with urgency, and I understand: *If I want to keep going, I need to stop making trouble.* I look at the pain on his face. He's just gotten a shock as well.

"Okay," I say softly. "Are you . . . ?"

"I'm fine. . . . I mean, I knew Doc wasn't going to win any father-of-the-year awards."

He's hiding his hurt, and for now I let him. We need to get back to his cell and wait for Ken. I charge forward, into the exercise yard—into chaos. People are running around wildly, trampling through tents and cardboard boxes.

"What's going on?" I ask Jacks, but he looks just as confused as I am.

"I don't—"

A woman runs at us, her hands scraped and bloodied. "It's here!" she screams. "It's inside!"

Jacks catches her and holds her arms. "What is it? What's inside?"

"A Florae!" She wriggles from his grasp. "Run!" she screeches before disappearing into a sea of panic.

CHAPTER TWENTY

I immediately reach for my gun with one hand and pull on my hood with the other, then push Jacks against the wall. My Guardian training kicks in, and I scan the yard for any signs of nearby Floraes, but all I can see are frightened people, some running around without direction, a few too terrified to even move. One man sits on the ground, sobbing into his hands. A woman is knocked to the hard concrete but manages to regain her footing before she's trampled.

"Do you have a weapon?" I ask Jacks.

He shakes his head. "I've never needed one."

I grab the knife I keep on my left thigh and hand it to him.

"If there's a Florae, you'll need this."

I'm surprised when I look at him—his eyes have gone glassy with fear. "Don't think about it. Just go for the neck or try to stab the brain through the eye." I take a step away from the wall.

"Where are you going?" he asks, desperation in his voice.

"I'm going to find the Florae and kill it."

"Are you crazy? You're going to die."

"I'll be fine," I call over my shoulder. "I've done it before. Trust me. Go back inside the wall."

When he doesn't respond, I stop and look back at him. He holds the knife limply at his side, his face slack. I can't just leave him there. He's petrified, and I have no idea if he'll be able to defend himself. But I can find the Florae and kill it before an outbreak occurs. I could save hundreds of lives.

I go to him and pull up my hood just far enough for him to see my eyes. "Jacks. Go back inside the wall. Circle around to the cellblock and close the door. I'll meet you at our cell. You'll be okay in there."

He focuses on me, shaking his head. "But it's a *Florae*."

"That doesn't matter. If you see one, don't think about what it is. Think about what you need to do to survive."

Jacks nods, steeling his face. "Will you be okay?"

"I'm trained for this." I put my hood back down. "You may know Fort Black, but I know Floraes."

"Good luck," he tells me, starting to sound like his old self. "I'll meet you at home."

Home. The word sounds so foreign to me, but I nod. He turns and disappears inside the wall.

I wade into the chaos of the crowd, searching for a flash of green, listening for the creature's distinctive snarl. It's next to impossible to move through the mass of people struggling to escape without the slightest idea where to go.

"There!" someone shouts off to my left. "He's changing!"

I fight through the tide of people fleeing the area and find a group of men beating another man. He's unconscious and bloodied, but doesn't look like he has begun to change, or even like he's been bitten. I try to step in to stop them, but I'm knocked to the ground and someone steps on my arm.

I roll to the side and up to my feet and again try to stop them, but there's no reasoning with the mob. Then another man is accused—one of the men who'd been beating the man on the ground. "His hand! His hand!" someone is screaming. I see only knuckles bloody from beating the first man, but the crowd sees a Florae bite, and they're immediately upon him.

I leave the fighting men behind, trying to focus on finding

the Florae. There could be dozens of them by now, but I can't find a single one. I make my way across the exercise yard, the tents and cardboard homes mostly trampled under the feet of the panicked masses.

Through the chaos, I still can't find a Florae. Did one really get inside? Someone must have seen it to sound the alarm, but then where is it? Feeding somewhere? It could still be consuming its first victim. I scan the exercise yard to see if there is a particular area that people are running away from, but everyone is fleeing without direction.

I hear a whimper to my left and turn to find a child peeking out of a tent—he's hardly more than a toddler, tears smearing his face. I dive for him and pull him out just before a man crashes through the tent, dragging it behind him as he runs.

The child clings to me and my heart leaps into my chest. He can't be any older than Baby was when I first found her. I search for a parent or anyone who can protect him, but everyone is concerned with their own safety, with fleeing or finding and killing the Florae. I carry the child to the wall, weaving around debris and bodies. Smaller fights are breaking out all over the yard as neighbors accuse one another of being infected.

I climb the steps to the top of the wall and find several others who've come up to escape the violence below. A woman clutching two children eyes me, her face wild with terror. I half-expect her to bolt when I approach her, but she just squeezes her children to her more tightly.

"Are these your children?" I ask.

"Yes, we were caught outside the cellblock. They wouldn't let us back in. My husband's a guard; I thought to come up here—"

"That's fine. Can you look after him?" I place the little boy down onto his feet and move him toward her.

"What?" she asks, taking him despite the hesitation in her voice. "Is . . . Is he yours?" She sounds like she's in shock, but she cradles the boy's head against her breast.

"No. I don't know who he belongs to. But he needs you."

I look around the top of the wall and wonder why more people haven't come up here. Out of the corner of my eye I see a man running toward us. I step out of the way and realize too late what he means to do. He takes a flying leap off the wall, landing on the ground outside with a sickening thud.

I turn back to the woman and see that she has crouched down and drawn the little boy and her two children tightly into her arms. "Now," she says, "we're going to play a little game and see who can keep their eyes shut the longest. No peeking or you lose."

I back off and run along the wall for a better view of the exercise Yard. Looking down at the erupting violence, the absolute disorder, I realize that it's a kind of madness. A Florae-fueled riot, without the Florae. I scan every inch of Fort Black within my vision and can't find a single creature.

I go back down the stairs and make my way along the wall of the exercise yard, keeping my eyes peeled for the phantom Florae and avoiding the many fights that are still breaking out throughout the Yard. I'm halfway to Cellblock B when an announcement comes over the loudspeaker.

"Fort Black. This is the Warden. There is no longer a Florae threat. Please, stand down. The Florae has been dealt with."

The announcement does nothing to lessen anyone's aggression, and the riot continues to rage on. I'm even more convinced now that there was never a Florae, that it was all a mistake—or a calculated lie.

When I arrive at the cellblock, it's a different place. People have locked themselves in their cells and wait patiently for the commotion to end. When I reach my cell, though, it's empty. I should have stayed with Jacks. I'm debating whether to go find him, when he arrives at the cell door, breathless.

"Amy!"

I pull off my hood. "Jacks, I'm sorry I left you. . . . I thought

I could help, but it was a false alarm."

He stares at me for a second, then rushes to me and folds me in his arms. I'm startled, but as confusing as it feels, it also feels good.

"*I* should be sorry. I acted like . . . I should have gone with you. You could have been hurt." He holds me tighter. Through my synth-suit, I can feel his arms, his chest. We're the right size for each other—our bodies fit together perfectly.

"If something had happened to you . . ."

He pulls away and looks at me for a moment, studying my face; his dark eyes shine with a fierce intensity. And then it happens. Jacks is kissing me.

I can't say I haven't thought about what it would be like. Lying in my bunk at night, listening to him breathing, or watching his flexed back, marked with tattoos. I've thought about kissing Jacks. Even though I knew I shouldn't. Any distraction is a bad distraction. And then there's Rice, who creeps into my thoughts unbidden. I don't know where I stand with Rice—he hasn't tried to contact me, hasn't kept his promise of keeping Baby safe.

But these thoughts vanish because now Jacks's lips are on mine, his tongue uncertainly searching. And I can't help it. I press into him, kissing him back, hard. It feels good. Right. And something happens to my legs—left to stand on my own right now, I know I'd drop to the floor.

He pulls me closer, his arms moving down my back.

"Ahem." Someone clears his throat loudly and I jump back out of Jacks's arms. My legs *do* work, but the skin on my face, my body, is hot and tingling. A man stands in the doorway, smirking. "Sorry to interrupt. That looks like it could have gotten . . . interesting."

"Who the hell are you?" Jacks demands.

"I'm here for Amy." He looks at me. "That's you, right?"

"Yeah? What do you want?" I ask, my voice shaky.

"I'm here to take you to Ken Oh."

CHAPTER TWENTY-ONE

"You can't go," Jacks says, turning back to me. "Not now. Not with all those people killing one another out there."

"I'll be fine." I don't look at him. My face is still burning, but I've snapped out of the spell. "I'm not a Florae."

"Do you think that matters anymore? They're out for blood. No one is safe."

"I'm going," I say forcefully. I can't waste time right now. This is the chance I've been waiting for.

"What if it's a trap? What if Doc sold you out to that Reynolds guy?"

The thought had crossed my mind. "It's not, Jacks. Doc said Ken would be contacting me. This is it." And if it's not . . . I'm willing to take the risk.

"Then I'm coming with you," he says.

"Sorry," the man from the doorway says. "I was told to bring her only."

"I'm ready," I say. Jacks grabs my arm, but I wrench it from him.

"I won't let your feelings get in the way of what I have to do. You know what I'm here for."

Jacks steps back, that stony look returning. "Yeah. I do. Because you don't let me forget it for a second."

"Well, maybe for a second," the messenger chortles, listening. "She seemed to be concentrating pretty hard on you when I got here."

"Let's go," I say, before things get uglier. I look at Jacks. "I'll see you later."

"Sure," he says with a cold nod.

I follow Ken's messenger down the stairs and out into the Yard. Things have quieted down a little, though it looks to me as though nearly all the makeshift homes have been demolished.

The messenger leads me away from the Yard, back between the cellblocks. There are more agitated people here, and their screams echo off the concrete. Two men wrestle on the ground and I skirt around them.

We go all the way to the back wall, where the messenger nods to a guard and opens a door, the same door I saw Ken disappear through a few weeks ago. The door through which they take the Pox victims. I expect to see a dark, dank holding cell, filled with the dead and the dying. Instead, when I step inside, I am blasted with cold air. Air-conditioning. The door thunks shut behind me. The corridor is well lit and smells of lemon cleaner. Standing here, you have no idea of the turmoil raging outside.

"Where are all the sick people?" I ask the messenger.

He tilts his head, considering what I've asked. For a moment I think he's going to ignore my question, but then he relents. "We have beds for them in the rooms back here. We try to keep them comfortable." He holds up his arm, showing me the POX mark above the square tattoo on his wrist. "I tend to the weak and nurse the survivors back to health. What survivors there are, anyway."

I nod. "And Ken?"

"This way." The messenger leads me past several doors

until we reach the one he wants. He pushes it open and motions me inside.

Inside is an office, much like Doc's. The man sitting at the desk looks up at me. He's Asian and has a heart-shaped mole on his left cheek.

The door snaps shut behind me.

I'm filled with so much joy, I can't help but grin. My pulse is up so high, I think I'm going to rocket out of the ceiling.

Finally.

"You're Ken?" My voice is shaking with anticipation.

He taps his pen on his desk. "Yes, and you're Amy. You desperately needed to see me. What do you want?"

His abruptness throws me off. "I . . . I'm friends with Kay."

"Friends? Right." His lip curls meanly. "Because of you, my sister was demoted. I was briefed all about you when you escaped from the Ward last month. You're paranoid delusional with a disposition toward violent outbursts. You killed an orderly, and somehow my sister was blamed for it all. You are *not* Kay's friend."

I take a deep breath. "I know what they probably told you, but I didn't kill anyone. The orderly's death was a lie," I say, making myself speak in short, calm sentences. Losing my cool now would only make matters worse. "I'm not delusional. I was placed in the Ward because I found out about the Floraes, information that you all don't want New Hope to know. Dr. Reynolds wanted me silenced. He wanted me out of my mother's thoughts. He wanted me gone. I had to escape. Kay helped me because she cares about me."

He shakes his head. "Kay doesn't care about you. Kay cares about one thing, and that's Kay."

"Then why has she been contacting me to make sure I'm okay?"

"If that's true, she's taking another pointless risk."

"It's not pointless. She does care about me. She cares about you, too. She told me not to put you in danger."

"And you've done a fantastic job. Threatening Doc with a knife? After that stunt, he had to tell New Hope that you were here. Dr. Reynolds was very eager to hear that bit of information."

I take a step back and have to fight an overwhelming urge to run. Will he come for me now that he knows I'm in Fort Black, or is he just glad I'm out of his way?

I hold my ground. I have to see if Ken will help me with Baby, or at least tell me about her. "Kay said to tell you, 'Ted doesn't need you.'"

Ken looks at me a long time, his face unreadable. Then he

stands, places a finger to his lips, and moves around me to the door. He opens it, waves for me to follow, and walks down the corridor. I follow him to another door and into a tiny, closet-sized room packed with a cot and a dresser. On the sparse dresser is a single notebook and a picture of two children, a boy and a girl, about ten years old. Their arms are around each other's shoulders. The boy has a heart-shaped mole on his cheek.

Ken reaches to his ear, takes out his earpiece, and turns it off. He places it on the dresser next to the photograph. "This room is clean," he tells me. "It was a broom closet, but I made it my bedroom in case I needed a quiet place . . . with no one listening."

"Won't they be worried you turned it off?" I ask.

"If they were listening in at that exact moment, maybe. Or if they try to contact me while we're talking, but I'm not due for another check-in until tonight. I'll take the risk."

He's still staring at the picture. Gingerly, he touches it, caressing the girl's face, then looks back at me and produces a single laugh so quiet, I think I might be imagining it. Then he takes the notebook, tapping it absently on the dresser.

"Ted," he says. "Did she tell you who he is?"

I shake my head.

"Ted's a bear." That little, nearly soundless laugh escapes

him again when he sees my confusion. "Kay's older than me, by all of twenty-three minutes. She always thought that meant something, that I had to do what she told me to. When we were little, I had this teddy bear. Ted. I loved that stupid bear so much, but Kay never saw the point of loving an object. She would take Ted, make me beg for him back, you know how children are. I would cry and tell her that Ted needed me, but she'd never budge. She would say, 'Ted doesn't need you. You need Ted.' I'd usually have to do all her chores before she gave him back.

"When we got older, the few times she really wanted me to do something for her, she would always say, 'Ted doesn't need you, but I do.' She hardly ever needs me now, though. Or if she does, she doesn't ask." He looks at me narrowly, then shrugs. "She's asking now. She wants me to help you." He puts down the notebook he is fiddling with and faces me. "If Kay trusts you that much, then I do too. What is it that you need, Amy?"

A wave of relief washes over me. "I need to know about Baby. She was taken by Dr. Reynolds," I tell him. "They think she was bitten by a Florae and didn't change."

"You mean Hannah O'Brian?" he asks. I nod at Baby's true first name, though this is the first time I've heard her last name. "She's all any of the researchers are talking about. I have a sample of her blood in the lab."

"Kay thinks you might be able to help me save her."

Ken gives me a sharp look. "Kay must not understand. Hannah was part of the original experimentation process that produced the bacteria that created the Floraes. She was in the group that tested the vaccine. She's the only human that we know of to have been bitten by a Florae and not turn into one. I've made a new batch of vaccine based on her blood sample."

Something comes to me then, something Amber told me after she arrived in New Hope, after I saw her for the first time and nearly strangled her for what she did to Baby and me. I'd put her in the hospital. A flash of anger is dissipated by the memory of her in the Ward, her lobotomy scar across the side of her head.

"Someone told me there are children in Fort Black with the same mark Baby has, the triangle on the back of her neck." It marked her as a test subject. It marked Rice as well, but Dr. Reynolds must see more value in him as a researcher than as a lab rat. Or is it possible that Dr. Reynolds doesn't know Rice was injected with the original vaccine?

Ken shakes his head. "We had a facility near this prison. Not the same one that Baby was in, but we were performing similar tests there. When the infection broke out, we evacuated the children from that facility to Fort Black. The walls offered better protection. That was years ago, though. We hadn't anticipated the chaos that Fort Black was in. We lost track of those children. . . . Not one of them made it to New Hope. That's why Hannah is so important. Of all those children, all those locations, she's the only survivor we know about."

My jaw tightens. So they don't know about Rice. How did he get the scar on the back of his neck? How has he kept a secret? I don't dare say this to Ken. Instead I ask, "And how did Dr. Reynolds regain contact with Fort Black?"

"He never lost it. Like I said, after the infection, there was absolute chaos, but Reynolds already had the Warden on the payroll. Hutsen-Prime was doing some testing on the prisoners here before the outbreak. The Warden was more than accommodating. He just saw dollar signs. When we lost all our test subjects, that's when Reynolds decided to use Fort Black as his ready-made petri dish."

"And now? There's no money anymore. But the Warden's still allowing all the people of Fort Black to be experimented on without their knowledge. What does he get now?"

"Food, gasoline, power. He lets us conduct our research, and we help him remain king of his crumbling castle."

It makes sense. It makes it hard for me to breathe, but it

makes sense. Ken may be Kay's brother, but the offhand way he delivers this awful information makes me want to . . . I don't want to think about what it makes me want to do to him. I know that they're trying to save the human race, but can't they see that they've lost their humanity in the process?

I breathe and try to focus. "I understand that your research is important," I say, "but they're hurting Baby . . . Hannah. Your vaccines aren't working. You have to try something else."

"The replication isn't working because the bacteria has mutated from its original strain."

"My mother told me that. She said it went airborne, then changed again."

"To a pathogenic bacterium . . . which can only be spread with an exchange of bodily fluids, such as saliva or blood."

"Right, so if the bacteria itself has changed, what good is Hannah? You have the original vaccine; you can modify it without her."

"Hannah is a medical miracle, one that researchers are trying to duplicate. We've given the vaccine to test subjects, but they still aren't immune. They change when we introduce the bacterium, just like everyone else. There is an answer, though, and it's somewhere in Hannah's blood. If we can figure this out, no one else will change. I can assure you that Hannah is well cared for. She's very valuable."

I swallow. How many people have they changed trying to test a useless vaccine? "Kay thinks she's in danger."

"Kay doesn't have all the information. She doesn't have the clearance."

"Kay knows more than you think." But I don't tell him how I know this. I can't put Rice in danger. I change tactics. "Maybe you could request that Baby be sent here. Then you can have full access to her. It will only benefit your research."

"I have her blood. That's all I need."

"Kay said you'd want her for yourself."

"How many times do I have to tell you?" he asks, his voice getting louder with frustration. "Kay knows only a fraction of what she thinks she knows. I have Hannah's blood. I don't physically need her here with me."

Despite myself, my eyes well with tears.

"But . . . you have to help me." My heart has dropped into my stomach. He's been no use at all, after trying so hard to find him. I wanted so badly for Kay to be right, for Ken to be the answer. He was my only option. And now I have nothing. All this wasted time and energy for a dead end.

"Look, I know you care about Hannah deeply, but she's just

one child. What is one child for the future of humanity?"

"I'm not willing to sacrifice Baby for the good of humanity. I don't care how selfish that is. She doesn't deserve to be tortured so others can live." I look at him, into his eyes. "What if it were Kay?"

He stares back at me for a moment, then looks down with a sigh. "I'll try to find out more for you, but that's all I can promise."

"Thank you." I can't help it. Despite the fact that I'd just been fantasizing about breaking him in two, I step forward to hug him. He tenses, so instead I hold out my hand for him to shake. Kay isn't comfortable with hugs either.

Ken picks up his earpiece off the dresser, turns it back on, and places it in his ear. He pauses, staring at the notebook resting next to the picture of him and his sister. Without looking at me, he puts one finger on the notebook and pushes it toward me, giving it one last tap. I nod my thanks and grab the notebook, quickly shoving it into the pocket of my sweatpants. But I wonder why Ken wants me to have it.

He opens the door and walks me down the corridor, talking now for his earpiece's benefit. ". . . so you see, Amy, I have absolutely no information to give you. I'm sorry. You'll have to leave now." He opens the door that leads back into the prison, mouthing, *Be careful.*

I nod and step out of the wall and into the prison, back into the sunlight.

The door closes behind me, and I take about five steps before I'm suddenly grabbed from behind. A massive arm clamps my waist and arms, and another encircles my neck. I was careless. Stupidly careless. The riot must have picked back up again. Someone—some huge, reeking man—is taking advantage of finding a girl alone and unarmed. But I'm not unarmed. If I can just get free for a second, I can reach my gun.

I stomp down hard on my attacker's foot, but he doesn't even flinch. I feel hot breath on my ear and even before he speaks, I realize with an icy spike of terror that I know only one creature on Earth who produces this unmistakable stink.

"Not this time, cupcake," Tank says. "Got steel-toed boots on."

Panic floods my body as I struggle against his bulk, but he's so much stronger than me. I'm powerless.

"I'm going to enjoy this," he tells me, hefting me up. With my feet dangling, he carries me toward the wall. I don't make it easy for him and I kick against his shins. He bends down so my feet touch the ground and tightens his hold on my chest, making me gasp for breath. I fight desperately, but Tank's grip is ironclad. I try to think of a way out but have nothing. A cold, terrifying realization comes to me: I might not win this fight. But I know I can't give up.

Because if I do, Tank is dragging me to my death.

CHAPTER TWENTY-TWO

Tank is impossibly strong.

And the more I thrash around to break free, the clearer it becomes that my struggle against him is useless; his hold becomes that much tighter. I twist my head to bite his arm, but I can't get the angle right. I barely pinch him with my teeth. All I'm left with is the rank taste of his salty sweat in my mouth.

"Go ahead and open the damn door, Pete," Tank says, grunting. Out of the corner of my eye I see his crony scuffling past us, helping Tank snatch me away. They're dragging me from the back wall toward an entrance in the side wall. It's too much to hope that anyone will stop them. Not with the riot still raging and Florae-panic still clouding everyone's minds. And anyway, who would care about a guard having a little fun with the new girl?

So it's up to me.

I go slack as if I've given up. It takes a few seconds that feel like an eternity, but when I feel him relax just the tiniest bit, I land a forceful kick to Tank's knee. He doesn't drop me, but he has to adjust his hold, hoisting me up in his arms to get a better grip, his hot, labored breaths blowing down the back of my neck. I duck my head down as far as I can, then whip it back, hard. My skull makes contact with Tank's face, and I hear his nose rebreak with an ugly, satisfying crack. Then he lets out a wounded howl.

For a split second my heart freezes in my chest—he's not letting go. Then I feel hot liquid spill down my back; he drops me to stanch the flow of blood from his nose.

I fall to a sitting position, the force sending shock waves up my spine, but I recover and quickly roll away. Tank, one hand on his crimson, swollen face, lunges after me screaming, "You little bitch!"

I skitter away just in time, but then someone else is on me—someone small and light. Pete. I feel a sharp pressure in my chest, like a punch but more precise. He has a knife. He brings it down again and again. The blade rips through my shirt but glances off my synth-suit underneath.

In another second Tank will be on me again. I grab the blade of Pete's knife and shove it off to the side, my synth-suit protecting my hand, then drive my other fist into his neck. As he clutches at his throat, gasping, I snatch the knife from him and kick the side of one of his knees, toppling him to the ground.

Then Tank is in front of me again, his face and hands covered in blood. He looks like an oversized Florae splattered in gore. I hold on to the image, as it occurs to me that if Tank were a Florae, I would have already killed him. It'll be easier to get the job done if I think of him as something less than human.

My gun is out, and I hold Pete's knife in my other hand, but still Tank takes a step forward. He's going to make me kill him.

"No!" Pete screams hoarsely. He's dragged himself to his feet and is holding up his hand. "No," he croaks between desperate gulps for oxygen. "Lay off."

Tank turns to glare at Pete, but I don't wait to see if he's going to take his advice. I sprint back to the Yard, cutting in and out of the thinning crowd and ducking into the first door I find, to Cellblock C. Then I lean against the wall, my heart pounding out of my chest.

"You okay, honey?" a man asks, his Texan accent thick. I can barely see him in the dark, moving toward me out of his cell. "Y'all get caught in that mess out there?" I don't even have to answer him. He sees the gun and knife and backs away, retreating to his cell.

Once I can breathe normally again, I check my chest for damage. Pete stabbed me maybe a half dozen times, and my shirt is shredded, but the synth-suit held. I'll be bruised, but there's no real injury. Amazingly, Ken's notebook is still in the pocket of my sweatpants.

I discard my ruined shirt and am wondering what to do with Pete's knife—I already have my Guardian knives in their sheaths on my thighs—when the man's voice comes out of the dark again. "You sure you don't need nothin', honey?"

I sigh and glare into the dark at him.

"A shirt, mebbe? You can't walk around like that, I wouldn't think. I got a shirt, if . . ."

I take a breath, letting down my guard slightly. He just wants to barter. And he's right: I still have to get back to

Cellblock B, where Jacks's cell is, and I have no idea where Tank and Pete have gone. It *would* be good to get something that covers my arms and head. Something that would make me less recognizable.

"If what?" I ask him.

He takes a step into the muddy light of the entryway. He's a little man, tucked inside a hoodie. He nods at the knife. "That looks like a mighty fine blade."

I look at the weapon still in my hand, then back at the man again. "I'll trade for that sweatshirt," I tell him.

"Yes, ma'am." He peels off the hoodie and holds it out to me.

"Drop it on the floor. I'll leave the knife."

He looks doubtful.

"Do you want it or not?" I push. He drops the hoodie and backs away. I take the knife and throw it far down the hall, where it clatters to a stop on the concrete floor. The man shakes his head, then moves slowly to retrieve it.

I quickly snatch the hoodie off the ground, pull it on over my head, and push up the hood. I crack the door, then put my hand to my ear and turn on my sound amplifier to check if the coast is clear outside. It all sounds good until I catch a snippet of conversation from the Yard.

". . . I *know* I stabbed her." It's Pete's voice, raspy from my punch to his throat.

"I told you, she was mine," Tank's voice cuts through. "Anyway, you must'a missed her. Did you see how fast she ran off? No one with a knife in their gut could move like that."

And that's what I should do again now—run. Run to my cell and lock the door. I know where Tank and Pete are now; it would be easy to avoid them. But then what? Live in constant fear? I scan the Yard for either of them, but they're out of my line of vision. I tense my body up, ready to bolt for Cellblock B. Then:

"It doesn't matter anyway. It's not like she has a lot of places to hide."

"But we can't do it when Jacks is around," Pete croaks. "He says . . ."

I pull the hood down lower over my face and walk outside, heading in the direction of their conversation. Maybe their attack was motivated by something more than Tank's bloodlust.

"Well, doing it when Jacks isn't around is going to be tough. She's always with him or in their cell."

"But that's how Doc wants it," Pete insists. "When she's

alone. He said the Warden will have our asses if sumpthun' happens to his nephew."

Spotting them across the Yard, I duck behind a trampled tent, my heart racing. So Doc wants me dead. Is it because I found out about the testing and he thinks I'll tell everyone? Or is this coming from New Hope, from Dr. Reynolds? Or from Ken?

I peek out behind the tent and see Tank and Pete still walking, their backs to me. They haven't seen me, so I continue to trail them. It looks like they're headed for the front wall, to the guards' quarters.

"Doc also said to get it done by the end of the day," Tank says, "but that ain't gonna happen."

Pete looks up at Tank, giving a panicked little hop as he hurries to keep up with him. "What are we gonna do? Doc's gonna be pissed. You saw him angry, what he done to Freddy that one time."

"I saw him."

"Made him into a damn *Florae*!" Pete shouts.

"I said I *saw* him. Shut the hell up." Tank looks around. "Everybody in this place is going crazy 'cause they think one of those things got inside, and you're gonna go around shouting about what we saw Doc do?"

That's what Doc meant when he said sometimes he had to "create an opportunity" to test the vaccine. Poor Jacks. He has no idea what kind of monster his father actually is.

Pete nods. They're almost at the wall. "I know, I know. Sorry. But if we don't make this happen, we're the ones gonna end up dead."

"It'll happen. Trust me. When Doc came to us and told us what he wanted done, I thought it was my damn birthday! I ain't gonna let that little bitch slip through my fingers," Tank assures him.

He opens the door and nearly collides with the Warden. "Oh, sorry, boss."

"It's all right." The Warden steps out. "Did you boys take care of that thang yet?"

"Oh no, not yet, boss. But don't worry. I'll get it done," Tank says before they disappear through the door in the wall.

The Warden sighs and mutters, "Useless," before continuing on his way. He's heading straight for me, so I duck behind some cardboard boxes, crouching low, hoping I look like one of the helpless masses from the Yard.

I peek around the box to find the Warden continuing toward me, and I pull my hood down low. He pauses a few feet away from me. My body thrums with fear.

"Did you," his voice booms across the Yard, "just spit on my boot?"

"No, boss," comes a frail voice. "I didn't see you was standing there."

"You didn't see me?" the Warden asks, pulling the man up by his raggedy shirt. He's so painfully thin, he shakes in the Warden's grasp. "Or you didn't spit on my boot?"

"I . . . I don't . . . know," the man stutters out a reply.

"Well, then, clean 'em." The Warden pushes the man to the ground. A crowd has gathered now, and everyone is staring and laughing at the unfortunate man singled out by the Warden.

"Clean 'em good," someone calls.

He tries to wipe the Warden's boot with what's left of his shirt, but someone else yells, "Spit-shine 'em!"

The Warden laughs and glances around the crowd. I realize this is all for their benefit, to assert his dominance. To put on a show, a spectacle. New Hope was about hiding the bad away from its citizens. Fort Black puts it all on display and lets the people lap it up.

"Spit-shine!" the Warden calls. "Maybe that's what he was trying to do! I like the sound of that. You, lick my boot clean."

My stomach drops at the humiliation the man is suffering

at the hands of the Warden. Only a coward would treat such a harmless man so cruelly. The man reaches out his tongue and touches it to the Warden's boot. The crowd erupts in shouts and clapping, laughing at the man's embarrassment. The Warden pulls his foot away and uses it to kick the man aside. Still laughing, he walks through the crowd, which parts out of his way.

I stare after him for just a moment before I disperse with the crowd and hurry back to Cellblock B. Whether Doc has told Dr. Reynolds I'm here, he wants me dead. Even the Warden is behind him. I guess they realized I wasn't as good a companion for Jacks as they'd hoped. I should have known they'd want to get rid of me after exposing Jacks to the truth.

My decision's made. Fort Black isn't safe for me anymore, if it ever was. Ken's promise of information isn't enough to make me stay. I need to get my pack and find Jacks.

When I get back to our cell, though, Jacks isn't there. I don't have time to wait for him. I grab a piece of sketch paper and a pencil. A note will have to be good enough.

I'm still staring at the blank paper, unsure of how to say good-bye, when Brenna appears in the doorway. "Jacks here?"

"No. I . . ."

Brenna takes in my wild eyes, the pack on my back. "What's up, Amy?"

"It looks like I have to leave."

She blinks at me. "For good?"

I nod. "I think so."

"Where you going?"

It's probably better for her if she doesn't know. "Pretty far away. I guess I'm glad I at least have my bike."

"I know where there's a car lot and a mechanic's shop out there," she tells me. "I heard Dwayne bragging about it. Maybe we can get you a car."

"A car won't be hard to find. There are a million out there, just rusting away."

"Yeah, finding a car ain't the problem. . . . It's finding a car with gas. The Scrappers have sucked all the ones around here dry."

My eyes widen. I hadn't even thought about the lack of gas. "Oh, Brenna. You mean you know where to find a *working* car? That would be amazing. Can you tell me where that lot is?"

"I can take you there. When do you want to leave?"

"Right now." A car would be a game changer. But I can't put Brenna in danger. "Do you know how to survive out there?"

"Sure. You know, I used to be a Scrapper. I make a better living at the fights, though. I'll show you where it is. I'm real good at being quiet, when I have to be."

"We don't have to be quiet. I have a gadget that scares off the Floraes." Immediately I know I've said too much. I'm not thinking—or really, I'm thinking of something else, what to write to Jacks.

Brenna is silent for a couple of seconds. "Are you serious?" she asks slowly, her brow furrowed skeptically.

I don't answer right away. I feel like smacking myself. How could I be so careless? If word gets out about the advantages I have, I'll be dead within a day. Though it hardly matters now; I'm leaving Fort Black for good. Who cares if Brenna blabs when she gets back? "Yes, I . . . You won't say anything to any-one, will you?"

She takes another step closer. "Really? Like I'm gonna tell anyone," she says with a roll of her eyes. I look her in the face, and I believe her. I have to. "Amy, that has to be the most valu-able thing in Fort Black. Hell, on the whole planet."

I shrug, trying to play it off. "So we'll be safe on the way there. Fine. But, Brenna, just to be clear: I'm not returning to Fort Black. You'll be on your own on the way back here."

"Don't worry about me," she says with a grin. "You bet your

ass I can take care of myself. Maybe I can even find something good to bring back and trade."

"Okay, then," I say, and return to staring at the blank page, contemplating my last words to Jacks. Finally I scribble:

Jacks. I'm in danger here. I have to go. Thank you for everything. Really.

I know it's a lame note. Especially after all that's happened between us. The fact is, I don't know *how* I feel about Jacks. But I can't let anyone into my life right now. Not in that way.

Besides, Jacks could never go with me—not with what I have ahead. He's too afraid of the world outside the walls of Fort Black. Too afraid of the Floraes. And I'm afraid too, but I can't let that stop me from doing what I have to do.

I put the note on Jacks's pillow and look at Brenna. "Get what you need and meet me in the parking garage at my bike. You have one too, right?" As I ask, I remember she showed me hers the day I got mine. I'd never thought to ask her why she needed one. If she used to be a Scrapper, it makes sense she would have one.

"Yep, and I don't need to pack anything. It's not far. I should be back by nightfall."

"Oh, wait." I remember Tank and Pete were last at the front wall. "Is there any other way to get out of here besides through the front gate?"

"Yeah, there's the back entrance, out the garage where our bikes are. But . . . Amy, *what* is going on? Why are you in such a hurry to leave?"

I look at her. "Brenna, has anybody ever wanted to kill you?"

Brenna pauses and then gives me a wicked grin and raised eyebrows that say, *Look who you're talking to here.* She snorts out a laugh.

"Just every damn day," she tells me.

CHAPTER TWENTY- THREE

After the constant noise of Fort Black, the silence on the outside is deafening.

Brenna and I leave the prison without incident. As we make our way through the garage to our bikes, I'm sure we'll be spotted by one of Doc's minions. But our departure is quiet, effortless. We unlock our bikes, check the tire pressure, and ride off. It's not against the rules to leave; when I look up nervously at the top of the wall, the guard just nods and waves to Brenna. It all seems so easy.

Too easy.

We ride across the dusty flats, side by side. Before, this would be kind of a good time—the breeze rustling my hair, the sun beating down on my face. As I listen to the wind whistle in my ears, I can almost imagine everything is like it was Before. It feels . . . free.

"This is fan," I say with a smile.

Instead of sharing my delight, Brenna responds, "Aw, shit. Look left."

I swivel my head to where she's pointing. In the distance, a Florae has spotted us and is making its way over, brought by the sound of our voices.

"So you sure this Florae gadget of yours is going to work?" Brenna says nervously, looking from side to side. Because of Fort Black's intentionally rural locale, we're forced to ride in the wide open. Aside from a few clumps of houses, there's nothing around for miles.

"It will work. I was out here for months before I came to Fort Black and never had a problem." I was also sure to keep it charged and turned it on before we left.

"I hope it doesn't crap out now," she mumbles. I can feel Brenna's fear through her sudden silence as the Florae lopes toward us, gaining speed.

"Shit," she says again, pedaling faster. As if that would help.

But at a hundred feet, the monster begins to tremble, its pale yellow-green skin shimmering in the brilliant light. It flinches back and veers away in the direction it came.

"There," I breathe, slowing down. "See?"

"Holy crap," Brenna says. "You got any more of those things?"

"No, only the one," I tell her as she gives me a strange look.

We ride for another half hour. The deflected Florae has given Brenna confidence, and she begins to ask more about me, my past, and my family. Not wanting to reveal too much about my mother, I tell her about my father. All the things I loved about him. How he went on and on about buying organic and not wasting water.

"An eco-nerd, huh?" Brenna says. "Well, he sounds like he was a good guy."

"He was." There's a tug in my chest, but the tears don't start this time. I wonder, after all this death and sadness, if my tears just dried up. "What about you? Your family?"

Brenna just shrugs. "I never had a family, really. Hey, this car lot's a little farther out than I thought," Brenna says, distracting me. We stop to drink some water. I guzzle mine greedily before I hear Brenna curse.

"My water bottle's got a hole in it." She holds it up. A few drops fall from a pin-sized hole in the bottom of the bottle and onto the ground, splattering the pavement.

I shake my canteen, but I've drunk all my water. "Hang on," I say. Water's usually not hard to find, if you know where to look. I stop, flip my pack from over my shoulder, and check my supplies. "I've got a filter, but we've got to find a source." I scan the horizon with my binoculars. "There's a farmhouse over there," I say, pointing. "Maybe there's a stream or a well. If you think we have a few miles, maybe we should hit that."

"You think it's safe?"

"Safer than you passing out in this heat and me having to wheel your ass around. Let's go."

We make our way quickly over the parched, scorched ground, slowing down as we get close to the farm's gate. Before, it must have been a lovely home. The gingerbread trim is still intact, as is a porch swing, drifting back lightly in the almost nonexistent breeze. But it's only a shell of a house now. The paint is peeling, and the windows have all been shattered. Trash litters the yard—empty cans, wooden chairs, an old trampoline.

Brenna leans over and picks up a pink hairbrush.

"Think I can trade this for something?" she asks, rubbing her shaved head.

"Well, I don't think you'll be using it," I say, grinning. "Hey, let's stay away from the house. There might be a well back here."

"Hell no," Brenna says, walking up on the porch. "Let's see what else is inside."

"Brenna, I'm telling you, the place could be–"

Quick as a flash, a figure shoots out the door. Before Brenna can move, the attacker has her by the neck and holds up a rusty kitchen knife. It's a woman, thin, with dark rings under her eyes.

"Occupied," she whispers hoarsely. She's so filthy, it's impossible to tell her age, but she looks at least as old as my mother. Her hair is plaited in two greasy gray braids.

Brenna yells in frustration and struggles to free herself. The woman holds the knife closer to her neck.

"Be quiet, girl!" she shrieks between clenched teeth. "Do you want those *things* to come? I have nothing to lose by killing you."

"Except that I'll kill *you*," I say, purposefully loud. The volume puts her on edge.

The woman narrows her eyes and looks at me.

"How?" she sneers.

"It will take me exactly one second to take out my gun." I lay my hand on it at my side.

The woman grits her teeth but holds tightly to Brenna. "What do you want?"

"Water," I say. "That's it."

She looks at me warily.

"I'll stay right here with your friend while you get it," she says. "And don't think about going inside. My man'll kill you in a second."

"Well, she'll kick *his* ass," Brenna says. "I've seen her level dudes bigger than whoever you've got back there."

The woman looks at me again. I notice that her hand is shaking. She's terrified of us, that we'll bring the Floraes.

I nod and slowly make my way around the house. The well, like she said, is easy to spot. When I look inside, the water is murky but filterable. "Found it!" I yell.

There's a grunt from the front of the house. When I look in the direction of the noise, I let out a small breath. The entire back of the house has been burned away. There's no way anyone could be inside.

"It's just gonna take another minute," I call, then silently make my way to the house. Without taking the time to look around, I walk through to the front and rush through the door, grabbing the woman's arm and yanking the knife away from Brenna's neck.

The woman doesn't scream as she tears at me. She's survived this long by being quiet. But within a second, Brenna has her pinned to the floor. To my surprise, she doesn't struggle at all. She just lies there, limp, on the rotting porch. Up close her face is red and cracked, her nose permanently red, as if she's been crying for years.

I check the front windows to make sure there's no one lurking around. Through one of the downstairs windows, I can see one room that survived the fire. Purple walls and what looks like a poster of a teen star from Before. I can't help but smile when I realize who it is—Kay, holding a microphone, her eyes shut, her short hair streaked with blue and her body wrapped in a spangled leotard. It's hard to think of the Kay I know as the same person as this clichéd teen superstar. My eyes dart around the rest of the room. It's mostly trashed, but I can make out some other items. A broken princess mirror, a canopy bed on its side.

A girl must have lived here, Before.

I return to the front. "There's no one there. Nothing inside really."

"Go ahead and kill me," she says, as loud as I've heard her speak yet. "I don't care anymore." She stares at us pathetically.

"Why would I kill you?" Brenna asks. "It was just, you know, a misunderstanding."

The woman turns her empty gaze to the sky.

"Everyone kills everything," she whispers. I look at Brenna, whose face is carved into a deep frown.

"This your house?" Brenna asks.

The woman nods.

"Kids?"

"Not anymore." She closes her eyes. "We used to be three, and now I'm one," she says flatly.

We stare at her, unable to respond to her sadness.

"My husband was bitten, infected. He killed our girl. Ate her. Now I hide in the cellar to keep him from killing me when he wanders back."

She sits up and wipes her face angrily. "Take as much water as you want. I don't care. I'm surprised the creatures aren't here already, with how much of a racket you all are making."

"Go back to the cellar," I say. "We'll leave soon, and you'll be safe from the Floraes."

Brenna holds out the pink brush to the lady. "I guess this is yours."

The woman looks at it. "Keep it." She turns and walks into the shell of her house.

"Wait!" I call to her, but she hurries into the house and disappears, though I see her peeking through a burned-out window frame. I leave the woman as many protein bars as I can spare on her front steps. "These are for you . . . for the water," I call out to her.

She pokes her head out of the door. "What's wrong with them?" she asks suspiciously.

"Nothing. . . . Please, take them," I tell her.

She bends down and gathers them up in her arms. "Thank you," she says hesitantly. "I forgot . . . you know. That people can be kind." She backs away and ducks inside.

I stare after her for a while, sad, but Brenna calls to me and breaks my trance. We stay just long enough to fill up our water bottles. Then, after bleakly surveying the ruined landscape, we get on our bikes and slowly ride away.

I'm quiet for a long time. Brenna, seeming to sense my mood, doesn't bother to talk until we're a few miles away.

"She's been out there a while," Brenna says. "It's hard to

remember, isn't it? That Florae are people. We're so glad when they die, but those are ex-humans that get blown away."

I don't say anything. Actually, it *isn't* that hard for me to remember. Because my mother started it all. Because I was forced to kill a Florae that used to be a friend.

And this is what Jacks doesn't understand. Or Rice. Or anyone, really. I don't have the luxury of starting a life in Fort Black. Or New Hope. Or anywhere. *We used to be three,* that woman said. Families have been torn apart because of what my mother did. I owe it to them to try to stop the cycle—to stop whatever Dr. Reynolds is pulling now.

But first thing's first. I have my own family to think about. And Brenna's helping me get closer.

"Hey, there it is," Brenna says, pointing to an old strip mall next to the abandoned highway. "That's where the mechanic's shop is. . . . Dwayne said there were plenty of gassed-up cars."

We pedal faster toward the strip mall, containing the auto shop, an old frozen yogurt shop (judging from the remains on the plastic chairs and tables, clearly a site of a huge Florae attack), and a sporting goods store, thoroughly looted. My pulse speeds up as I see the parking lot filled with vehicles. We drop our bikes, running from car to car. Most have keys in the ignition, but the gas caps are all hanging open. The fuel has been siphoned. There are plenty of cars but no gas to get them going.

"Shit," she says, slapping the open door shut. "They got to this one too."

I kick the tire of the car nearest me.

"Sorry, Amy," Brenna calls from the last car in her row, and the last one on the lot. "I didn't think a Scrapper would have gotten all the gas already. I wonder how he carried it back? He was really on top of that shit."

I manufacture a smile. "It's okay. I appreciate your help. I guess I'll just go on from here on my bike. Are you going to be able to– What are you doing?"

Brenna has pulled a knife and is running straight at me.

I blink, trying to make sense of what I'm seeing, but there's no mistaking the look on her face. She's trying to kill me.

No, not Brenna.

She can't be working with Doc too. But they wanted me away from Jacks, and Brenna just coincidentally showed up to help. Is she going to kill me out here, where no one will ever find me? Or was this just an elaborate trick to get my emitter? She always admired my synth-suit and asked what other gadgets I had.

Well, I won't give it up without a fight.

I've been too slow to grab my own knife when Brenna is upon me. Except she flashes past. I whirl just in time to see her tackle a man to the ground. I get it now—but there's no time to feel guilty for thinking she'd betrayed me. She needs my help subduing the man on the ground.

Except she doesn't. By the time I've tossed my pack aside, Brenna already has him in a chokehold and has pushed his head to the side with a bone-wrenching crunch. She releases him and he slides to the ground, his head bent at an impossible angle. I swallow my horror and compose myself. I recognize him, despite his mangled appearance. Pete. Tank won't be far away.

"We should go," I say. "Now."

"Why was he trying to kill you?" Brenna asks, unmoving.

"I don't know—habit? He and Tank have had it in for me since I got here." I frantically scan the auto yard. Tank could be hiding anywhere. I don't have time to explain everything to her, and even if I did, it wouldn't help her any. She still has to live in Fort Black. The more she knows, the less safe she'll be there. "I didn't think they'd follow me outside the walls."

They're guards, not Scrappers. How did they make it out here without the Floraes finding them? They must've followed us close enough to be protected by the emitter. I'd have seen them, though. Had they just gotten lucky, riding in the wake of the emitter?

I look down at Pete. "Tank must be here, too. He's . . ."

"Right here, cupcake."

I turn to find Tank standing ten feet away, a rifle leveled at me. His nose is swollen, his face purple. He looks like a monster, not a man.

"If you fire that gun," I tell him, "the Floraes will find you and they'll kill you."

Tank harrumphs. "We've been trailing you since you left Fort Black and you two haven't shut up once. I don't see what all the fuss is about with the Floraes. If it's this easy to avoid them, I could be a Scrapper. It ain't that hard."

It's pointless to reason with him, so I try to pull my gun, but Tank doesn't hesitate to pull the trigger. I'm on my back before I hear the crack of the gun echo through the air, pain exploding from my chest where the bullet hits my synth-suit, the wind knocked from my lungs.

I hear Brenna cry out, "No!" as Tank laughs.

"Drop it, girlie," he says to Brenna. Her knife falls to the ground next to where I'd been standing. She takes a step back, but Tank yells for her to stop. "We ain't in Fort Black anymore, and this ain't the Arena. I could kill you now and no one would ever know."

I can tell he's getting closer by the sound of his footsteps on the loose gravel of the parking lot. "You killed my buddy Pete, and I'm all tore up about it, so I need some cheering up. I was also looking forward to what I was going to do to cupcake there. I know you'd rather fight men than be with one, but we'll see how much fight you have left after I'm through with ya."

The pain in my chest is subsiding. My lungs scream for oxygen, but I make myself draw in a silent breath instead of gulping in air. I wish my gun were still in my hand. I turn my head slightly, but I don't see it on the ground. It must have flown off, out of sight, when I fell. But as soon as Tank's familiar foul smell hits my nose, I jump up, onto him, going for his rifle.

"What the . . . !" he screams. He's shocked that I can move, that I'm not bleeding to death on the ground, so I do manage to get a hand on the gun, but he just covers both my hand and the rifle's action with his enormous mitt and clamps me tight to him with his other arm.

"You ain't *dead*?" he says, grunting. "Oh, cupcake, you're gonna *wish*–"

A pair of arms wrapped around Tank's neck cuts off his words, along with his oxygen. He needs at least one arm to fight Brenna off, but he's not giving up the rifle. He heaves me aside with his other arm and starts clubbing away wildly over his shoulder with it. He throws me too hard, though: Both the rifle and I are torn out of his grip. I hit the dirt on my back again, this time accompanied by a horrible crack.

I sit up and see that Tank has stopped struggling, and Brenna has stepped away from him. Both are looking with shock at Tank's left shoulder and the spreading bright-red bloom on his dirty white shirt. He places his hand over his heart and looks up at me, confused. I stare at the rifle, still in my hand. The gun either fired accidentally when I dropped it, or I pulled the trigger without even realizing it. Tank stumbles to the side, almost falling. He gives me one last look of pure hatred before loping into the distance, leaving a trail of blood behind him.

I hop up, trembling. Suddenly the feel of the rifle in my hand is repulsive. I set it down on the ground, then, spotting my own Guardian gun, grab it. I look at the place Tank disappeared to in the distance. I've never shot a person before. I've killed Floraes, though, but it's just not the same.

"Are you okay?" Brenna asks.

I shake my head. "He's going to die out there."

"Good. He should die."

I try to tell myself that he's a murderer and deserves to die. But what does that make me?

"You've never killed anyone before, have you?" Brenna gives me a look that's almost motherly. It's so out of character, it jolts me from my trance.

"I did. A long time ago." I don't recognize my own voice, it's so eerily calm. I lick my lips and try to recover. "When everything first happened and I was just trying to survive day to day. I was alone and then had finally met another survivor. But he was going to hurt me, so I rigged a car alarm and set it off. The Floraes got him."

"Well, Tank was sure as shit going to hurt you too," Brenna says, her moment of tender concern gone. "He thought he *did* kill you. . . . Hell, *I* thought he killed you. Why aren't you dead?"

At the mention of me being shot, the pain floods back to my breastbone. I touch the hole in the sweatshirt I am wearing over my synth-suit and wince. Pete pounded my chest with a knife, but the bullet was ten times worse. I'll have bruises upon bruises. I cough experimentally, sending a sharp pain through my ribs. It stings when I move, but I don't think there's any internal damage. I may have lucked out again.

"It's that ninja suit you wear, isn't it?" Brenna asks. "Where can I get one of those? That might be even more useful than that Florae repellent sound thing you have."

The emitter. I frantically scan the ground for my pack, spotting it a few feet from where I'd left it. Someone must have tripped over it during the scuffle. I spring over to it, my chest burning as I bend over to grab the emitter. I let out a groan.

The emitter is broken in two.

It takes a few seconds for the fear to hit me, but when it does I can't move.

"That doesn't look so good," Brenna whispers, looking around. "You think it still works?"

I stare at the broken emitter, my legs heavy. I've relied on it so much these past few months. Now it's gone. We're sitting ducks.

I will my limbs to work and quickly sling the pack over my shoulder and, ignoring the pain that shoots through my ribs, spin in place with my gun. "We need to find shelter, now," I hiss. Two loud gunshots had gone off. Maybe there weren't any Floraes around to hear them. Maybe we're still okay.

Yet out of the corner of my eye, I catch a flash of green streaking across the parking lot.

The world seems to slow. And now I see it—a Florae. It rises slowly over a car. Its eyes are milky and unseeing, but its ears—or earholes—are a hundred times sharper than our own. I know it's heard us. And if one has, there will soon be many more.

Brenna and I look at each other. Our instinct, of course, is to run. But that would only make things worse. We'd go in different directions, and the Florae, with all its inhuman speed, would hunt us down in seconds. Our only hope is to stick together.

The two of us stand there as if time has stopped. I wish I could sign to her, like I did so many times to Baby. I hold up a hand to try and convey we should be still. She shows me she understands with a small, stiff nod.

And then everything happens at once.

I raise my arm and shoot the creature with my silenced Guardian gun before it can figure out exactly where we are. It falls, but there's no time for relief. Another appears to our left from another car, attracted by the minimal noise. I turn to Brenna and put my fingers to my lips. She again nods her understanding.

We can make our stand here; there are plenty of abandoned cars to hide behind. But I don't know how many are coming, and they could attack us from any direction. It would be pointless to use the rifle, as the sound of the shots would just bring more. They are only a few now, and far enough away for us to find someplace where we can be quiet and wait for Them to disperse.

I point behind us, to the shelter of the strip mall. We need someplace secure that we can hide.

Another creature appears a few hundred feet behind Brenna, listening. I take aim and silently mouth one word at her.

Run.

CHAPTER TWENTY-FOUR

We sprint past rows of cars toward the strip mall. I run silently, like I used to years ago, in New Hope, my mouth gaping. Brenna, on the other hand, makes a lot of noise, loping heavily along. She's fast and strong but not light on her feet. Her loud shoes banging on the pavement will only bring more Floraes. I shoot three before we make it to the auto shop.

The door is already wrecked, the wood shattered by Florae claws. Whoever tried to hide in here before didn't last long.

The floor is covered in rust-colored bloodstains. Auto parts are scattered everywhere inside. A car is perched high up on a lift—a great place to hide, but I have no idea how to get us up there.

"Can you shoot?" I ask Brenna.

She gives me a hard look. "I *am* from Texas." I hand her the gun, and she aims it at the open doorway. There's about twenty bullets left in the clip, and I hope Brenna doesn't waste them. A Florae appears and she gets off two shots before bringing it down. She grins. "See, no problem."

I pull a knife and search the shop for a ladder or anything of use to fight the Floraes or help us hide. At the back is an office separated from the shop by a counter used to transact business with customers. Useless. I look wildly around for another advantage, and then it hits me.

Whoever used to own this place would want to lock up their money at night. There's got to be a way to barricade this office. Then, looking up, I spot it—a metal gate that can be pulled down from above.

I hop up onto the counter and slide into the office. The actual office door is solid, made of steel, not wood. The outside windows are high up; a Florae couldn't get through those. Leaping back on the counter, I stretch for the handle at the bottom of the sliding door. I jump and miss it, landing with a blinding shockwave of pain.

Chest throbbing, I check on Brenna. She's holding a shooter's stance, gun trained on the doorway. Two more Floraes lie dead on the threshold. She's no taller than I am, but she's more athletic. Maybe she can jump higher.

"Brenna, I need you here," I whisper-yell, my voice echoing through the shop.

She backs toward me, gun still on the doorway, as I hop down from the counter. I take the gun from her and motion with my head at the gate. "Pull that down. It's too high for me, but if we don't get it, we're dead."

Brenna swings herself up onto the counter, eyes the handle, and leaps, grabbing it on her first try. The door comes crashing down, metal runners shrieking, but it jams to a stop halfway.

I run to help her, only to spot a trio of Floraes drawn by the screeching of the metal. I drop them each in turn with a head-shot, but the closest one made it to within ten feet of us—and two more are jostling with each other in the doorway.

"Get that thing *down*," I say, growling.

"I'm *trying*." She slams it with the bottom of her fist in frustration, and it falls another few feet. I duck down to continue to shoot Floraes through the opening. It's a bad angle, though, and one makes it all the way to us, slamming into the counter and wedging its head and neck between it and the bottom of the rolling gate. Its black-blue tongue flicks out of its mouth and it thrashes its head, razor-sharp teeth bared. It's so close, it can almost taste us.

I shoot it and it slides back off the counter as another creature rams the gate. I pull the trigger but nothing happens.

I'm out of ammo.

There's no time to retrieve another clip from my pack. I draw my knife and am just about to stab it in the eye when Brenna pushes the Florae away and jams the door down the last few inches. She closes the mechanism on the counter and locks it in place, grinning.

I slump against the wall. The Floraes scratch and scramble wildly against the rolling door and the other, regular door, but it looks as if, for the moment, both will hold.

"Amy–" Brenna starts to speak, but I shush her. We just have to stay silent until nightfall. They'll wander away by then.

"But, Amy." She's panting loudly and I look at her closely. She holds up her left hand, its flesh ripped and bloodied. Her ever-present grin has disappeared. "I think one of them got me." Her voice is surprisingly calm, but the look on her face betrays her horror.

"Was that from a Florae or from the gate?"

She turns her hand sideways. Gashes run across her middle and ring finger. The gate would have cut her palm, not the outside of her fingers. It wouldn't have made such a deep wound. It looks like she was cut with a knife.

Brenna has been bitten by a Florae.

"What are we going to do?" she asks, eyes wide. "I don't want to turn–"

"You won't," I tell her, stepping toward her and pinning the wrist of her wounded hand to the counter so that she can't move. She twists her head to look at me, her eyes filled with terror.

"Amy, please. Don't," she whispers.

"I have to make sure you don't change." I look at her shredded, useless fingers.

"Don't do it." Her voice is unlike that of the Brenna I've come to know. The fear is taking over.

"My knife is sharp," I say, willing the tremors out of my voice. "You'll barely feel it."

The truth is, I'm probably more scared than she is.

She takes a deep breath and nods. "Do it," she says, resigned.

"Brenna, I'm so sorry," I tell her as I bring the blade down.

CHAPTER TWENTY-FIVE

After a few hours, the Floraes stop beating on the door. I look at Brenna, lying like a rag doll where I deposited her, lifeless, on a beat-up couch. I had to do it.

I had to remove the infected area. It's a long shot, but those "flu" injections Doc gave to everyone could actually be a vaccine. The instructions he showed me said to remove the infected area. I only cut off the fingers that had been bitten, her ring and middle finger on her left hand. It sickened me to do it, but I couldn't let myself chicken out, not with Brenna in real danger.

After it was done, Brenna passed out, probably from the shock. I let her sleep for a few hours, making sure the bandage I made from an old shirt I found on a hook stanched the bleeding. Luckily, I found an old first aid kit with some painkillers in a desk drawer. They're expired, but they seem to be doing the job.

"How are you feeling?" I ask when I notice her eyes are open.

Brenna sits up woozily on the shabby couch and looks at her bandaged hand, blood seeping through the dressing. "Like crap."

"Well, hopefully this worked."

"Yeah. I'll be pretty pissed if you cut off my fingers and I still turn into a green flesh-eating freak."

I move closer and sit on the arm of the couch. I explain the possibility of Doc's vaccine. "And it was only two fingers. I thought you were tougher than that." My joke comes out hollow, my concern clear in my voice.

Brenna laughs feebly, though. "Lucky it didn't get my arm . . . or my face."

I let out my own strained laugh, but we both know what

will happen if Brenna turns into a Florae: I'll have to shoot her. I've reloaded my gun and been watching her for signs of any change, but so far she's been fine.

"Do you think those shots that Doc gave me really made me immune?"

"I don't know," I tell her honestly. "But it looks good so far. And it's been a couple of hours." I don't have a lot of faith in the vaccine working, but I want Brenna to believe that it will. I don't want her last hours to be full of fear.

Brenna wobbles and lies back with a moan. "I don't feel so good." She's starting to look a little green, but not Florae green, more like about-to-vomit green. I give her some water to sip, which seems to help. "Am I starting to change?"

"No. I think you're nauseous because I cut your fingers off."

I frown, thinking. Are you supposed to keep people who are in shock awake? Or is that just for a head wound?

"Are the Floraes still out there?"

"No, I think they've forgotten about us." I glance up through the window at the darkening sky. "We'll probably be okay if we whisper." Not too long ago, I was afraid to speak at all, afraid to make any noises. Now I know Them better. I know what They are, how They work. "They're more active during the day."

Brenna's eyes begin to flutter and I wipe the sweat off her

forehead with the remains of my shredded shirt. "Brenna, stay with me."

She opens her eyes, focusing on something over my shoulder. "It's not easy, you know."

"What isn't?"

"Being a fighter . . . having to be twice as good because you're a girl." Her eyes settle shut again. She sounds like she's whispering to herself as much as to me. "I can't just be myself. I can't just be Brenna. And now I'm dying."

"You're not dying," I tell her, trying to inject my voice with confidence I don't feel. "Soon you'll be back in Fort Black, making out with that redhead you have a crush on."

She laughs weakly. "How'd you know about that?"

"I saw you staring at her, after we went to get my bike that one day. I can put two and two together."

"Well, don't tell anyone about that. Her man would be real angry."

"Like you care."

Brenna's wicked smile slowly drops and then we're both quiet. Brenna can't die. Not now, not here, without knowing what it's like to be wanted.

My mind wanders to Rice, holding me in the sunshine of New Hope. And then Jacks, his body pressed against mine in a prison cell. The way he kissed me, I'd never felt anything like that before. Not even with Rice. It was as if my entire body was on fire, being consumed by my want for him. What would have happened if we hadn't been interrupted? I let my mind go there briefly, then shake my head, blushing. I can't think about that now. I can't afford to.

Brenna's shock is showing itself—she's starting to tremble. I've got to keep her mind busy.

"How did you make it to Fort Black, anyway?"

"I was brought there. The caretakers at my foster care facility packed us all in a van and drove us over to Fort Black. I was only eleven. . . . I don't remember much."

"They brought you to a prison?"

"Yeah, I guess they thought the walls would protect us or something."

I study her face. Her eyes are closed again, and her features are peaceful. I can see the little girl in them.

"Where are all the other kids?" I ask. "Are they still around?"

"Naw. They disappeared. I ran away from the doctors. . . ." Her brow furrows. "Wait, that can't be right. I must be remembering it wrong. Our caretakers put us all in a room, but no one was telling us what had happened. One kid wouldn't stop crying. I didn't want to be with them anymore, so I ran into the exercise yard and hid. I never saw them again. I've been on my own ever since."

There's a ringing in my ears. Children gathered together, transported somewhere. Ken had said the children, children like Baby, were brought to Fort Black but got lost in the chaos. I slide my hand around the back of Brenna's head and lift it slightly to look at the spinal column tattoo on the back of her neck.

"Brenna, why did you choose that tattoo?"

"Oh, I thought it was badass." A tiny grin. "And I wanted to cover up an ugly old scar I had there, from foster care. I try not to think about back then, but the caretakers used to take blood, give us shots, make sure we were healthy in case someone wanted to adopt us. Even then I knew I was too old to be adopted. People just want babies, not preteens with too much attitude."

My mind churns with the new facts. If Brenna was part of the experimentation group that Baby was, she could be immune. She might not change. Baby was bitten years ago, infected by a different strain of bacteria. Could Brenna now be fighting the new, mutated bacteria? It's such a long shot. Ken said they'd tested that vaccine and it's not effective. I try not to get ahead of myself, but a new spark of hope has permeated the air.

I let Brenna go back to sleep. Hours pass, and I nearly fall off the arm of the couch when I start to doze off. I move to a tattered chair across from Brenna, set my sound amplifier to maximum, and tilt my head toward her. If she moves, I'll hear her. I try to get comfortable, but something is digging into my side. I reach into the pocket of my sweatpants and find Ken's small notebook.

I'd completely forgotten about it. I open it and skim the pages. It's his personal journal.

Day 46 in Fort Black: I am no closer to finding what I am after than I was in New Hope. Dr. Reynolds insists that there are answers here, but all I see are dead ends. I have even halted my main research, barring any new discoveries, and started working on a side project. This "Black Pox" that runs rampant here is easily treated. I am hesitant to share my findings, as I know I will be chastised for working on anything that is not a Florae vaccine. Even so, I've insisted on creating a quarantine zone, an area of my allotted space in the back wall, where those infected with the Pox can rest and die in peace. It's a small comfort, but it's something.

I flip ahead a few pages.

Day 52 in Fort Black: I still have not been able to speak with Kay. I am only allowed to contact the research staff in New Hope and discuss matters that relate to our research. I am concerned for her after her demotion, a fact I had to hear about secondhand from a lab assistant as passing gossip. The news was a shock. I'd been briefed on the escape of the girl those months ago, but no one mentioned my sister was blamed. I'm grateful for the information the assistant let slip, but if we were monitored, she'll be punished. I hope she isn't sent to the Ward. She's a good worker.

Day 55 in Fort Black: Instead of sitting on my cure for the "Black Pox," I decided to broach the subject with the Warden during one of our rare meetings. He was adamant that I keep my findings to myself, unwilling to give the people here even the slightest reprieve from the fear that binds them to him. I'm sure that as soon as he is able, he will report me back to New Hope. I should have known better than to suggest anything that would endanger his position.

Day 56 in Fort Black: As expected, I received a call about my non-sanctioned research and a long talk from Dr. Reynolds about the importance of my project. As if I didn't know. I believed, just for a second, that the actual saving of lives might counterbalance the possibility of a Florae vaccine. But I was wrong.

Dr. Reynolds doesn't see life in the same way others do. In his eyes, the good of the whole outweighs the good of the few. I can't say I disagree. I just wish I could do more for the people who are dying around me every day. I can help them, and yet I do nothing. Dr. Reynolds has spoken. My hands are tied.

After thumbing through his journal, I understand Ken a little bit more. What Kay was trying to tell me—he's not bad, he's trying to do some good, but he has to play by so many rules, and he feels like he can't make waves. She said to convince him to take Baby as his own test subject, but maybe I don't have to. Maybe Brenna will be the key.

I turn to the end of the journal and I see an entry that makes me pause.

Day 73 in Fort Black: I came across a transcript today of a conversation between Doc and one of the guards, a man named Ellis Lawson—Tank. Doc recommended I take him on as a door guard, but his file is too disturbing. I have requested another guard with a less troubled past.

A few loose sheets of paper are tucked inside these pages. It's a psyche-eval of Tank, and a lot of it is him talking about how much he likes Fort Black and wants to keep a place there. Eventually Tank mentions Jacks's sister, Layla. I nearly rip the paper as I read.

I guess the one thing I'd complain about is I ain't seen any action in a long while. Not since that sweet thing Layla got herself killed in that fire. Now, just between you and me, it wasn't the fire that done it. I'm only telling you this because I've taken care of people for you before and you know that if you want someone gone without a fuss, I'm the one to come to.

I know some things about this place. Some nasty things. So I know if I unburden myself a bit, it stays between us. Just don't tell the Warden, because he had a talk with me about how I was to leave Layla alone and the importance of family and whatnot. I wasn't going to cross him—I know better than to go against the Warden—but everything worked out so perfect. I don't see how you can put a glass of water in front of a man dying of thirst and tell him not to drink. And that Layla, she sure was a sweet thing. Not like all the women around here now, all tough and worn from hard living. No, she was soft and fresh. I'd just stare at her sometimes when no one else was looking, just drinking her in.

Well, Jacks had her locked up real good and, like I said, I didn't want to piss off the Warden, so all I could do was look— that is, until the night of the fire. Jacks let her out then, and I saw her in the crowd. . . . Well, I waited until it was all chaotic- like, and took my chance. I pulled her behind the cellblock and, well, let's just say I showed her what it meant to be a woman. And that part was amazing, but it was nothing compared to what came next.

I can still feel her neck in my hand, the way she struggled for breath.

I stop reading then, my own breath coming in short, ragged gasps. Tank, not the fire, killed Layla. I force myself to read the rest, to learn what happened.

I didn't let her go quick. I'd ease up a little and let her have a bit of air, then squeeze again. There's nothing like the feeling of having a life in your hand, but it ain't the same as killing a man. Killing those girls is like every good thing that ever hap- pened to you happening again all in that moment.

When I was done with her, I threw her body in the Yard with the others who died and the fire did the rest. Jacks and the Warden never knew it was really me who killed her. No one ain't never going to know about this, right? It's just between you and me? Good. I wouldn't want the Warden to know. He wouldn't like it. It's nice to tell someone, though, someone who understands.

With shaking hands I fold the papers up again and stick them in between the pages of Ken's journal, placing it in my pocket.

I sit back and stare at Brenna's still form. She was right. Tank deserved to be devoured by the Floraes. He's more of a monster than they are.

I try to rest, but broken images flash through my mind. Fire. A young girl's body, beaten and broken. Tank's evil sneer. Jacks's pained face whenever he mentions his sister. Eventually I drift into a fitful sleep.

When I wake, Brenna is moaning. I jump up. She's shaking, sweat beading her neck and forehead. I put my hand on her head; she's burning up with fever. I check my watch—twenty hours since she was bitten. I feel more confident that she won't change, but I still can't be sure.

I wake her to give her more pain medicine and a sip of

water. Her eyes flutter open for a moment and then close. What she really needs is antibiotics. Her wound is probably infected, and this auto lot office isn't the best place to recover.

Suddenly Brenna opens her eyes wide and stares through me. "They're gone now. All the Floraes. There ain't any around for at least a mile."

"Shh—you need to rest. Besides, how do you even know they're gone?" I whisper, stroking her head, trying to calm her.

"I can't hear them anymore."

I pause, my hand resting on her head. "What do you mean?" I ask slowly.

"Since I was bitten, things have gotten . . . clearer. I can hear things outside really well. It doesn't make sense."

I study her for a long moment. "What *can* you hear?"

"There's a stream about a half mile that way." She motions with her eyes. "And the wind has picked up. Can you hear it, through the leaves?"

I shake my head. "I can't," I say.

But I know who could.

Baby.

CHAPTER TWENTY-SIX

Twenty-four hours, and Brenna still hasn't changed.

Still, she's in bad shape. Her clothes are soaked through with sweat, and she shivers uncontrollably. I found an old, musty blanket to cover her with, but she kicked it off, burning up, then begged for it back, telling me she was freezing, only to throw it off again twenty minutes later. She's been in and out of consciousness. She needs medical attention. She survived a Florae bite.

I've been thinking about it, while I've watched her fitful sleep, waiting for the cover of night. There's only one option. I have to get her back to Fort Black. I don't know the area, and I don't know if I can find a pharmacy or grocery store to get her meds. Even if I did, they might all be scavenged this close to Fort Black.

Going back there is a deathtrap for me. Pete and Tank are gone, but Doc and the Warden are still out to get me. If I show up again, they'll try to find some other way to kill me. But I owe Brenna my life. If it wasn't for me, she wouldn't have been out here; if it wasn't for her, I'd be dead.

And if we go back, I can get back on track with Ken. Maybe he can help protect me. Plus, Ken will want to study Brenna. It's possible his vaccine was effective or she's naturally immune, but I don't think so. I think she's immune because she was experimented on as a child, given the same injection that Baby received.

My mother told me the scientists tried to perfect a vaccine, but were now having trouble because the bacteria has mutated so many times since then. Baby might not even be the key to a cure, since she was bitten so long ago. But Brenna was just bitten, and her body still managed to fight off the new Florae infection. The researchers would die to have her.

Her dressing has turned the rust color of old blood, and there are no more bandages. I'm not sure if I should move her like this.

But I don't have a choice. I kneel down next to her. "I'm going to take you back to Fort Black, to get you some help, but you have to be quiet," I whisper. "Do you hear any Floraes out there now?"

She opens her eyes, barely able to focus on my face. She's too sick to talk. I pull on my synth-suit hood and walk to the office door. It creaks as it opens, and I freeze, my reloaded Guardian gun drawn. I still have nearly all the ammo Kay left me with—the clips are slim and light, and each carries an impressive number of charges—but still, I have to conserve.

After waiting a long, silent moment with no Floraes in sight, I take a step out of the office, then another, into the comforting darkness of night.

It's been a while since I was out in the After, unprotected. I have to be the Amy I was before New Hope and Fort Black: silent, wary, stealthy. There's no other way if I want to live.

With some difficulty, I transfer Brenna from the couch into the bike trailer. She moans and mutters, and her wound reopens, staining her already bloodied bandage a deeper shade of red, but she finally settles in.

I take off on the bike, pulling her behind me. She's heavy, so the pace is slow. I do what I can to keep my pedaling even so that the noise is a constant hum, but I still have to shoot a Florae before we've gone a mile. I wonder how many more we'll see along the way, drawn to the area by yesterday's rampant gunfire.

We pass a gas station, and I stop for a moment, silently entering and surveying the store. My Guardian glasses act as night-vision goggles, and I'm thankful again to Kay, for what she's given me to ensure my survival. All the good supplies have been scavenged, of course, but there's a first aid kit hidden behind the counter that's better stocked than the one I have from the auto lot office.

I rebandage Brenna's wound, cleaning it with hydrogen peroxide first. The skin on her hand looks papery and is streaked with red marks. I make her swallow eight pain pills, though they expired years ago.

Before we get back on the road, I use a pair of scissors I snagged from the office to cut my hair short, leaving it a little longer on top, just like Baby cut it for me. Then, turning my head over, I dump the rest of the peroxide on what's left of my hair. I hope the color will change—if not to blonde, to orange.

After all, Tank and Pete likely aren't the only thugs Doc sent after me, and I don't want to be immediately recognizable.

I debate whether to try to change Brenna's appearance, but her short hair makes it harder. Pete and Tank aren't going to tell anyone that I was with Brenna. I think back to our leaving Fort Black. . . . Only a few people saw us together. Even if they tell the Warden that Brenna is with me . . . I'll have to take that chance.

I check Brenna before we head out again. The moonlight reflects off her damp skin. She looks so pale, but she's at least a little coherent for the moment. She smiles weakly, then snaps her eyes over my shoulder, holding up four fingers on her good hand.

I turn and see the Floraes, too—shuffling along the road toward the gas station, hunting. I slip into the bike trailer with Brenna and pull the flap over us. Moving my head from side to side, through my amplifier I hear a low snarl, a damp huffing, the unmistakable scrape of Florae claws on pavement as They approach.

I stay completely still, curled next to Brenna, who thankfully remains quiet, no longer shivering. The Floraes pass us, but still I wait. I could shoot them, but if we can take cover, I'd rather save my bullets for a more dire situation, for when hiding isn't an option. It's how I survived so long in the After, by being patient and careful. Finally Brenna opens her eyes. "They're gone," she whispers.

I carefully remove myself from the bike trailer and stretch, searching the road behind us. There's no sign of Them. Getting back on the bike, I pedal on, slow and steady, in the direction of Fort Black.

As I scan the horizon for Floraes, my mind slowly turns over my options. First I'll find Jacks, who can help me. Then I'll bring Brenna to Ken. He'll study her blood, maybe develop a cure from it. Or maybe he already has the cure—maybe it *was* the latest vaccine that's saved Brenna.

But why didn't my mother find the formula sooner? Why didn't Rice? My mother created the original bacterium strain that started all this, and Rice is the smartest person I've ever met. The labs at New Hope are well equipped and staffed. How could Ken, working alone in his Fort Black lab, succeed where they failed?

No. Like Baby, Brenna has to be immune because of that long-ago testing.

After a few hours, the prison walls are in sight.

I circle around to the garage entrance and stop the bike

outside the door. Brenna's lucid enough to keep up on her feet when I haul her from the trailer. Supporting most of her weight, I lug her to the door and kick at it.

I feel eyes on us through the door, and then the guard cracks it open.

"Oh, *hell* no," the guard says. All I can see are his wide eyes and the end of his rifle barrel. "You're not bringing her in here. She looks like crap. She's bitten, isn't she?"

"Get Jacks," I say, leaning Brenna against the wall. "Hurry."

"But–"

"Now!"

The door shuts, and Brenna slides down the wall into a sitting position. I give her some water, thinking it might already be over. If the guard goes to Doc instead of Jacks–and that's probably protocol, with a probable infection at the gate–it will be. Long minutes pass before the door opens again, but it's Jacks who's standing on the threshold with the guard.

My heart presses against my chest. To my surprise, my eyes fill with tears.

"Well," he says. "I don't usually like blondes, but . . ." His eyes flick to Brenna and his smile fades. "Brenna? What happened?"

"She's sick. Help me with her."

The guard still doesn't like it. He keeps his gun trained on Brenna while Jacks and I hoist her to her feet and bring her inside. His eyes bore holes into our backs as we make our way through the garage. Sweat beads on my forehead. How long will it take him to call the Warden?

Jacks and I take Brenna around the wall to one of the examination rooms and place her on a bed. "I'll go get Doc," he says, turning to leave, but I grab his arm.

"No, wait. Not Doc."

"Why?"

"Well—" How do I explain that his father wants me dead? But before I say anything, he pulls me in for a hug.

"When I read that note, I thought I'd never see you again."

The hairs on my arms are standing on end. "Brenna was bitten by a Florae," I whisper into his ear.

He releases me, eyeing Brenna, and then a needle on a metal tray across the room. The potassium chloride.

"You don't understand." I put myself between him and the tray. "Brenna was bitten yesterday afternoon." He stares at me, uncomprehending. "Jacks, it's nighttime now. It's been about thirty hours since she was bitten. She hasn't changed. She isn't going to change."

Jacks shakes his head. "That's impossible."

"It's not impossible. It's happened." I step closer to him. "Don't you see? Brenna could be the key to a cure. She could end it all–New Hope, Fort Black . . . People wouldn't have to live like this anymore."

I watch as he struggles with what he's just heard.

He looks over at Brenna. "Amy, this means . . . ," he says, understanding dawning on his face, "humans can take back the world."

CHAPTER TWENTY-SEVEN

"I have to get Doc," Jacks is telling me for the third time. "If her wound is infected–"

I cut him off. "Can't *you* help her?"

"I'm not a doctor, Amy." Jacks stares at me for a long time, then looks away. "I don't know what to do. I know finding out about all his experimentations bothered you. . . . It freaked me out too. But he's still a doctor. He still helps people."

"But–"

I stop myself. Doc and the Warden are trying to keep Jacks safe. If Doc is taking orders from Dr. Reynolds, Jacks will be a lot safer if he doesn't know about the failed assassination. Even his father may not be able to protect him from Dr. Reynolds. Because if I tell him, he'll definitely confront Doc about it. That's just Jacks.

"Doc is unreliable. You know that better than anyone else. Can't you just find Ken?"

"It took you three weeks to find him before, and that's only because he wanted to see you." He looks at my bleak gaze and softens. "But I can ask Doc to contact him. Tell him I need to ask him about an incoming patient, or something."

"Okay." That could work. If Jacks doesn't mention me, Doc won't know I'm still alive. "Just don't tell Doc that I'm here. Tell him something happened to Brenna, something that Ken will want to know about."

"And Doc? Shouldn't he look at her wound?"

I hesitate.

"What happened, anyway? It looks more savage than a normal bite."

"I cut away the infected area."

Jacks grimaces. "You cut off her *fingers*? Damn. I'm surprised she didn't kill you. Just by reflex." He shakes his head. "Doc's got to see her."

"But—"

"She could die, Amy."

I look at Brenna. She's trembling again, her clothes soaked through with sweat. When I place my hand on her face, her skin burns against mine. I wish I could help her myself, but I don't know what to do.

"All right," I say, reluctantly.

Jacks hurries from the room. Within minutes, he rushes back in the door, Doc trailing behind.

When Doc sees me, he blanches. Even with all that's at stake with Brenna, I have to say, I take some satisfaction in his reaction. Clearly, he thought I'd be dead by now.

Doc composes himself and goes to Brenna's side, unraveling the blood-soaked bandage from her hand. Jacks sucks in air at the sight of her missing fingers.

"It's a clean cut," Doc notes. "How did she lose them?"

"A knife," I tell him. "I think it's infected, though."

"Yes . . ." He's still staring at the wound and shaking his head as though something doesn't make sense. Then his eyes snap to me. "Those fingers have been removed. This wasn't from any knife fight or accident. The cuts are too precise."

When I don't say anything, he presses. "I can't help her if I don't know what happened."

"I had to take them off," I explain, "but I did everything I could to sterili–"

"*You* took them off? Why on Earth–"

"I had to remove the site of the infection."

"She's infected *because* you–" He stops short, his eyes widening. "She's been bitten, hasn't she? How dare you bring her here! She must be removed at once. These rooms aren't strong enough to hold a Florae." His hand goes to his ear to make a call, but I slap it away.

"No! You don't understand. You have to help her get better, then Ken needs to see her right away." I don't want to tell Doc anything, but how else am I going to get him to help Brenna, to call Ken? "She was bitten more than twenty-four hours ago."

Doc looks at me dumbly, then studies Brenna.

"Are you certain?" he asks.

"I've been with her the whole time."

"How do I know you're not lying?" he asks.

I narrow my eyes at him. "I'm not exactly dying for her to turn into a Florae, am I?"

Doc glares at me distrustfully, then goes to the cabinet and takes out a tray with medical supplies. He takes a sample of

Brenna's blood, then hooks her up to an IV.

"These antibiotics should help. Jacks, go see when Brenna last received a booster shot." Jacks nods and leaves the room.

I stare at Doc, who is doing a remarkable job of ignoring me. He takes more of Brenna's blood, and I realize that I'm not scared. Even though he tried to kill me, even though I'm in an examination room, surrounded by medical supplies. Maybe my anger is overpowering my fear of the clinical setting. I'm not shaking. I don't feel overwhelmed or unsettled. It's about time I feel like my old self again.

"Why did you want me dead?" I ask pointedly. "Did you tell Dr. Reynolds I was here? Did he tell you to kill me?"

He doesn't look at me, just nods. "The Warden and I talked it over. We thought telling New Hope the truth was the only way to salvage the situation. Dr. Reynolds now knows of your presence here. I was only trying to help," he tells me, not bothering to look up at me, as if this is any kind of explanation.

"And having me killed . . . Who was that helping, exactly?"

His head snaps up, and he looks at me sharply. For a moment I see Jacks in him, his expression. The resemblance fades when he begins to speak. "I wanted to report you from the beginning, but my brother thought we could use you. He also thought you'd be good for Jacks, but I knew you'd be trouble. The Warden is always pulling stunts like that. Good old Johnny. Skirts the law and never gets punished for it.

"Not me. I always get caught. I always get punished. I made one little mistake when I was a doctor. I wasn't even supposed to be on call, but . . . What was I going to do? The man was dying anyway. He was a goner; it wouldn't have mattered if I was stone-cold sober. I did my best. One of the nurses reported me, said I was acting strangely, and a drug test later I was done. They searched my office, found some wayward pills. Lawsuits and divorce, and the only place I could get a job was as an orderly at the prison my brother ran. And he only hired me because he knew I would help with the late-night experiments. He knew I wouldn't tell anyone. . . . Who would believe a washed-up drug addict? He also knew I didn't have anywhere else to go.

"Well, they sure needed me, in the end. When the infection broke out and there weren't any 'real' doctors around, you bet your ass they wanted me to practice medicine then. And so what if we still help New Hope out with their experiments? So what if a few people die? People die every day for no reason. At least here, I can collect data and make their deaths worth something."

I've heard it all before, this rationalization. "You don't have to be their puppet," I say through gritted teeth.

"Do you think I can just ignore orders from New Hope? Not with my track record, not after the debacle of the fertility study last year. I'm already in enough trouble as it is. And now you're here. You're supposed to be dead. If Dr. Reynolds knew you were still alive—"

"What? What would he do?"

He looks at me, his mouth open to answer, but then Jacks returns to the room with a clipboard. "Brenna just received a shot," he says, breathless from running, "last week."

Doc grins maniacally. "That's the latest formula. I knew it. It worked!"

"That's just one possible explanation," I say. "Maybe the most recent vaccine worked, maybe Brenna is immune, maybe cutting off her fingers stopped the spread and kept her alive, but . . ." He doesn't let me finish with my second theory. The one that involves Brenna being part of the original test group . . . the one that sounds crazy, even to me.

"After all this time, we've gotten it right!" He puts the blood samples on the metal tray. He reaches over and hugs Jacks. "This is my chance, my boy."

Jacks gives Doc an uncomfortable half hug. "Chance for what?"

"Vindication! I'm going to run some tests. There must be more tests, life tests, but I know what they'll show. I knew it!" he says again, heading for the door.

What is a life test? How can Doc be so convinced the vaccine was effective? It's just what he wants to hear. "What about Ken?" Ken will listen to me.

"What about him?" He's looking at me, but it's as if he can barely see me.

"He needs to examine Brenna."

"Yes, yes. I'll tell him to come see her," Doc says, brushing me off as he disappears through the door.

"I don't trust him," I tell Jacks as I return to sit at Brenna's side. Already the color is returning to her face. I wonder briefly what, exactly, is in that IV.

"He's just excited there's a vaccine that works."

"But there isn't," I say. "Or, at least, he can't know that it works. I don't think that's what's going on with Brenna at all." I fill him in on all the medical testing Hutsen-Prime had been performing on children before the outbreak. I explain my theory that Brenna was part of the original test group. That she, because she was bitten more recently, could be the key to finding a cure. "I don't know the science, but I think there was something special about that first batch of vaccine. Something that Baby and Brenna got, that they haven't been able to reproduce since. If they have Brenna, they won't need Baby anymore!"

"But won't they just torture Brenna instead?"

"It won't come to that, not if she's the answer. They'll be able to develop a vaccine quickly, maybe even a cure. Brenna was bitten more recently than Baby; her body has combated the mutated strain of bacteria. Besides, Brenna is strong. Baby is just a child."

I know I'm trying to convince myself as much as I am him. The fact is, I know in my heart I would trade Brenna for Baby. I would sacrifice anyone, including myself, if it meant that Baby was safe.

"Why were you even out there?" Jacks asks.

"Tank attacked me in the prison. I was going to make a run for it, and Brenna said she could take me to get a car with gasoline."

"What?" Jacks says, clenching his fists. "I'm going to kill him. Now."

"Too late."

"Why?"

"He and Pete followed us out there. They're both dead. I . . ." My voice catches. "I shot him. The Floraes must have gotten him."

"Good." Jacks looks at me, taking in my guilt. "If anyone deserved to die, it was Tank. Do you know how many girls he's probably tortured? Girls who couldn't defend themselves like you could. Girls like my sister."

I stare at him, his stony face and dark hair. He holds on to so much pain about his sister's death. My eyes trace the snake tattoo on his arm while I debate what to do. Would knowing Tank was at fault ease his pain? Would knowing be better than not knowing?

"Jacks, there's something I have to tell you."

He looks at me expectantly. I take a deep breath.

"Your sister's death . . . wasn't your fault–"

"I should have been watching her," he cuts me off.

"No. I . . . It was Tank," I say, struggling to find the right words. "He was obsessed with her. He used that night, the night of the fire, to take her. He killed her, Jacks. No matter how carefully you watched her, he would have found a way."

Jacks stands up, approaches me with shaking hands. "He told you this, Amy?"

"Yes . . . no, but, Jacks, Tank is dead."

Jacks grabs my shoulders, shakes me. "How do you know what happened?"

"I read it, in Tank's psyche-eval." I realize I made the wrong decision, and fear flashes through me. Jacks collapses onto the floor. He puts his head in my lap and sobs softly. I stroke his hair. "I shouldn't have said anything," I whisper.

"No." He lifts his head and looks up at me. "I'd rather know everything that bastard did to her. She shouldn't have to suffer alone."

"But she's gone."

"Amy." He puts his hand in mine. "I want to read it too. Whatever it is you read to find out the truth."

I shake my head. "It's not a good idea, Jacks." It's too horrible; I can't let him read it.

"I need to."

Reluctantly, I pull out Ken's journal, handing Jacks the loose pieces of paper. I watch him silently while he reads, his mouth slowly dropping. I expect him to rant, to break things, to hit the wall or kick a chair. Instead he sits motionless for a long while, rereading the words.

"Oh God." A tear escapes the corner of his eye. His pain is so great that for the moment, it drowns his anger.

"It's not your fault," I tell him softly. "You had no way of knowing what Tank was up to."

He rubs his face, wiping away any trace of tears. "I couldn't protect her. I couldn't protect either of you."

"I'm not exactly easy to protect. That's why I have to take care of myself. And Tank's gone now. He's not coming back."

I reach out my hand to his and hold it gently.

"I've got to tell Doc. I've got to tell my dad."

"Do you think that's such a good idea?" I ask. "It might be better if he doesn't know."

Jacks stands, clutching the paper. "He was still her father."

I know I can't stop him, and he leaves without another word. I wait, wondering if knowing is better. Was my life better when I was ignorant of what the Floraes really were, and my mother's part in their creation? Was it better to not know if Baby was safe or not? No. Knowing is always better.

Jacks returns a while later, looking grim.

I jump up and ask, "How'd he take it?"

"He . . . He acted like he didn't even hear me. He's working on analyzing Brenna's blood. He didn't even stop to talk about what I was telling him. He . . . He may have been high. He just kept saying that I should go away and he'd come get me when he was done."

I make Jacks sit and get him some water. He drinks it slowly, staring at the wall. I stay next to him, trying to be a source of strength he can use.

Jacks and I sit with Brenna in silence. Every minute that passes she looks more like herself, and I silently will her to get better. She may be the only hope that Baby has.

Hours later, we're deep in the darkest morning.

I'm exhausted, but my mind is racing and I'm too wired to sleep. Too much is at stake; too many people I care about are in danger. Still, my body's shutting down. My eyes are just beginning to close when Ken comes into the room.

He looks from me to Brenna to Jacks.

"What are you doing in here? I saw the light on, but this room is supposed to be empty."

"Doc didn't send you?" I ask. "He said he was going to get you a long time ago."

"No, why would he?" He looks curiously at Brenna.

I scramble up, overcome with gratitude for this stroke of luck despite Doc's efforts to thwart us.

"Brenna was bitten by a Florae and didn't change," I say hurriedly.

Ken freezes for a second, his mouth open. Recovering, he rushes over to examine Brenna. "Are you certain?" He feels her head, looks in her eyes, and unwraps and studies her wound. He has the same wild look on his face that Doc had. Their single-minded obsession has ruled them, and now that the end is in sight, it's as though a fever has taken over. "I have to see what's going on in her blood."

"Doc's already on it," Jacks tells him.

"He took Brenna's blood," I add.

Ken looks up from Brenna for the first time since receiving the news that she was bitten and didn't change. "But I just saw Doc in the exercise yard. He had a line of people he was giving shots to. I wondered what he was up to so late at night, but I just assumed it was the newest vaccine."

"Giving shots?" I say. "He's not even looking at Brenna's blood?"

Jacks leaps to his feet. "Where's that clipboard Doc had me get?" He's frantically searching the exam room. "The one with the names of the people who've already had the shot?"

"I don't know. Doc must have taken it," I say.

"What are you doing?" Ken asks as Jacks tears the room apart.

"That list," Jacks says, giving up and staring at Ken, eyes wide. "Doc took it. He's lining those people up, he's injecting–"

"You're not making sense," Ken says. "Why would he be vaccinating people who've already received the vaccine?"

"He said he was going to do some 'life tests,'" I say. "What does that mean?"

Ken looks at us, his excitement replaced in a flash by fear. "Life tests? *Life test* is the term we use for experimenting on human subjects." He gives his head a shake. "No. He must just be inoculating them. Then he'll test this subject's blood."

In Doc's mind, the vaccine is effective. Removing Brenna's fingers stopped the spread of infection while the vaccine suppressed it in her blood. I think of all I know about the infection, and for some reason the Black Pox springs to mind. People can survive the infection and still spread the disease. Doc was already unhinged. Jacks said he thought he was drugged up. Could the possibility of a vaccine and the news of what really happened to Layla push him over the edge?

I remember Doc's look, his feral glee at the thought of having found a vaccine. I shake my head just as Ken did, trying to rattle that mad image out of it. No. Not even Doc is crazy enough to risk injecting Florae-infected blood into the veins of people he only *thinks* have been successfully vaccinated. If he's wrong–

Then the blood in my own veins turns cold, remembering Pete's panicked whisper to Tank about the fate of another of Doc's thugs.

Made him into a damned Florae.

I can barely say the words. "Doc *is* testing Brenna's blood," I say. "He's testing it on those people in the Yard."

CHAPTER TWENTY-EIGHT

"Show me where he is," I order Ken. "Now."

"Amy, calm down!" Jacks yells.

"Don't you understand what's going on?" I scream. "We've got to stop this before it's too late!"

Ken nods but eyes Brenna. "She shouldn't be left alone."

I turn to Jacks. "Can you stay with her?"

"If you're going out there, I want to go with–"

"No," I say. "I can fight a Florae if I need to. Brenna can't. You need to protect her."

"I need to protect *you*," he says, grabbing my wrist. "You're the one I–"

He stops himself, hesitates, and then leans in. My heart leaps to my throat as I think he's going to kiss me again.

But then he just whispers, "Just . . . get back here alive."

He's so close, a strange, tingling sensation pours through me, all the way to the ends of my toes.

"I will," I tell him. "I promise."

I follow Ken into the corridor and around a corner. There's a surprising lack of guards around, but when we head out into the Yard, I see why.

Doc has tasked the guards with rounding up people and keeping them in line. He's set up lights, utilizing the power from the wall. The standing lamps look out of place and cast an eerie glow across the yard. We watch as Doc administers a shot on a woman, then pushes her to a guard to move her along. As Ken and I approach, one man refuses the injection. Doc nods to a guard, who brings down the butt of his rifle in the man's face. Doc injects him, and the patient is dragged to the side.

Ken and I run past the guards. One tries to stop us, but Doc waves us through. "Ah, Ken," he says, "you've come to participate in my case study? I can use the help." Doc's eyes have gone glassy, a sickening grin plastered to his face.

Ken eyes the syringe in Doc's hand. "What the hell are you doing?"

"The vaccine. It's effective. I'm injecting all these people with that bitten girl's blood. A meaningless test, but protocol is protocol. The *i*'s need dotting, the *t*'s crossing. I know she's immune. And if she's immune, even though she's a carrier, everyone else given the vaccine is also immune. I mean, I couldn't go out and get a live Florae, could I? Much too dangerous. Believe me, I know."

"How does that make any sense?" Ken asks desperately. "The girl didn't change, but that doesn't mean the vaccine was effective. There could be any number of other factors in play. But one thing we *do* know is that she's a carrier."

"Oh yes, she is, certainly," Doc tells us happily. He takes a bottle out of his pocket, pops the top, and pours some pills into his mouth. He pauses and swallows with a shake of his head. He turns back to us. "I ran her blood. The same bacteria we find in the Floraes is in her, fully developed, and yet she remains unchanged."

I cringe as he gives another man a shot. "If the vaccine is

ineffective," I say, "doesn't that mean that all these people are now infected?"

The man who was knocked out with the rifle begins to shake where he lies, unconscious. I pull out my gun and take a step back from him. "Ken . . . ?"

"It's started," Ken whispers, unbelieving.

I look around the Yard. How many has Doc infected? Some people change in minutes, others hours. How can it be contained? Another man drops to his knees, his hands to his ears. He screams, his skin turning from sunburned-brown to dark-yellow to yellow-green. When his hands fall away from his head, one ear tumbles to the ground, bouncing off the hard concrete. The other ear hangs loosely, attached by a thin piece of flesh. I stare, horrified. I've never seen anyone actually change before.

Ken comes to his senses before I do. "We can't contain this, not now. Our only hope is to leave."

"Leave? Where?" There's nowhere left to run.

"I'll contact New Hope, tell them about Brenna. They'll send a hover-copter for us." He grabs my hand. "Come with me. Kay would want you safe."

"And Jacks," I say, and he nods. We'll get out and take Brenna to New Hope.

Ken pulls me back toward the wall, but the panic has begun. Someone runs into us, knocking me onto my stomach. When I roll over, Ken has disappeared, and a man stands over me, salivating. He hasn't changed completely yet, but he's close—his ears and nose are gone, his skin a pale pea-green. His eyes are tinged with yellow, but they aren't yet milky and useless. They burn with a fire I've seen before in Floraes who haven't yet lost all their sight. Hunger.

He is no longer a man. He is a monster. He's one of Them.

CHAPTER TWENTY-NINE

He lunges greedily for me, and I don't allow myself to hesitate. I can't consider the fact that this creature was a man just seconds ago. I grab my gun, take aim, and shoot. His head snaps back from the impact and he falls over. Another Florae rushes to his side and begins to feed on him.

I scramble to my feet, pull up my hood, and prepare myself for a fight–knife in one hand, gun in the other. In the increasing frenzy, the lights that Doc had set up are knocked over and extinguished. I wish I had my Guardian glasses, but I left my pack with Jacks in the examination room. In the bottom of my belly I feel a familiar quivering.

Fear.

I'll be fine, I tell myself sternly. I lived for years in the shadows. I'm not afraid of the dark. It will make it easier to avoid the Floraes and get back inside.

Suddenly the Yard is filled with a burst of brightness. The spotlights in the guard towers have been turned inward. I silently curse the light. The guards are at least trying to destroy the Floraes, though. The sound of gunshots fills the air, making it hard to hear anything, to remain alert.

I sidestep a man on his knees, holding his ears, his face contorted in pain. Auditory sensitivity, one of the first signs he's been infected. I level my gun, but I can't bring myself to shoot him. He's still a person. A man rushes toward me on my right, and I prepare for his assault, taking the fighter's stance Kay taught me, but the man is only trying to escape. He dashes past me and starts banging on the door behind me to get inside the walls. I throw my back against the wall a few yards away from him, every muscle tingling, ready to fight any Florae that attacks.

One moment the man is pounding on the door, screaming in panicked desperation, and the next another volley of gunfire assaults my ears and the man drops to the ground. I sprint down the wall away from the door–the guards are taking down every threat to their quarantine. I can only hope Ken made it inside before the guards decided to shoot anyone trying to escape past the wall.

I need to reach my cellblock and figure out what to do from there. Jacks and Brenna should be safe inside.

Keeping my back to the wall, I circle the exercise yard, which has deteriorated into utter chaos. Only a few of the bitten have turned into full Floraes; most are in varying degrees of change and writhe on the ground in pain. One man I pass stares at his green arms, unbelieving. Another holds his nose in place as he pulls clumps of hair from his head.

I hurry along the wall, my progress interrupted by others infected who have not yet begun to change, pleading for help. I ignore them, though each appeal cuts through me like a knife, leaving a sharp pain in my chest. It is too late for them, though. They're doomed.

I reach the chain-link fence that separates the Arena from the Yard. Half of it has been torn down. A determined Florae now feasts within the crumpled fence, surrounded by bodies.

I continue on past the damaged area of the fence before the creature can focus on me, but another Florae has homed in on the smell of his blood. It might have passed me in the dark, but a spotlight sweeping the yard highlights me for a fraction of a second, just long enough for this new Florae to focus its weak eyes on me. It speeds toward me, and I manage to shoot it in the neck—only enough to slow it down. It plows into me, driving me against the half-erect fence. Weakened by its wound, though, it merely pinches at my synth-suit as it tries to bite my shoulder. I work my knife into the hole my bullet opened in its neck until the blade finds the spinal column, and then I pull it out for one final thrust. The knife severs its spine with a sickening snap, and the creature falls to the ground, twitching.

Freed, I move past Cellblock A, pushing through a crowd of people fighting to get inside. Cellblock B is no better. There's a man at the door with a rifle. I survey the twenty or so people between us, unable to tell if they're infected or not. I don't see any bites or gashes, but I understand the man not wanting to take any chances.

"Get lost or get shot," he tells a man pressing close to him.

"My cell is in there!" the man shouts. "My wife is waiting for me."

"Too bad," the armed man says, knocking the man back with the butt of the rifle, then sweeping its barrel back and forth before the crowd. He's trying to contain the infection to the Yard. Understandable, but I have to get inside. That's where Jacks would look for me. I step up, putting away my weapons and pulling down my hood so he can see my face.

"I just want to go to my cell and lock myself in," I say, looking at him over the end of the rifle barrel now trained on me. "I haven't been bitten, and if I had, I wouldn't do much damage from inside my cell."

The people around me murmur their agreement and, pushing in around me, move me to within inches of the rifle barrel's cold black eye.

Lowering my voice, I say, "You're not going to be able to hold all these people for much longer, not if they decide to rush you." I can see the fear in the man's eyes, but he holds his ground. "It's admirable, what you're trying to do," I tell him, "but don't you think you'd be better off going to your own cell and locking yourself in?"

He considers this, nodding just perceptibly, then takes a step back into the cellblock. "All right. Y'all got thirty seconds to get to your cells and lock the doors. If I catch anyone out, I'll shoot. I ain't getting bit by no damned Florae."

I rush past him and sprint away from the others, up the stairs to my cell. Jacks isn't there, and there's no note from him.

Buzzing with adrenaline, I can't just sit and wait. Besides, the Floraes are outside and I can do something to stop them. I doubt anyone in the Yard will survive, but maybe I can help the guards prevent the infection from taking out everyone in the cellblocks, too.

I decide to go up to the roof and scout out the situation, take out a few Floraes from there. I'll also be able to spot any hover-copter arriving. I scribble a note to Jacks, telling him to meet me on the roof, and then I lock up. I'm about to run for the staircase when a sob escapes from the next cell over.

I go to the open door and peer in. What I see hits me like a punch to the stomach.

"Pam?"

CHAPTER THIRTY

Pam looks up at me from where she sits on the floor, eyes red and puffy. In her lap is a man, bloodied, breathing in short gasps. His shoulder has a chunk of flesh missing, the gouge dripping a dark puddle onto the floor of the cell.

"Mike, he . . . he was bitten," Pam says. "He came to find me. . . ." She stares at me, unseeing. She holds a bunched-up shirt to Mike's shoulder to stanch the flow of blood. Her hands are covered in green-black goo.

He's already begun to change.

I draw my gun and Pam's eyes focus in on the weapon.

"No! You leave him alone!" she screams.

"Pam." I have to calm her, explain to her what she doesn't want to admit to herself. "He's changing. Soon he won't be Mike anymore. He'll just be a Florae. He won't know you."

"I don't care," she says quietly. She wipes her tears with the back of her hand, smudging dark blood across her face.

I watch Mike. His hair has almost completely fallen out, his skin tinged a pale green.

"He'll kill you," I say.

"I. Don't. Care," she says to me in little more than a whisper.

I think of all the people still out in the Yard, fighting their way back to the cellblock, hoping to lock themselves into their cells and ride out the infection. Finally getting there, that close to safety, and finding Floraes waiting for them. "I can't leave you, Pam," I tell her. "Either he'll kill you or turn you. I can't endanger everyone in the block."

Pam's head drops as she digs through her clothing. She produces something from the pocket of her skirt and tosses it at me. It's heavy and metallic—a large, opened padlock.

"Lock us in," she commands.

I want to plead with her, but I know it's pointless. She is determined to stay with her man until the end. "Where's the key?" It kills me to ask, but I can't take the risk that she'll open the door after I'm gone.

Pam takes a key from her pocket and throws it to me. This time I don't catch it, and it skitters across the concrete walkway and over the side, falling two floors down.

Once I snap the lock on them, there'll be no turning back. My resolve breaks. "Pam, please," I try one last time. "You don't need to die."

"If Mike dies, I don't want to live." She gazes at his face, stroking his head, pulling away the last wispy brown hair as she does so.

I place the padlock between the two bars of the door and the cell. "Last chance," I tell her.

"Do it." She doesn't look up. I close the padlock with a click that echoes through the cellblock. I have sentenced her to death.

Mike reaches up as though to scratch his nose, then rubs it so hard it begins to come off his face. His mouth twists into a snarl, baring his teeth, sharp and yellowed.

"If you love him," I say quietly, "you'll let me end it."

I don't think she hears me, but just as I turn to leave she responds. "He's still my Mike. I'll be with him until he's no longer the man I love. After that, I don't care what happens."

I force myself to walk down the hall, my limbs heavy. As I make my way to the roof, my body shakes with rage. I tell myself the screams I hear below aren't Pam's. And they might not be. So many people are dying right now, it's impossible to tell who owns what cry of pain.

When I pull open the door to the roof, I see that dawn is breaking. With the light, the Floraes will become even more aggressive, even more lethal. As I look around, I inhale, startled to find a figure cowering by the door. It's the Warden, clutching a rifle to his chest and muttering to himself.

"Warden?" I say. But he ignores me, too overcome by fear.

I step around him and head to the ledge, searching the chaos below for signs of Jacks, Brenna, or Ken. No hover-copters have come yet; the only things of note in the sky are a few clouds and the pink-orange color that marks a new day.

I turn my attention back to the Yard where so many have changed. Those still human are being slaughtered. I check my gun. My backpack lost to me, I only have the one clip with no more than thirty rounds remaining, and I shot at least three Floraes on the way to the cells. I wish I could do more. The Warden whimpers. I glance at him and consider the rifle he's cradling. Depending on how many shots he's taken, there could be as many as thirty more bullets, and a rifle would be more effective this high up.

I go to him and reach for the gun, but he twists away from me, clamping it to his chest.

"I need this," he whimpers again. "For my own protection. My men are dead."

"What men?" I ask to keep him talking while I calculate how to go about overpowering him. He's not large, but he's scared out of his mind, which could make him unpredictable. Especially with that rifle in his hands.

"My personal guards."

I shake my head, unable to drum up any sympathy. He's the one who let Hutsen-Prime experiment on his prisoners. He's the one who continued to deal with New Hope after the Floraes appeared, selling out the people of Fort Black as lab rats. The only way he got to where he is now was by standing on the backs of the people he was meant to protect.

He's not a threat, I say to myself. *He's a pest.* I reach for the rifle and quickly pluck it from his hands.

I'm about to head back to the ledge when Ken bursts through the door armed with a rifle of his own. Looking relieved to find me there, he reaches back through the doorway and guides Brenna through it. Her eyes are open but flat, uncomprehending. Ken eases her to the ground and looks at me.

"I'm glad we found you. Jacks said you'd probably go back

to your cell. When you weren't there, I thought you got trapped in the Yard."

"Jacks." I look to the doorway, expecting him to step through, but it remains empty. "Where is he?"

"I don't know. . . . We got separated. I contacted New Hope, a hover-copter is on the way."

"We can't just leave Jacks—"

A figure fills the doorway and I wheel toward it, rifle raised, hoping it'll be Jacks, but fearing it will be a Florae.

Instead it's Doc who stumbles toward me, his lab coat covered in brown-red stains. He's followed by a huge bulk of a man, his left shoulder covered in blood.

I freeze in panicked shock. "You—you're dead," I say, disbelieving.

"Not just yet, cupcake," Tank growls, lurching toward me.

CHAPTER THIRTY-ONE

I raise my gun, but before I can shoot, an arm snakes around Tank's neck and he's jerked backward. Jacks's face appears. Relief floods my veins but is instantly replaced with fear. All of Jacks's focus is on Tank as he pounces on his chest. He punches Tank's already broken nose.

"You killed her!" Jacks screams as he pummels Tank's face. Tank reaches up and pushes Jacks off. He struggles to his feet, holding his damaged shoulder. Jacks jumps at him, but Tank uses all the strength in his good arm and connects a sweeping punch to the side of Jacks's head. Jacks entire body recoils at the impact.

Jacks shakes his head woozily and looks as though he's about to fall before he gets himself straight. He leaps at Tank again, and Tank tries to sidestep but is too slow. Jacks punches him in his wound, and the pain brings Tank to his knees.

"You killed her," Jacks repeats, his voice guttural.

"Yeah, I killed her." Tank grins, exposing his blood-soaked teeth. "And she was sweet."

Jacks brings his knee up to Tank's jaw, and Tank's body falls backward. Jacks kicks Tank's head again and again, his blood pooling beside his body.

"Jacks. Enough," I say. Jacks looks up at me blankly, then slumps down beside Tank's body, his head in his hands. I go to his side, but Doc holds out an arm to stop me.

"Give him a moment," he says, his voice filled with tenderness.

My blood churns at his touch. Where was that compassion when he decided to start his experiment? Unable to control my anger, I grab his slight body and drag him to the ledge.

"Look at what you've done!" I scream.

"I had to!" he says, trying to push me off. "Mistakes were

made, but none of them were my doing."

Likely sensing how close he is to being thrown over the edge, he stops talking. When I don't let him go, he starts again.

"I had no choice. They were going to replace me! Dr. Reynolds made it clear I needed this to work or I was done! Do you understand? Failure isn't tolerated. Do you think Dr. Reynolds wouldn't punish me through my son? If I am not successful here, the only place for me in New Hope would be in the *Ward*! And my son would be there too. Do you want that for Jacks?"

He twitches his head down toward the madness in the yard with disgust, as though he weren't responsible for it. "Time was running out. They were coming for me in the morning! Brenna would redeem me. Brenna *had* to be the answer."

It feels good to tighten my grip on his arm, to drive my fingers through his flesh to the bone beneath and feel him squirm. The man was going down and didn't care who he took with him, didn't care who he killed. He's whimpering in pain, and I notice for the first time the trail of red we've left across the roof.

I drop his arm and back away. He isn't covered in his victims' blood. He's covered in his own.

"You were bitten."

"Yes, but it doesn't matter. I've taken the vaccine."

"Look around you," I tell him, stunned by his self-delusion.

"The vaccine *doesn't work*." I hear a hollow thud behind me, a sound I've learned to recognize as an otherwise completely silent hover-copter landing.

"Are you coming?" Ken shouts.

Doc moves to go around me, but I shake my head and step in front of him, raising the rifle.

Ken appears at my side. "We've got to go now. Doc can come if he wants. We'll let New Hope sort it out." As fitting a punishment as being committed to the Ward would be for him, I can't let Doc come with us. "He's been bitten," I tell Ken.

"Leave him then," he says simply. "Let's go." He puts his hand on my shoulder and nudges me toward the hover-copter.

"I can't go without Jacks," I say, continuing to stare at where Doc stands by the ledge, still believing he has done something good. I run to Jacks's side. He looks up at me. "We've got to go. Now, Jacks."

He shakes his head. "I can't leave here."

"You have to. It's not safe," I plead.

"It's not safe anywhere." His eyes have begun to clear. "You're going back to that place, where they have your sister? Where they tortured you? No." He shakes his head. "I can't come with you."

"But Fort Black is dying," I tell him. "It's infested with Floraes."

"My father . . ."

"He's been bitten. I'm so sorry."

"I'm not leaving him here alone. And my uncle? They're the only family I have."

I don't know how I can make him understand. He refuses to budge. He's in shock.

I take his hand. "Jacks . . . your father is infected."

Jacks looks to where his father stands by the wall. He walks slowly over to his father, with me in tow.

"Dad?"

Doc looks at his son. "I . . . I'm sorry. For everything. For the years I wasn't with you and Layla, for what I did to your mother, for all of this."

Jacks nods. "I forgive you." He drops my hand and reaches to my other hand, taking the gun.

Doc eyes the rifle. "What happened to Layla was never your fault. You did more for that girl than I ever did. You were a better role model, a better provider. It wasn't your fault, son."

"I know," Jacks tells him. "I love you, Dad."

Doc stands up straight. "I love you too, son."

Jacks raises his gun and fires into Doc's chest.

Doc stumbles back, clutching his wound and staring at Jacks, his face torn between pain and love. Then he falls backward and disappears over the railing.

I turn to Jacks and take the gun away from him. "Jacks, I . . . Are you okay?"

He nods once, tears streaming down his face.

"It's now or never, Amy," Ken calls to me.

"Jacks, please. Come with me." I reach out for his arm and slowly lead him to the hover-copter.

Ken looks at Jacks, covered head to toe in blood. "No," he says simply.

"I'm not leaving him," I say.

"Then stay. I was only letting you come because of Kay. . . . But taking him—the risk is too great. What if he's infected? And you . . . You're not supposed to be anywhere near New Hope. Do you want to get caught? Because the more people we take, the more likely it is that you'll be found out."

I look at Jacks, who is slowly regaining his senses. "Amy, go. I'll be fine."

I shake my head. "You'll die."

"I won't. I said good-bye to my father. I'll go back to my cell and lock myself in. I'll be safe there."

"If you live," I say, tears streaming down my face, "your uncle knows how to contact New Hope. That's where I'll be."

"New Hope," he repeats, nodding. "I'll find you in New Hope. I promise."

He hugs me to him, brushes his lips with mine, and then pushes me toward the open door of the hover-copter. Before I know what is happening, the door has closed me inside. I collapse onto the floor of the hover-copter and hug my knees.

The ache in my chest worsens the farther we get from Fort Black. I realize that all those feelings for Jacks I had buried deep down inside are now being ripped from their hiding space and are rushing to the surface. I cry into my knees and for the first time in a long time, let myself feel.

PART THREE

THE END

CHAPTER THIRTY-TWO

We land outside of New Hope, and the door to the hover-copter opens. Kay steps out with me.

"You remember what I told you, sunshine?"

I nod. "Wait until dark. Then go to Building Nine, climb the fire escape to the fourth floor. The window will be open."

It was pure luck that Kay happened to be on patrol near Fort Black when Ken radioed for help. She was piloting, and when she stepped back to check on me and her brother, she found me crying on the floor of the hover-copter. She didn't try to comfort me. Instead she acted as if we'd never been apart, and started talking tactics. It worked, pulling me from my sorrow. I wiped my tears and listened to her strong, able voice.

Kay laid out the game plan to get me into New Hope, that it was too dangerous to bring me in all the way. Instead I would walk in, Kay letting me know the best route since the new cameras have been set up around the perimeter.

Kay looks at me for a moment. "How are you holding up?"

"I'm . . . fine," I tell her, hiding the truth. I'm far from fine, but I can't break down again, not now when I'm so close.

She puts a hand on my shoulder. "Don't get caught."

"I won't." I pull up the hood of my synth-suit. I'd abandoned my sweatshirt and pants miles ago, tossing them out of the moving hover-copter, leaving me wearing only the black synth-suit. I used to feel naked wearing the thin fabric, but now I feel like I am wrapped in a layer of protection.

Kay steps back into the hover-copter, and before they take off, I offer Brenna a small, hopeful wave. She's too far gone to wave back. I hope that Ken knows what he's doing. I can't shake the feeling that I'm abandoning her, but she should get the best medical attention in New Hope, before she's subjected to anything worse. I hope I can help her before then.

The hover-copter rises noiselessly and disappears over the tree line. I back away into the shadows and wait for the cover of darkness.

CHAPTER THIRTY-THREE

For weeks I'd been desperate to get back to New Hope. I thought all the waiting was over, that it would be time for action. But now that I'm here—nothing.

I sit on the floor of the studio apartment and wait. I've been waiting three days. Three days of hiding. Three days of delay. Three days without action. I thought I felt confined in Jacks's cell, but now I really am caged. Kay made it very clear—I'm not allowed to leave for any reason. Twice a day, Kay or Gareth bring me food and try without success to deflect my questions.

Gareth lived here before he became a Guardian, and they never reassigned the apartment. Kay made sure of that, so they could have somewhere to meet, away from the Rumble Room, away from the other Guardians who were more loyal to Dr. Reynolds and his crony Marcus. Dr. Reynolds has no idea I'm here in New Hope. For all he knows, I'm dead by order of Doc or killed during the Florae outbreak.

Though I've been instructed to stay away from the window, I can't help myself—I creep up to it and pull back the curtains, peeking my head only slightly over the windowsill to survey the area. New Hope seems shockingly peaceful compared to Fort Black. We're not near the center of activity, at the Quad or labs, but a lot of people still walk below, kids in color-coded jumpsuits, researchers in lab coats, and normal citizens whose apparel is what anyone would wear Before. A girl in a yellow jumpsuit catches my eye and for a moment I think I see Baby. The Baby who was so excited to wear yellow and was actually happy here when we first arrived. I pull the curtain closed and shake off my nostalgia, reminding myself that New Hope is not our home.

I pace the small room, my frustration starting to get the better of me. I haven't been able to see Baby, much less figure out a plan to rescue her, and Rice hasn't been able to get away long enough to come see me.

Rice.

Usually the thought of him calms me, but now, for some reason, the idea of seeing him agitates me further. Actually, I know the reason—Jacks. What if Jacks had been able to leave Fort Black? Would he be here with me now, cooped up in this tiny apartment? He would understand my agitation, my need to do something other than wait.

I think of our last moments together, Jacks covered in Tank's blood. Is he still the Jacks I knew? He defeated Tank and then had to turn around and kill his own father. I hope he knows it was a necessity. I hope he's safe.

I collapse onto the bed.

I want to fight, but all I can do is wait.

CHAPTER THIRTY-FOUR

When Gareth finally comes in, I practically pounce on him.

"Any news?"

"No, honey, nothing has changed since yesterday." He pulls a sandwich from his backpack and hands it to me. He's wearing a T-shirt and jeans, his off-duty clothes. It means he may be able to keep me company for a while.

Sure enough, he turns the TV on to the cartoon channel and lounges on the bed. Uneasy, I sit next to him and nibble on my sandwich. It's impossible to relax when I know Baby's so close.

"Amy," Gareth says without looking my way, "I can probably get you some regular clothes." It's not the first time he's offered. He thinks I should change out of my synth-suit, but I'm hesitant to remove it. I even showered in it, though wearing it almost eliminates the need for showering. When I stepped out of the shower, the suit was dry within a few minutes. I know it seems like I'm being overly cautious, but the outbreak at Fort Black just proved that I could need the suit at any time. It also feels right to wear it, a layer between myself and the world. It makes me feel safe.

"I'm fine," I tell him, though that's far from the truth. The silly cartoons on TV are starting to irritate me. "This is bullshit," I say. "Why don't they talk about the situation at Fort Black? Send a convoy to search for survivors?"

Like Jacks, I want to say. But I can't push the words past my lips.

Gareth eyes me. "Dr. Reynolds doesn't care about the people there."

"What about Ken's lab? His research?"

"They'll probably send us back out to gather what we can."

"When? After they think everyone will be dead or changed?"

Gareth just shrugs.

My sandwich has turned to cardboard in my mouth, and I place it on the counter. I can't stop thinking about Jacks.

"And what about Brenna? Have you heard anything?"

Gareth shakes his head. When they landed in New Hope, Ken whisked Brenna away to the labs and disappeared along with her. Neither Gareth nor Kay have the clearance to access information about their whereabouts.

"This is killing me," I say, growling. "I need to do something."

"There's nothing you can do." He sits up and rubs his face. "There's nothing any of us can do right now. We just have to wait for an opportunity."

Gareth's impassivity galls me, but then I think about all he's done for me, and I can't help but feel grateful. If he knew a way to help me, he would. He saved my ass when Dr. Reynolds found me coming out of the Rumble Room. He helped Kay break me out of the Ward. He was even there when Fort Black was imploding, piloting the hover-copter that carried us away.

A question comes to me.

"Were you with Kay when she picked me and Baby up on the lakeshore?"

"Yeah, I was flying the hover-copter." He grins. "I have never seen Kay as pissed as she was after you shot her."

"I've always wondered why you guys used the Florae net on us. Why didn't you just land and ask us to come with you?" I learned standard procedure in my Guardian training, and scooping up post-aps like fish wasn't part of it.

"There was a group of Floraes nearby. We thought it was too risky to take the chance of making noise while we explained ourselves to you. Kay said it was better to grab you and apologize later."

"Kay apologize? Yeah, right."

Gareth huffs a knowing laugh.

"I bet you guys wish you left us to the Floraes."

Gareth shakes his head. "And miss all the excitement? No way. You sure do know how to get yourself into trouble, though."

"And out of it," I say in my defense.

Gareth just smirks. "But mostly in."

"Hey, I did help the Guardians when Floraes were let into New Hope. I took care of myself then."

"Yeah, that's true." The smile fades from his face. "Seriously,

Amy. I admire you. I don't know if I could survive the things you've survived."

I wonder which parts he means. The After? The Ward? Finding out my mother kick-started the apocalypse?

Before I can ask him, there's a loud knock at the door. Gareth and I look at each other, then he jumps up and peers through the peephole. When he sees who it is, he cracks the door enough for Kay to step through. She's wearing her synth-suit, meaning she's either on duty or in training. She'll have only a few moments.

"Amy," she says, walking to me, "you have to see this." She takes a tiny thumb drive out of one of her pockets and hands it to me.

"What is it?"

"Footage of Baby. Ken got it to me."

"Is she okay?"

"She's alive." Kay backs away toward the door. "I have to go before I'm missed. I'll come back later, sunshine, so we can talk." She looks at Gareth. "Make sure she's okay after she watches that." He nods and Kay disappears through the door.

Gareth goes to a drawer, pulls out a laptop, and turns it on. Numb with anxiety, I hand him the thumb drive and he plugs it in.

I don't know what I expected, but when Baby's face pops up on the screen, I let out a long, relieved sigh. She is alive, or was this morning when the video was taken, according to the time stamp at the bottom.

But the relief stops there. Baby is so pale that at first I think the recording is in black-and-white. Then I see she's wearing her bright-yellow jumpsuit. Swimming in it, would be more accurate. Her face is gaunt and her eyes are shadowed, giving them a sunken look. She twirls a hair around her finger, then plucks it from her head. I flinch as though the hair had been attached to my own scalp. She did the same thing when we were in the After, right after we lost our home and before we came to New Hope.

Someone off-camera says, "Hannah," and Baby looks up blankly.

"Yes?" she asks hesitantly. It's so strange to hear her voice after our years of silence together. I didn't even know she could speak until Rice revealed that he knew her true name, shocking her into repeating it. That was just moments before I was taken to the Ward. After that I was allowed to see her only while I was heavily drugged.

"Hannah, we're going to ask you a few simple questions." My chest constricts. I recognize the voice now. It's Dr.

Thorpe, my Ward psychiatrist.

"What's your full name?" Dr. Thorpe asks.

"Hannah O'Brian," Baby replies softly.

"Have you ever gone by any other name?"

Baby looks off-camera, confused, and shakes her head.

"How old are you?"

"Six." Baby tugs at another strand of her dull blond hair, then yanks it out.

"And where do you live?"

"New Hope."

"And do you have any family in New Hope?"

Baby looks at this camera this time. "New Hope is my family."

"Yes," Dr. Thorpe's voice prompts. "But any family members living in New Hope?"

Baby scrunches her face. "No . . . my family is gone. I have no one."

I take a step back and sit on the bed, utterly deflated. I feel the pieces of my heart shattering in my chest.

Gareth pauses the recording. "You okay?"

"Yeah," I lie, then swallow. "What are they doing to her?"

"I think . . . with all she's been through, Baby is weak. She's not thinking straight. They're letting her forget the truth and filling her head with lies. They're trying to change her history."

"Brainwash her?" I ask. "When I was in the Ward, Dr. Reynolds once threatened to tell her I had died."

Gareth sits next to me and puts his arm around me, resting his head next to mine. "Amy, I'm sorry, honey. I think they're going a step further than that. They're trying to convince her that you never existed."

I close my eyes for a few moments, and we sit in silence. "Let's watch the rest," I tell him, opening my eyes.

"Are you sure you're up for that?"

"I have to see what they're doing to her."

He pushes play and I listen while Dr. Thorpe asks Baby more questions, planting the seeds of lies in her head. I watch as Dr. Thorpe tries to unmake me.

CHAPTER THIRTY-FIVE

Hours later, when Gareth has gone, there is a knock at the door. I assume it's Kay, but I look through the peephole just to be sure. When I see who it is, I fumble with the lock and yank the door open with shaking hands.

"Rice," I whisper, not really knowing what else to say.

"Amy," he says breathlessly, the expression on his face caught between worry and joy.

A moment passes, and I realize he's standing there, waiting for me to let him in.

"Come in," I murmur, stepping back and motioning him inside and out of sight. When he's closed the door behind him, he just stands there with that same weird look, adjusting and readjusting his glasses.

"Amy, I'm so sorry I couldn't come sooner. I've been–" He stops and stares at me. "I couldn't get away. And also, I've been scared to come."

"Scared?" I ask in a soft voice.

"Yes. I missed you so much. . . . It really freaked me out. When you left, I didn't know if I'd ever see you again. So it took me a little while to find the courage to get over here."

I don't know what to say. These past months I've thought about Rice, about the moment I would see him again. Now he's here, and it doesn't feel real.

"Does that make sense?" he asks softly.

"I've . . . I've been waiting here. Not knowing anything. And you were too *scared* to come?" Did he think telling me that would make me feel better?

"I know, I'm so sorry. Please, Amy. Can you forgive me?"

Instead of answering, I take a step forward and tentatively reach out to him. Before I know what I'm doing, I wrap my arms around him. He's thinner than I remember. I can feel his ribs. Everything I missed about him comes racing back—his solid reasoning, his quiet nature, the way he always makes me feel safe. I always feel *right* when I'm with Rice.

He runs his hands softly through my short hair and, taking my face in his grasp, he brushes his lips against mine—tentatively at first, then pressing more firmly.

He's kissing me. And suddenly things no longer feel right—they feel horribly wrong. I break off our kiss abruptly and back away from him.

"I'm sorry, Amy." He looks confused and under that, exhausted. "I just can't believe you're here," he says.

"You must have known I'd come back."

"Yes, of course you would." He looks at the floor. "Baby's here."

"Yeah, Baby and . . ." I trail off, embarrassed. I'd thought about him so much, but what was truly between us? He helped me and promised to help Baby.

Baby.

I move away from him to peek out the window. No one's out there.

"Rice, I saw a video of Baby. Kay brought it to me. It was awful. What are they doing to her?"

"I haven't been able to get her away from Dr. Reynolds," he says, pulling me from the window to sit on the sofa.

"Well, you have to try harder," I tell him. Frustratingly, tears are starting to well up. I wipe them away angrily with my synth-suit-covered hands.

"I've tried, Amy," he says gently. "It's not a simple thing."

I look at Rice in his lab coat and glasses. He's so different from Jacks. It took some convincing, but once Jacks was on my side, he was there. He wouldn't hesitate to help me break Baby out. He wouldn't think about it.

I take a breath, collecting myself. Jacks isn't here. For all I know, he's dead.

"Have you been working with Dr. Reynolds, testing Baby's blood?"

Rice seems again confused by my cold tone. "Yes, of course. It's my job, and it lets me keep an eye on her."

"Right. So you can watch them hurt her. Watch them brainwash her. How could you let this happen?"

"Amy—"

"You promised to protect her." I'm taking out my frustrations on him, but I can't stop myself. "If they needed a test subject, you should have volunteered yourself."

Rice looks at the floor, his face pinched. He's gripping one hand with another, but they're both shaking.

"Dr. Reynolds doesn't know, does he?" I ask him. "He has no idea that you took the original vaccine, too. Were you part of the original experiment? Were you a test subject?"

He sighs and shakes his head. "After my parents died, Dr. Reynolds took me in. He kept me out of the foster care system, out of the group homes. I . . . I helped him with his experiments, but only because I didn't know what kind of a man he really was."

I flinch away from him, horrified by his admission.

"Amy, he was like a father to me," he tells me, desperately wanting me to understand. "When the original infection broke out, I was scared, and I injected myself with the vaccine. Reynolds never knew. Before you, the only person to know was Katie . . . the girl I told you about. The one who died setting up the emitters with me." He looks up at me, his eyes haunted. "I would've told him if I thought it would make a difference. Just because I injected myself with the original vaccine doesn't mean that I'm immune. Do you know how many times we've tested it since then? How many people we've sacrificed?"

"Rice, I really think there was something about that original batch that was different. Something that got into the mixture or wasn't accounted for."

"It was created in a lab, Amy, not some guy's basement. We've replicated it thoroughly. We've modified the original, and still nothing. I've tested my own blood, and I can't see anything in it that would suggest I'd be immune. Should I let myself get infected on the off chance that it will work, like it did for Baby? If I were gone, who would help her?" he asks quietly. "And besides, I don't even know if Dr. Reynolds would let me take her place. He's been training me since I was a child. He's invested too much time and effort to let me go. He sees me as an *asset*," he hisses, as if he hates the word. As if he hates himself. "He'd make me continue to test her and probably test myself as well."

I feel my anger dissipating, like air leaking slowly out of a balloon. I'm left feeling guilty and ashamed of questioning Rice's motives. Rice's eyes are filled with hurt.

I reach out and take his hand. "I'm sorry," I say quietly. "I know you've done everything you can."

"Maybe," Rice replies after a few moments. "Maybe I could speak with your mother, tell her you're here."

"No." I shake my head slowly. "She can't be trusted. She sold me out to Dr. Reynolds, left me to rot in the Ward." Even as I say it, I know it's not as straightforward as that. My mother also told Kay where I was, and tried to protect me from Dr.

Reynolds for as long as she could. "It's better if she doesn't know."

"What about Dr. Samuels?" I ask. "He got you a message when I was in the Ward. He gave Kay Dr. Reynolds's key card to break me out."

"I don't know, Amy. I don't even know if I can approach him without being found out. Everyone is so afraid of being put in the Ward or simply getting expelled. Dr. Reynolds went overboard after your escape, questioning everyone's loyalty."

"But not yours?"

"No. He thinks of me like a son." His voice is full of bitterness. "More like his trained monkey."

"Rice? What happened? What made you start to doubt him, and then . . . help me?" I almost said *betray him* instead of *help me*. "Was it Marcus hauling me away to the Ward?"

"That was part of it, but before that I found something. . . ." He stops himself, rubbing his hands, hard, over his face. "I found evidence that Dr. Reynolds . . . had my parents killed so he could adopt me. So he could use my brain in whatever twisted way he saw fit."

His hands have fallen from his face. His eyes are huge, his face a mask of such pain and self-loathing that I want to forget all the resentment I feel for him and wrap my arms around him again. But then the horror of what Rice has said sinks in, and I place my hand over my mouth in shock. It shouldn't be surprising, the lengths that Dr. Reynolds would go, but I can't imagine the pain that Rice must have felt when he found out. I place my hand on his shoulder, trying to be a comfort.

"I don't know how I ever thought he was a great man," Rice says quietly. "Now he just seems like a madman."

A madman who has Baby. I pull away. "Are you sure I can't get in to see Baby?"

"I don't know how, not without giving yourself up to him."

"Do you know anything about Brenna?" I ask. "Are they doing the same things to her that they're doing to Baby? I'm the one who brought Brenna to Ken. Any harm that comes to her is my fault."

"Ken is working with her. He hasn't told anyone that she's immune. I only know he has her because Kay told me." He drops his face a little closer to mine. "He won't hurt her, Amy. He isn't bad. He hasn't told anyone about you being here, either."

"I don't think he's bad," I say. "He's the reason I'm here. I think he's just obsessed with finding a cure, or at least a vaccine."

"Just like every other researcher here," Rice says. "Even I . . . If I could just catch a break. There's something I'm not seeing."

"I understand the need for a Florae vaccine, but I wouldn't trade Baby for one."

Rice looks away, and I get the eerie feeling that he *would* choose a vaccine over Baby.

But then he says, "We have to be careful," and I know he's still on my side. "Dr. Reynolds is out of control," he goes on, studying me. "It's like you're a ticking time bomb, Amy. You want to help Baby so badly, it's all you see. If you let yourself go off, you'll only make things worse for her. You know that, don't you?"

"I know, but I feel so powerless. These last few days I've been bouncing off the walls. I think I'm going to lose it."

"Remember when I told you to be strong, when you were in the Ward?"

I nod.

"And that worked, didn't it?"

"It did."

"So, again. Be strong."

I look at him, into his pleading eyes, and I nod.

Rice stands to leave and we hug again, but my arms feel heavy and awkward. I don't want him to go, but I don't know why. I make myself step away and say, "Come back when you can."

"I will," he tells me. He leans in, and I think he'll try to kiss me again, but he almost immediately changes his mind. He straightens up, gives me a curt nod, and then he's gone.

During the next twenty-four hours, I can't sleep or eat the food that Gareth leaves for me. All I do is think of Baby's face in that video, pale and resigned. A ghost of the happy, vibrant girl I knew.

I sit cross-legged on the floor and close my eyes, trying to think of nothing. My mind automatically goes to Rice. The way he's always cleaning his glasses and how his shaggy blond hair always ends up in his eyes. His striking blue eyes—intelligent, caring eyes. Part of me wishes that I could have kissed him again before he left, wishes I'd not let him leave at all.

My mind skips past Rice, and all I can do now is imagine the worst. All the people I know are in danger. And Jacks. The image of his face forces itself into my mind—his brown eyes clouding over into a milky yellow, his tattooed skin slowly turning green. I try to shake it from my imagination. I can't think of Jacks right now. I just can't. Surely, he fought them off. He wouldn't have let his fear endanger his life.

But still, it wouldn't matter, would it? Even a trained Guardian eventually would have been overwhelmed by the Floraes.

The image of the monsters taking Jacks down returns; he's changing into one of Them—

I shake my head.

I don't care what Kay and Gareth say. I can't wait for them, and I don't care what's out there. I can't stay in this room a minute more. I go to the door, open it wide, and walk out.

CHAPTER THIRTY-SIX

When I step through the door I nearly run into Kay, dressed in her synth-suit. She stares at me for a moment before whispering, "Amy, what the hell are you doing out here?" She grabs my arm and tries to pull me back in. "You know you can't be seen."

"I'm going to get Baby. It can't wait any longer."

She shakes her head. "Don't be stupid. Do you think you can take on Dr. Reynolds and half the Guardians? You could die."

"I would die for her, to give her a chance."

"And what was your plan?" She raises her eyebrows.

"Break into the lab. I've done it before. Find where they're keeping Baby . . . get her and escape." As I say it aloud, I realize how ridiculous I sound. I have no real course of action, just a desperate need to make sure Baby is safe. "Kay, I can't lose her."

"I know, Amy, but have a little faith." She holds something out to me. It's a key card, Level One. "Ken gave this to me. We have to get into Dr. Reynolds's office and see where he's holding Baby. This card will give us access to anywhere in the lab. We should be able to sweep in and get her. We'll stash you both just outside of New Hope, but within range of the emitters. Then we'll figure out what to do with you from there."

"What about Marcus?" I shudder slightly, remembering his ferocity and skill in all forms of combat, a result of his military training, as well as the ruthlessness of the Elite Eight–the Guardians loyal to him.

"Gareth is going to keep Marcus occupied, and we have someone on the inside who said Dr. Reynolds will be in psyche-evals all morning."

"Rice?" I smile.

"No, he's too close to Dr. Reynolds. We thought it was

better not to involve him, so he can have plausible deniability. He's our plan B."

I nod, knowing that Rice won't like being cut out of the loop. But at least now I have my chance. I'm going to get Baby.

Kay has me pull down the hood of my synth-suit and walk next to her, out of the building and across the Quad. I know I won't pass for any of the male Guardians, the synth-suit is too tight fitting for that, but at a glance I might resemble Jenny, though she's a little smaller than I am. Hopefully no one is paying close attention, and most of the people we pass don't even spare us a second glance.

It brings back a strange feeling to walk to the lab where my world was shattered. I'd stolen Rice's key card and broken in to confront my mother, who admitted her part in the Florae apocalypse, the creation of the bacterium that caused the infection. I shudder as we reach the black door, marking the lab as a restricted area. I glance up and find a newly installed camera staring back at us. I hold my breath, hoping our ploy will work.

Kay swipes the clearance card and the door unlocks. I release the breath I didn't know I was holding. We walk right into the lab building as if we belong there, and take the elevator to the bottom floor, Level B5, where all the research happens.

Kay leads me through the hall. With my hood pulled down, I'm just another Guardian. Marcus's cronies, the Elite Eight, have been conducting random inspections under Dr. Reynolds's orders, so no one questions us.

We walk the labyrinth of hallways, through doors to restricted areas, and past an open doorway where a group of researchers is gathered around a table in a conference room. I falter and let out a small gasp.

One of the researchers is my mother.

She looks ragged, her face lined with stress. Kay sees her too and grabs my arm to get me moving again. I can feel my mother's eyes on me as we hurry away. Can she recognize the shape of my body? My gait? Will she raise the alarm?

When we've turned a corner out of sight, Kay murmurs, "Do you think she realized it was you?"

"No." I shake my head, willing it to be true. "She would've said something."

"We can circle back a different way, hide you again."

"No. Let's stick to the plan," I say.

Dr. Reynolds's office is near my mother's. I keep checking behind us, worrying that my mother has followed us, but the hall remains clear. Kay turns the handle and it opens.

A feeling of alarm tickles my senses. It wasn't locked? We

did have to go through multiple security checks, but still . . .

We slip inside the office, and Kay points to a camera mounted in the corner. "Last night I distracted Marcus while Gareth got into the surveillance room. I set a ten-minute loop of the empty office. No one can see us."

"That's why the door wasn't locked: Dr. Reynolds would rather see what people are up to than prevent them from entering altogether."

Kay nods as I shuffle through the papers on Dr. Reynolds's desk. There are stacks of manila folders, names written neatly on the tabs at the side. Each folder represents a patient in the Ward. I open one: It details a course of treatment for a woman with "paranoid delusions of conspiracy." I grimace, seriously doubting that the woman's paranoia is a delusion.

I put the folder down and riffle through the rest, checking the name on each. No Hannah O'Brian.

Kay places an oversized sheet of paper before me. "Look." It's a map of the labs, just what we need. "Ken said Baby was in Florae Research."

There's a room at the center marked FR LEVEL ONE CLEARANCE—FPV ONLY. I jab it with my fingertip and look up at Kay. "FR—Florae Research? Has to be. But what is FPV?"

"I don't know. Ken didn't say anything about that. We didn't have much time to talk, though."

We study the map, trying to memorize the twists and turns that will take us to find Baby. After a moment of intense concentration, I say, "I think I've got it. Let's go."

Kay nods, placing the map back where she found it, under a pile of books. I make sure all the folders are on Dr. Reynolds's desk the way they were before I disturbed them and join Kay by the door. Stepping out into the hall, we navigate the lab. We pass a few researchers, but none of them appear to give us a second thought.

At the black door labeled FLORAE RESEARCH, Kay swipes the clearance card. Nothing happens. The door doesn't budge. Kay tries it again. Nothing.

"What's wrong?"

She touches a clear pad next to the card reader and sighs. "Well, now we know what FPV means. Fingerprint Verification. We need a Clearance One fingerprint to get in."

"What do we do now?" I ask, starting to panic.

"Well, we can start by not hanging out here, looking sketchy." She turns and walks down the hall. I run to catch up.

"Do we need Dr. Reynolds's fingerprint?" My heart sinks. If so, we'll have to turn back now, before we've even begun.

"No . . . just someone with clearance. I think I know who

we can ask." We turn a corner, and Kay stops at a door. Again, I instantly think of Rice, but obviously, Kay purposefully wants to keep him out of this. "Who?"

"The same person who told us that Dr. Reynolds would be busy all day."

She knocks, and after a moment there is a curt "Come in." We step through the door into a small office, and I'm relieved to find Dr. Samuels seated behind a cluttered desk. He still wears the same yellow bow tie and tweed jacket, but looks older than I remember. Everyone's appearance seems to have changed for the worse in the short time I've been gone.

Dr. Samuels stares at us, then reaches into a desk drawer and pulls out a pistol. I take a surprised step back as Dr. Samuels points it at us.

"You will *not* be taking me to the Ward," he says, his face oddly calm. He raises the gun's barrel to his temple, closes his eyes, and squeezes the trigger.

CHAPTER THIRTY-SEVEN

Nothing happens.

Dr. Samuels looks as shocked as I feel. Kay rips her hood off, and Dr. Samuels stares at her, his look of surprise giving way to one of glazed horror.

"I . . . I thought they'd finally come for me. . . ." He's wide-eyed, mouth gaping, and turns to the gun in his hand. He sets the weapon on his desk, then yanks his hand away as if he's been burned.

Kay steps over and plucks the gun off the desk. "Holy crap, when I gave this to you it didn't occur to me you'd use it for *that*." She checks the gun. "Good thing the safety was on."

"Yes." Dr. Samuels lets out a nervous sigh. "Quite." He places his hand on his chest and watches as Kay removes the clip and tucks it into one of her pockets. After checking the chamber, Kay sets the pistol on the desk. Dr. Samuels stares at it. "I just couldn't risk being taken."

My heart threatening to pound out of my rib cage, I pull down my hood. Dr. Samuels's mouth drops open. "Amy," he whispers. He takes me in for a moment. "I suppose I knew you'd be back, for your sister." He nods at the gun on the desk between us. "I thought you were one of Marcus's men, come to take me away because of what I did for you."

I'm still shaken by his attempted suicide, but if we want to get to Baby, we need to keep moving. "I know you've taken huge risks already, getting the message to us, stealing the key cards," I say. "I can't tell you how much I appreciate it. And I know you're worried about being caught. . . . But please, we need your help again."

Dr. Samuels looks at us silently for a long moment. "What do you need?"

"A fingerprint. To get into the section of the lab where they're holding Baby."

Dr. Samuels nods. "Yes, FPV. Put into effect just recently." He straightens his bow tie, rubs his hands through his sparse, white hair.

"Will you help us?" I ask.

He rubs his temples again, then eyes the gun on the desk. "Well, three minutes ago, I tried to kill myself." He looks up at us with a faint smile. "So obviously fear of death isn't my problem."

"I don't blame you," I say quietly. "If you thought you were going to the Ward."

"Torture," he says grimly. "That's what they're doing there, I know. That's what they're doing to that little girl, your sister. It's . . . it's an abomination. We're *doctors*," he hisses. "We took an oath to do no harm." He gives his head a sharp shake. "We're *human beings*." He slaps his palms onto his desk and stands. "Let's go."

We flank him on the way back to the restricted area, where he swipes his key card and pushes his finger on the pad. The door swings open and we're through it.

I have no idea which of the many doors hides Baby from

me, yet have to tell myself not to run down the hall ahead of them. I have to control my emotions, not let them take control, or I'll end up doing something stupid.

Dr. Samuels stops at a door, swipes his card again, and taps a code into the keypad. He scans his print. The door opens to a dorm-style room.

Immediately I suck in a breath, paralyzed by the sight of Baby sitting at a child-sized table, coloring in a book.

There are a few toys, a few books on her bed, but everything else about the room is clinical. Hard, cold surfaces. Her bright-yellow jumpsuit blazes in the glaring light.

I am unable to move or even react. My time in the Ward floods back to me. I would spend days at a time in my room there, living the same bare existence that Baby is living here, drugged and numb. I begin to shake, my limbs no longer under my control. I stare at Baby, who hasn't bothered to look up at the open door. I feel a hand on my back, Kay's reassuring touch, and I know I have to push through the pain. I can't fall apart now, not when I'm so close to saving her.

I step into the room and walk slowly to Baby's side, pulling off my hood so I don't scare her. She never used to want to color. The *swoosh*ing sound of the crayon across the paper unnerved her. I kneel next to her as she scribbles furiously on the page, oblivious to the noise she is creating. I circle her in my arms and pull her to me.

She's limp in my embrace. I pull back and examine her.

"Baby . . . it's me. I'm so glad you're okay." When she doesn't respond, I pet her head. "Baby?"

At last she seems to focus on me, and my heart swells—and then breaks again when she opens her mouth to speak:

"My name is Hannah," she says. "Who are you?"

CHAPTER THIRTY-EIGHT

She can't have forgotten me. It's not possible. I place my hand in hers and sign, *It's me, Amy.*

Her hand remains lifeless in mine. Her fingers are freezing, her skin chalky white.

Baby, I try again. *I'm here to take you away with me.* She still doesn't respond, so I say aloud, "I've come to get you. I'm going to take you away from here."

For the first time Baby reacts with something other than indifference. "But I want to stay," she tells me, her face scrunched in worry. She reaches up and twirls a hair around her finger. Before I can stop her, she tugs it free. I move her hair aside gently, revealing a pink bald patch on her scalp, agitated and raw.

"Oh, Baby. I'm so sorry. I should have come sooner. I tried, I really did." How have I allowed them to turn Baby into this zombie child? I blink hard, battling back tears.

Kay and Dr. Samuels are whispering at the door. Then Kay's calling to me. "Amy, what's the holdup? We've got to get going."

"She doesn't"–I turn to Dr. Samuels, swallowing my emotion–"she doesn't recognize me."

"Sunshine, I'm sorry, but you're going to have to make her come."

I nod, take hold of Baby under her arms and hoist her to my hip. Her six-year-old frame feels so light, as if I'm holding the shell that used to contain her. Pressed close to me, I can feel her heartbeat, weak and sporadic, through my synth-suit. She appears resigned to being carried until I've made it almost to the door, and then she lets out a scream so loud, I nearly drop her. Weak as she is, how can she make so much noise?

She keeps it up. There's nothing for me to do but take her back into the room. Cradling her head on my shoulder, I get her to quiet down, but when I move to escape with her again, she lets out another heart-wrenching wail.

"You've got to leave her," Kay commands.

"No." Now that I have Baby in my arms, I'm not letting her go. Not for anything.

"She's been compromised," Dr. Samuels explains quietly. "She won't go willingly."

"'Compromised'? What does *that* mean?"

"She's . . . She's not herself."

I start to ask him again what he's talking about, but I know. Baby isn't Baby. Dr. Reynolds has seen to that. I think of the video, and I shudder. They've made her into Hannah, New Hope citizen and willing test subject. I hope it's not too late, that Baby hasn't completely disappeared. I look into her cold, vacant eyes, and I'm not so sure.

"You can come back for her," Dr. Samuels says weakly.

Baby's shoulder cuts into my arm as I squeeze her to me. She's skin and bones. "By the time we get the chance, she could be dead."

"We can't drag a screaming child through the lab," Kay

tells me. "And even if we did manage it, how could we hide you both?"

"We can get some sedatives," I say desperately. "Dr. Samuels, you must have access."

"I don't know how her body would react," he tells me. "I don't know what they have her on, and she looks anemic. I don't think her liver, not to mention her heart, could take anything right now."

"Amy," Kay's voice warns. "We have to go. And Baby can't come with us."

I want to tell them to go on without me, just so I can spend a few more moments with Baby. I think of Pam, staying with Mike in their cell until the bitter end, unwilling to leave him to save herself. I have to do what's best for Baby, though, and her best chance is having me on the outside, working to get her out.

I ease her down into her chair, placing her purple crayon in her ice-cold fingers. "I'm going to leave now, Baby," I say, surprised at the strength of my voice when my insides feel like gelatin.

"My name is Hannah," she says, resuming coloring on her paper. "I'm not a baby."

"Okay, Hannah." The name sounds so strange in my mouth.

"Hannah, I'm going to go now, but I'm going to come back and get you. I'm going to find someplace for us, someplace we can call home."

She looks up at me, her brown eyes strangely serene.

"I am home."

CHAPTER THIRTY-NINE

Numb, I back away from her slowly, unable to absorb the fact that the Baby I knew is gone. But it's right there in front of me: That clever, fearless, lovely girl has vanished.

"Quickly, follow me," Dr. Samuels tells us.

"Amy, put on your hood," Kay says, and I do it, glad to mask the pain on my face. I'm the last one out of Baby's room, and I can't help but look back at her, clutching her crayon and scribbling robotically. The door closes and the click of the latch feels like it's severed something deep inside me, but I turn and follow them down the hall.

Dr. Samuels leads us quickly down a series of unfamiliar corridors and at last into some sort of meeting room. There's an oval table surrounded by several chairs and a projection screen on the wall. "Wait here until I'm sure the coast is clear," he tells us before ducking out the door.

I stand by the wall while Kay sits on the table. She gives me a moment before asking if I'm okay.

I nod only because I have to give her some response.

"We'll go back for her, Amy," Kay tells me, but this time I can't even nod.

Then Dr. Samuels opens the door but doesn't come in. He just stands there, staring at me for a moment. "Amy, I'm sorry. I had to."

I frown, looking at him, then to Kay. "What?" I turn and see that standing behind him is my mother.

I glance at Kay, whose look of horror confirms my fear.

"What did you do?" she asks through gritted teeth.

Dr. Samuels has betrayed us.

"Amy!" My mother rushes me and hugs me to her. She smells like flowers and cotton, and in my bewilderment, I hug her back. Then I regain my senses and break her hold, backing quickly away.

She sees my look of confused hatred. "Amy, please. You don't understand."

"What don't I understand?" I hiss. "How you left me to rot in the Ward, how you let them torture Baby?"

She shakes her head. "It's not as simple as that." She keeps her distance, but her voice is pleading. "I let him put you in the Ward because I thought it was the safest place for you. Then, when Dr. Samuels told me about what treatments you were really receiving, I went to Kay. I told her where you were."

I stare at her, disbelieving. "You're lying."

"Amy." I feel Kay move to my side. "She's telling the truth. She wanted you out of there."

"Amy, I couldn't stand up to Dr. Reynolds then. Not directly. I didn't have the support."

"And now?" I ask. "Why are you here now?"

She shakes her head again. "Dr. Reynolds has gone mad since you escaped. He thinks I'm purposely stalling in finding a vaccine. Insane. He's placed us all under surveillance. It's impossible to get work done. I can't leave the lab without being followed by that gorilla, Marcus. I'm sure he's looking for me right now."

I still don't trust her. And yet, there are tears in her eyes.

"Amy, Dr. Reynolds was convinced you'd come back and contact me. He's been waiting." She steps closer, grips my arms. "It's dangerous for you here, but when I saw you in the hall . . . I was so happy." She releases me, presses the backs of her hands to her eyes.

I want to hate her, but part of me knows she's telling the truth. She did her best. All the strings she pulled to keep me under Dr. Reynolds's radar, all the conversations we had about how I needed to fit in to be happy. She was trying to protect me the only way she could.

Still, I can't help but stay at arm's length from her. "I only came back for Baby," I tell her.

"Yes," she says, a look of fresh pain crossing her face. "Baby. I've tried to keep her safe, tried to keep her from him. And that meant acting as though she didn't matter, as though she were nothing more than an annoyance. I thought having her live in the dorms, distancing her from you, would be enough to keep her under his radar, but . . . one of the minders saw the injection scar on her neck and she was scooped up."

She's searching my face. I try to keep it frozen, but I feel my resolve melting.

"I had no idea who she was until then, but Dr. Reynolds is convinced I was keeping her from him. That I knew she was part of the original test group and I didn't tell him. He began to spread rumors that, after your breakdown and escape, I couldn't handle the strain. I know he wants me in the Ward."

"What?"

"He sees me as a threat, Amy. He always has, and now—now he's just unhinged."

The idea of my mother—my powerful mother, always in control—thrown into the Ward to be tortured and experimented upon. . . . I just can't wrap my head around it. "Is he . . . Is he going to *do* it?"

"Given the opportunity," she says, "yes, absolutely. But even as mad as he is, he's kept his political sense, knows not to push too hard too quickly. I'm a public figure, not just to the people of New Hope, but to the researchers. In their eyes, I'm still the director, their leader. If nothing else, it would be a blow to morale to have me committed." A quiet, desolate laugh escapes her lips. "So I play the political game too. I do what I can—what little I can—to keep him in check while pretending to be on board."

I'm stunned and terrified in a new way: Now I have my mother's safety to worry about too. It seems impossible, but it's true.

"As soon as I could," she goes on, "I looked at Baby's blood work and told Dr. Reynolds that I didn't think she could be useful–it's the truth; the bacteria that causes the infection has mutated too much. I don't even know that if she's bitten again, she would survive. There's no way to know how she survived the first time. But he didn't believe me. He thinks I'm trying to sabotage his efforts, as if I'd manipulate my findings just to trip him up."

Brenna was bitten more recently. . . . Was I right about her being immune to the new strain? If that's true, then Baby is useless to them. Maybe Ken can find a vaccine analyzing Brenna's blood. And if that doesn't work . . . Rice hasn't been bitten at all. I shake the horrific thought from my head. Would I trade Rice for Baby?

Kay interrupts my horrible thoughts. "The other researchers are unhappy too, right? They must want to get rid of Reynolds."

"I'm sure many do," she allows, "but they also know it wouldn't be easy. And there are others who see what Dr. Reynolds is doing, preserving the human race at any cost, as necessary. I used to be one of them," she says, then gives her head a shake. "But after they took you . . ." Again I think of Rice. Where does he truly stand?

"But like you say, you're the director," Kay cuts in, "their leader, not just another researcher. Surely, you can do something."

She sighs. "If I ever did have power, it's all but gone now. Reynolds brought me here from Chicago and made me director, thinking I'd inspire confidence among the citizens. I was non-military and, with my background in bacterial research, the person best suited to find a vaccine. He could hype me as the *hope* in New Hope. And I did do research work. At the start, I think it made obvious sense to him to bring me in: I'd created the bacteria we were fighting against, after all. But I also made him uneasy, and over these last few months all I do is speak at events, record updates for the news." She shakes her head. "Now I'm just a talking head. Whatever power I might've had, Dr. Reynolds gave me—and, after Amy's escape, he's stripped it away."

"But no one in New Hope knows you're just a figurehead, do they?" I say. "None of the normal citizens." After all, everyone in New Hope lives under the haze of the researchers' lies. "They don't know that the Floraes are people, or that you're experimenting on children. They don't even know how dominated they are by Dr. Reynolds."

I remember my talks with Dr. Reynolds, my psyche-eval. He wants New Hope to be perfect, but *his* version of perfection. No room for dissent or discussion. When the bacteria were released, he saw it not as a nightmarish tragedy, but as his opportunity to remake humanity according to his vision. He's manipulated every aspect of New Hope, using his background in psychology to prey on people's fears and make them blindly follow him. The last thing he wants is for people to know the truth.

"You should tell everyone in New Hope," I say quietly to my mother. "You should confess everything."

My mother shakes her head slowly. "Amy, no. Even if Reynolds didn't immediately silence me, it would do no good. It would only upset the general population."

"Well, it's time they were upset." I look into my mother's eyes. "It's time they knew the truth. All of it. The Floraes, the research, the Ward."

My mother is still unconvinced. "I don't think–"

"Then people could decide for themselves," I say, my voice shaking with anger. I'm so sick of the lies, the cover-ups.

"Decide *what*, Amy? This isn't a democracy! It's as if you think they can just vote Reynolds out."

"If the people knew the truth, it would rob Dr. Reynolds of some of his power," Dr. Samuels says from where he's been standing in the corner of the room, waiting quietly. "It would be a start."

My mother turns and looks at him, then she swivels back to me.

"I've thought about it," she admits. "But there's something else. He threatened . . . not in so many words, but he made it clear that if he ever found out I was plotting against him, he'd take Adam away from me. He could do it. He wouldn't think twice about hurting Adam to control me."

I think about my little half-brother. He's only three. Would Dr. Reynolds really take a child? Of course he would. He took me. He took Baby.

"Some of the researchers and I have talked around the issue. They're as alarmed as I am by Dr. Reynolds. But everyone is so careful. No one wants to be sent to the Ward. I have to be careful, too. For Adam."

"What would you do?" I ask. "If you weren't so afraid."

"I'd distribute my current lab notes. They're damning enough on their own. But I'd also release the records that would expose that I created the bacteria, that the Floraes are people. But, Amy: What do you expect people to do with that information?"

Again Dr. Samuels speaks up, this time more forcefully. "You could do more than simply release the information. You could set it all out for them, tell them what it all means, what's really been going on here. And you could put yourself forward as an alternative to Reynolds."

My mother laughs hollowly at this. "A coup, Dr. Samuels?"

He nods, his mouth set in a firm line. "Precisely. You're the only person in a position to influence one . . . and we have a secret weapon."

All eyes turn to me. "What?" I ask, not understanding.

"When you escaped," Kay tells me, "Dr. Reynolds told New Hope you were dead. It was a big deal, the director's daughter dying. There was a funeral and everything."

"It was macabre," my mother intones. "I knew you'd escaped, but I had to sit there and play the grieving mother, act as if my daughter . . . you were dead."

"But, if we show people you're alive," Kay says, "they'll know Dr. Reynolds has lied. They might be more willing to listen to what else he's kept from them."

"Fine," I say. "I'm in. Just tell me what I have to do."

At first I think my mother's just going slap down the idea. But she doesn't. "They could well choose to keep Dr. Reynolds in power, to find a vaccine," she says quietly.

"But at least they'd have a choice," I tell her. "And what makes you so sure that they'd value a vaccine above anything else? It's become an obsession among the researchers, and maybe Dr. Reynolds sees it as an end that will justify his methods, as the ultimate vindication, but what would the citizens of New Hope think? Sure, it would be reassuring, but would they truly be willing to sacrifice children to get it? If it were a cure, maybe . . . but you told me a long time ago that a cure was impossible, that the Floraes would never become people again.

"So isn't there already an alternative?" I continue. "You have the emitters to keep away the Floraes. You have other technology that can keep us safe, that can help humans reclaim the world."

Dr. Samuels nods his agreement. "A vaccine is not the only thing that can save humanity. It would only solve one problem. Let the citizens of New Hope decide what sacrifices they're willing to make."

My mother shakes her head. "What would you have me do? Make an announcement on the evening news? Show that Amy is still alive and then expose all of Dr. Reynolds's secrets?"

"Exactly," Kay says. "You'd have the support of at least half of the Guardians."

"It would be pointless. Dr. Reynolds would be able to distance himself from any research I've done. It would discredit me and make him look even more attractive to the people of New Hope." She sighs, closes her eyes for a moment. When she opens them, her face has changed, her jaw set.

"The only way it would work would be to release everything at once. We have to get *his* lab notes, as well. He'd have documentation of all the experiments. Then I could share everything at one time, send out a data burst to every computer in New Hope. I could have it coincide with an announcement on the news, so even if Dr. Reynolds shuts us down, he won't be able to stop the information from spreading."

"You would do that?" Kay asks. "You could still be blamed for everything."

She nods, then looks at me as she says, "I *am* to blame. I was responsible for the bacteria. It's about time I was made accountable. If everyone knows, even if I'm punished, Adam would be safe. Most people wouldn't want to hurt an innocent child."

"Maybe they'll understand," I tell her. "New Hope still needs a leader."

"I'll remain director, if they'll have me." Her eyes flick to Kay. "But we still need Dr. Reynolds's lab notes."

"I'll get them," I say. "I've already been in his office."

"Amy, you didn't!" She's horrified. "What were you thinking?

No. If he finds you, he won't send you back to the Ward. He'll kill you."

"I won't wait around for him to find me," I snap. "People have to start putting themselves at risk." I refuse to be ruled by fear. And I can see my mother is about to refuse to as well.

"His notes aren't in his office anyway," Dr. Samuels says. "They're in the lab, in a safe. You need Level One Clearance and his personal combination. I think . . . I think I can help get the notes."

My mother shakes her head. "It's too risky."

"What would I lose if I were caught?" Dr. Samuels asks, his voice heavy. "My wife is long dead. So are my children. I have nothing. I've already broken protocol several times. I'll go. If I'm caught, you will be safe to figure something else out."

"I'm going with him." I turn to him. "I'm not going to let you risk your life alone. You'll need protection."

"Absolutely not," my mother says, which almost makes me laugh. "It's too dangerous."

"I don't know why you think you can still tell me what to do," I say, more harshly than I intend to. Her face tightens. The pain is still fresh from Baby's rejection of me, so I know how she feels. "I'll be fine," I say, more kindly. "I can take care of myself."

"I'll go too," Kay offers. "It's time to bring that bastard down."

"There's a problem," Dr. Samuel tells us. "I don't know the combination to Dr. Reynolds's safe . . . and I know of only one other person who might."

My mother nods. "Richard."

Rice. We were trying to keep him out of danger, but there's no way now. We need him. If Dr. Reynolds is out of the way, Baby will be safe.

"Call him," I tell my mother.

She puts her hand to her ear. "Richard, will you please meet me in conference room 1B? I have some data I need to share with you." She listens. "Okay, see you in five." She drops her hand. "He's on his way."

"Good." Finally all the pieces are falling into place. I'm actually doing something.

My mother moves to me, puts an arm around my shoulders, and I let her. The anger I felt toward her has deflated. I know she was in a horrible situation. At least now she's trying to make it right.

When Rice steps through the door, he looks from me to my mother and back again. "I should have known you'd be up to something," he says with a slight smile. He takes off his glasses and cleans them, then puts them back on. His blue eyes shine at me through them.

"Well?" he asks. "How can I help?"

CHAPTER FORTY

Kay and I trail Rice down the hall. My hands are sweating inside the fabric of my synth-suit, even as its quick-drying fabric seeps the moisture away. I'm rubbing them together nervously when Kay tilts her head toward me, and even though her face is covered, I can tell she is giving me a look. I drop my hands to my sides and do my best to walk with confidence and look like a badass member of the Elite Eight.

It wasn't hard to convince Rice to join us in our campaign to overthrow Dr. Reynolds. After hearing our plan, he agreed without hesitation. Still, I can tell by the pinched expression on his face when he glances back at me in the hall that he's unhappy we waited so long to include him.

It was harder to convince Dr. Samuels that he was no longer necessary. Rice had the Level One Clearance we required, as well as the combination to Dr. Reynolds's safe. Eventually he relented when Kay flat-out told him that he would slow us down. Blunt, but effective. Meanwhile, my mother is back at her office, organizing information, trying to decide the best way to present it all to the people of New Hope.

Rice gets us into the general lab area with no problem. No one questions Rice as we move through, as everyone knows he's the assistant director and Dr. Reynolds's pet. I'm beginning to think things will all fall our way when a familiar voice from the far side of the floor calls, "Richard . . . why are those Guardians in here?"

We freeze. Heads turn to us all across the lab as an older woman with blonde-gray hair pulled tightly in a bun moves quickly toward us. My stomach turns. It's Dr. Thorpe, my doctor from the Ward. Though she didn't agree with his diagnosis of my psychosis and Dr. Reynolds's heavy-handed use of sedatives and experimental treatments, that didn't stop her from helping Dr. Reynolds torture me.

"Miranda," Rice calls to her, as though delighted to see her. Smiling too widely, he explains that Dr. Reynolds requested him to lead the Guardians through a routine examination of security measures.

Dr. Thorpe narrows her eyes and looks me and Kay up and down. "Marcus is responsible for security checks," she says.

"Marcus was called away," Rice tells her. "He had to check on the situation in Fort Black."

"I see," says Dr. Thorpe, nodding. "It's interesting that you're taking such an active role in security, Richard."

"I needed to step away from my research," Rice says. "Clear my head. Though what I really need is a night's sleep."

"Yes, don't we all?" Thorpe says. "Well, just let me check in with Dr. Reynolds about this change. If you'd please just stay put until I come back?"

"Certainly," Rice says calmly.

But as Dr. Thorpe steps through the door into her office, Rice slips in after her and, out of sight of the large lab, snatches her hand away from her ear before she can make the call.

"That won't be necessary," he says. His voice is calm, but his fingers bite into the flesh of Dr. Thorpe's arm.

Dr. Thorpe's eyes widen. "Release me at once, Richard." Her eyes dart to me and Kay, now standing in the doorway. "What is this about?"

Before Rice can answer, I step forward. I remember Dr.

Thorpe's concern while discussing my medications with Dr. Reynolds. She pushed back against him, but in the end she relented, too scared to cross him. We need her as an ally. Careful to position my body away from the security cameras in the lab behind me, I pull down my hood and flash my face at her. Her hand flies to her mouth, her skin draining of color. She takes a step back, speechless. I pull my hood back up.

Rice loosens his grip on her arm slightly but still keeps her in his grasp. "Miranda, I know you don't agree with all that you've witnessed here, everything we've been forced to become a part of."

But Dr. Thorpe is looking past him at me. "Dr. Reynolds said you'd be back," she says. "I thought he was just being paranoid. He's been so . . . unpredictable lately."

"He's more than just unpredictable," I say, "and you know it. That's why you have to help us stop him." Her eyes flash away to Rice, then behind her as though Reynolds might be lurking there. "I know you're scared of him," I say, "of what he can do to you, but he has to be stopped."

Dr. Thorpe shakes her head. "*Stop* him? What are you thinking?" she hisses. "You can't imagine he'll step aside willingly."

"Not willingly, no," Rice tells her. "But maybe without bloodshed."

Dr. Thorpe's eyes widen.

"It can be done," Rice says.

"Why are we wasting time trying to convince her?" Kay asks, pulling me inside the office with her and pressing the door closed with her back. "We need to figure out something to do with her before someone else comes along."

"*Do* with me?" Dr. Thorpe shrinks back.

"She's right." I wanted Dr. Thorpe on our side. I thought I had seen something in her when I was in the Ward, but maybe I was wrong.

"*Do* with me?" Dr. Thorpe says again, then turns to Rice. "Oh, Richard, they're not going to—"

"No," Rice assures her. "We won't hurt you."

A quick rapping on the door turns Kay and me around. A researcher stands on the other side of the glass, an armful of folders clutched to his chest. He's not even looking at us as he waits for the door to be opened; his attention is fastened on the chart he's holding. There's nothing to do but let Dr. Thorpe pull away from Rice and answer the door.

"Yes?" she asks.

The researcher hands her the chart and finally does take the rest of us in as Dr. Thorpe studies it. Like all the researchers, he looks like he hasn't slept in a week. His bloodshot eyes move over each of us in turn but give no sign of actually registering what he sees, or the way Dr. Thorpe's hands tremble as she makes a note on the chart and hands it back to him. "See to it that Dr. Reynolds gets that when he finishes with his psyche-evals."

"Of course," he responds, seemingly annoyed that she feels the need to tell him his job.

Dr. Thorpe takes a step after him as he trudges off the way he came, but Rice steps past us and takes her elbow gently, stopping her. Giving her arm a squeeze, he says, "Thank you, Miranda."

She doesn't look back at us, just responds with a curt nod. "I don't wish to be a part of this. I'll continue on my way and forget I ever saw you."

"I don't think we can just let her—" Kay says, but Rice cuts her off with surprising force.

"Miranda is free to go."

"Thank you, Richard." Dr. Thorpe takes a hesitant step and then another. She catches her stride and continues into the lab without a backward glance.

"That was a mistake," Kay whispers as we continue on our way through a black door.

Rice leads us down a long corridor that loops back around

the main lab, with window views inside. There's no sign of Dr. Thorpe, though we just left her moments before. In fact, the room is now surprisingly empty; it looks like my high school chemistry lab.

Finally we reach our destination, a smaller lab that has little equipment but is lined wall to wall with books, mostly medical journals. Rice motions us inside and shuts the door behind him.

"This is where Dr. Reynolds designs his experiments," he tells us. He moves some of the books off a shelf, revealing a wall safe. Rice punches in the combination, but the safe only beeps. He glances at us and tries again. "I don't understand. I know the combination. I retrieved notes only yesterday–"

An earsplitting screech nearly brings me to my knees, and I clap my hands over my ears. Everyone else is affected too; I see Rice slump against the wall for support. The high-pitched shriek continues, and I realize that it's coming through my earpiece. Before I can remove it, the noise stops.

A voice takes its place. A voice I know all too well. A voice filled with arrogance and hatred.

Dr. Reynolds.

"Just moments ago, Dr. Thorpe came to me with some very interesting information. I contacted all the researchers to evacuate the labs. . . . Not everyone followed my instructions, or at least they didn't do so quickly enough, but I suppose that can't be helped. Those left behind will be of use, certainly. More data is always useful."

"What is he talking about?" I ask Rice, but he just raises a finger as if he's telling me to wait and listen with him.

"I have decided to take a page out of a colleague's book," Dr. Reynolds goes on. "A coarse little fellow in Fort Black—I believe he preferred to be called simply Doc. I've started the clock, to measure how long this takes. The results will be very informative, in case of a future breach."

"What—?" I begin to ask, but stop myself when I see the horror on Rice's face.

Again Dr. Reynolds's voice is in my ear. "I expected more from you, Richard," he continues. "You were like a son to me."

Rice's hand goes to his communicator. "Dr. Reynolds . . . I . . . Dr. Reynolds?" He looks at me, seemingly frozen in fear.

Suddenly there is another high-pitched noise, though this time it's not in my earpiece; it bounces throughout the lab and is accompanied by flashing lights.

"That's the Florae alarm!" Kay screams over the noise. "A Florae has escaped."

Rice shakes his head. "Not escaped. He let it out."

"We won't be able to leave the lab!" Kay shouts. "Emergency

protocol shuts down all exits. We're trapped here, five floors underground."

I pull out my gun. I may have to play Dr. Reynolds's game, but I'm not going to lose without a fight.

"How many Floraes are down here?" I ask Kay over the wail of the alarm.

"I don't know exactly!" she screams back. "Ten ... twelve ..."

"Twenty-seven!" shouts Rice, and I can't help but give him a look of pure horror.

I turn to the door. "Will it hold?" I shout.

"Yes, it's Florae-proof!" he yells. "They can't *get through*."

His last two shouted words echo through sudden silence.

The alarm has turned off, and with it, the lights.

For a moment there is complete darkness, and then the backup lights flood the room with a soft glow, the yellow-green light turning our skin the color of a Florae. In the quiet I can just make out a scratching at the door. With an agonizing pop the door opens a few inches, and a green claw reaches through, scraping the wall with its knifelike fingernails.

CHAPTER FORTY-ONE

Rice looks from the Florae's claw to me. "The doors are electric," he whispers, his quiet voice shaky. "They won't lock while the power is off."

I drop into my firing stance. "Stay behind me," I tell Rice. He has no weapon and no training. He'll be useless against the Floraes.

Kay throws herself against the door, trying to ram it closed, but it's pointless: She's knocked back across the room as the creature blasts the door open wide.

It stands there just inside the doorway, snarling, yellow teeth gnashing—and listening. Kay stays motionless in the heap she fell into. I can feel Rice's breath hot on the back of my neck. Another silent moment, and the creature might withdraw. But then Rice exhales behind me, releasing a tiny rattle of fear deep in his throat as he does so.

The small noise is enough to catch the creature's attention. It rolls its milky eyes in my direction and then bolts forward, mouth wide in anticipation, its blue-black tongue tasting the air.

I drop it with one shot, and the next one that muscles through the door after it. There are more, clawing one another as they fight their way in. Somehow three of them break through at once and all of them speed at me. I manage to take down the first two, but I hit the third in the neck instead of the head and then it's upon me, knocking me to the side and twisting down to finish me—and then it simply falls to the floor, lifeless. I look up at Kay, who nods once and trains her gun on the empty door.

"Did you get them all?" Rice's terrified whisper comes from the back of the room.

I shake my head as I get to my feet. There are only five dead. The other twenty-two are still on the prowl.

Rice recovers and moves to my side, stunned but recovering. "When the electricity goes out," he whispers, "the backup generator is supposed to power all Level One areas."

"But this is a Level One area, right?"

He nods. "Reynolds must have diverted the power supply to specifically put us in harm's way."

"It doesn't matter. I have to go get Baby," I say, turning toward the door. "If the power is out in her area, she'll be in danger. She doesn't remember how to be quiet anymore. They've made her a sitting duck."

Rice grabs my arm. "Dr. Reynolds knows that's where you'll go. And even if you make it, he won't just let you walk out of here with her."

That's all true, but he and Kay can tell I'm still going.

"It'll be easier for me to go on my own," I tell them, giving them an out. "I'll be able to avoid the Floraes."

Rice shakes his head. "No one knows these labs better than me. I can guide you." I grimace under my synth-suit hood. Rice is still shaking slightly. He may use Floraes in his experiments, but he isn't used to being hunted by Them, isn't used to the fear they create, a fear I've learned to push down over the years. But he's still trying, dealing with his fear remarkably well.

"Hell, we've come this far," Kay says from the door. "And

besides, I'm a Guardian," she adds. "This is my idea of a good time, sunshine."

"Okay. I'll take lead. Rice in the middle. Kay will cover our backs. Let's go."

We start working our way down the hall, Rice making so much noise, I'm expecting a Florae to run at us at any moment. I'm so on edge I almost shoot a researcher cowering in the shadows. Rice puts his arm around her shoulders and coaxes her to stand, then guides her with us down the hall. He seems better, now that he's helping someone else.

"I thought it was just a drill," the researcher says, her voice echoing off the walls. "I didn't want to leave my work for a false alarm."

Rice shushes her and we continue our slow progress. When we reach a hall lined with open doors, I halt. Any one of those rooms could contain a Florae, waiting to pounce. The researcher is still sniveling, and although Rice is trying to help, he makes just as much noise trying to quiet her.

Frustration wells up inside me and along with it, guilt. I place my mouth close to Rice's ear and whisper, "Look for a safe place." I motion over my shoulder at the researcher. There's no choice: I need to find a place to stash her so I can go get Baby.

Rice nods and scans the hall, pointing out a door at the far end that remains closed. A film of light leaks out beneath it. That room, whatever it is, has electricity. Maybe it has its own generator. If the door locks, the researcher will be safe there.

I move ahead to check out the open rooms one by one before allowing the group to move forward. It's slow going, and in each lab there are too many places a creature can hide.

We are almost to the locked door when the researcher screams. There's a Florae hurtling toward her from the end of the hall. I must have missed it in one of the rooms. Kay grabs her and tries to pull her along, dragging her down the hall. With her free arm, she shoots the Florae, missing its head by inches. She pushes the researcher toward me and returns to dispatch the Florae.

The researcher breaks free and is halfway down the hall when another Florae appears before her at its far end. It reaches her before I can get a shot off, and it latches on to her shoulder, biting her neck. Kay separates the Florae's head from its shoulders in a single move and then is down the hall to the new Florae, focused on feasting on the researcher, and expertly shoots it. Green-black blood splatters all over the wall and the creature collapses. Kay puts a shot in the head of the now-still researcher before she can change into a monster.

Rice and I sprint down the hall. When we reach the only locked door in the corridor, Rice swipes his card and enters his code. The door beeps twice. "I can't get it open," Rice tells me as he desperately tries again.

"What's the holdup?" Kay asks.

"I don't know. This door shouldn't even be locked."

"We have to move on," Kay says, already halfway down the hall. As soon as the words are out of her mouth, another Florae appears in front of us. Kay tries to draw down on it, but the Florae is too close and is on her before she can aim. It bowls into her and knocks her down as it rolls over her. I can't fire on the Florae twisting next to Kay without risking taking her down too. Kay snaps to her feet with a knife in hand before the Florae's next charge. She sidesteps it and stabs it hard through the neck, pushing the knife into the creature's brain. It drops at her feet, a mess of green and black.

Just then the door Rice struggled to unlock finally opens. Ken stands in the doorway, looks at the carnage in the hall, then back at us. "What the . . . You mean that evacuation order was real? You'd better get in here."

We push past him into his lab and he closes the door behind us, locking it. The lab looks like a scaled-down version of the main lab, with equipment I couldn't even begin to understand. At the far end is another closed door.

"How do you still have power?" Rice asks.

"I rerouted it from the main lab using my laptop." Ken taps his computer. "When Dr. Reynolds made his announcement, I thought it was a drill, and when the power went out, I figured no one else would need it. . . ." He stares at Kay and me in our synth-suits. His eyes flick from me to her.

"Tell me one of you is Kay."

Kay pulls down her hood. "You know I'm always showing up to save your ass."

"I didn't know my ass needed saving." He motions around the well-lit lab. "As you can see, I'm doing fine here." Ken grins, and I'm amazed at how similar they look. Before, when I saw them together on the hover-copter, I was in so much shock, I didn't have time to process their similarities. They're even the same height.

They may look alike, but I know there's a huge difference in their priorities. I face Ken. "Where's Brenna?" I ask. If she's down here, she's in danger too.

"She's safe," he assures me.

"And the camera?" Rice asks, motioning to where it hangs in the far corner of the ceiling. He looks at me. "Dr. Reynolds will know we're in here now."

As the words leave Rice's mouth, the power fails and the door pops open.

Ken shakes his head. "No," he says petulantly and too loudly. "I made sure I'd have power so I could finish my work."

"Dr. Reynolds turned off the power," Kay tells him. "He released the Floraes to kill us."

Ken refuses to understand. "He wouldn't do that. Not to me. My work is too important." He folds his arms.

"Where does that door go?" I ask, motioning to the far end of the room.

"It's . . . nothing."

Kay steps up into his face. "There are at least twenty Floraes running around, if not more by now," she tells him. "Where the hell does that door lead?"

"It's . . . It's my personal office. Oh, just go. It's open. There's a manual lock inside. There aren't any cameras. I didn't want anyone spying on my results." As I head to the door, I feel a twinge of guilt over scrambling for cover when I should be rescuing Baby, but I know we have to regroup and formulate a plan.

Rice gets the door open and goes inside while Kay and I wait at the door for Ken. He opens a drawer and takes out a folder.

"The Floraes aren't interested in your data," I tell him. "You're wasting time."

"These are my notes." Somewhere in the maze of the lab, someone screams. "I don't know why Dr. Reynolds is doing this. . . ."

"Ken, hurry!" I shout. I can hear Them snarling from the hall. Ken runs to us and shoves his notes at me.

"Hold these. . . . I have to get the blood samples. They might destroy those if they smell the blood."

"No–" Kay tries to grab his arm to haul him in the room, but he shakes her off. He doesn't even make it halfway across the room before a Florae flashes in from the hall and takes him down. Kay rushes to his side and I try to go and help her, when Rice yanks me into the back room and slams the door shut, leaving me with a horrible snapshot of the creature perched atop Ken, ripping into the side of his face and lapping up his blood.

I push against Rice, who is latching three separate bolts. "I have to help Kay!" I scream at him, forcing him from the doorway. My hands shake as I undo the bolts while Rice pleads with me.

I can still hear Ken's screams, until he falls abruptly silent. Rice is at my back and whispers, "I was just trying to save you, Amy. I wanted you to be safe."

I pull open the door and am knocked aside by a figure in black. Kay. She enters the room and collapses onto the floor, her hood pulled aside. I join her on the floor. Dazed, I try to comfort her as she weeps into her hands. She looks up at me. "I couldn't save him," she whispers and, for the first time, I see Kay's pain. Rice is with us now and pulls Kay to a cot in the corner. He makes her sit down so she can collect herself.

"Just . . . Let's give her a moment," he tells me.

My hood is stifling, and I pull it down to get some air. I feel numb. It's as if seeing all this death has turned my insides to ice.

"Amy?" a voice behind me says, pulling me from my thoughts. I turn and find a familiar face staring back at me from a chair in the opposite corner.

"Brenna?"

She's alive, and she looks healthy, her skin no longer a deathly paper white.

"It's about damned time you showed up," she tells me with a grin.

Maybe I'm not numb after all—when I see her, I'm so happy, I let out a tiny sob of joy.

CHAPTER FORTY-TWO

I rush to Brenna and hug her. She still looks more fragile than before, but she's better. Her skin is cool to the touch, meaning she's probably beaten her infection.

Suddenly there is a frenzied scratching at the door. My head snaps around.

"They can't get through," Rice assures us.

I glare at him, still angry that he prevented me from helping Kay when she needed me most. Even if Ken was already bitten, I could have been at Kay's side.

"Where's Ken?" Brenna asks. "I can't believe he let you guys in here. I haven't seen anyone but him for days."

"He didn't make it," I say softly, glancing at Kay. Her face tightens, but she closes her eyes and takes a breath. I know she is fighting her pain, trying to push it down until later.

"Oh, hey." Brenna's eyes widen. "You must be Ken's sister?" Brenna asks. "Holy crap, you look just like him. Sorry about what happened. . . . I mean, despite the fact that he kidnapped me. He talked about you a lot. He wished he could have spoken with you more."

Rice nods. "He was a good guy. He was a brilliant researcher."

"Yeah, he was great," Brenna says. "You know, except for the whole holding-me-against-my-will thing."

I push Brenna with my elbow and shush her, but Kay just stares at us. For a moment I think she's going to break down again, but instead she lets out a small bark of a laugh. "Ken was . . . complicated," she says, her voice strong and clear.

"He was a genius," Rice says quietly. "When I first met him four years ago, when this was still a university, he was one of the few people who was nice to me. Over time, though, he just got more and more secretive, more locked down into himself.

Dr. Reynolds tends to bring that out in people." He looks at me. "Amy, what do you have there?"

I'm still clutching Ken's notes to my chest. "He wanted to save these. . . ."

Kay stares at them, then says to Rice, "Well, have a look. See what Ken thought was more important than his life."

I hand the notes over to Rice, who takes them back to Ken's desk and starts reading.

"I guess he did try to make me comfortable," Brenna tells us, eyeing Kay. "He brought me books, which were way boring, but at least he tried. He talked to me about you, too," she tells Kay. "The stories were pretty exciting. He was proud of you."

"Maybe," Kay tells us, her jaw tight, "you should all stop trying to comfort me about Ken for a moment and spend your energy trying to figure out how we're going to get the hell out of here alive."

We listen to the Floraes scratch and snuffle at the door and watch Rice riffle through Ken's notes.

"This is pretty remarkable," he says, bending low over them, oblivious. "He was getting somewhere." He looks up at Brenna. "Did any of the other researchers visit you?"

Brenna shakes her head.

Rice looks around at the room and the door with its triple

locks. "He was keeping you all to himself. If he'd collaborated, if he'd set a team to work . . ." He shakes his head, flips back a few pages, then starts forward again with growing excitement. "There's an antigen found in both Baby's and Brenna's blood. I think the antigen, in conjunction with the original vaccine, is what saved them both when they were bitten. It makes them carriers, but immune to the effects. That's why they didn't change. This antigen is rare; do you know how remarkable this is?"

"I knew there was something different about the original batch of vaccine. . . ." I say. "But it wasn't the formula–it was the patients!" That's why they could never get it to work. The problem wasn't in the replication. It was having the correct subjects.

"I'm one in a million?" Brenna says with a smirk. "I always knew I was awesome."

"It's actually more like one in ten thousand. . . . But this is just . . . amazing," Rice continues. "That's why we never caught it before. We could vaccinate thousands of people and try turning them all and not one could have the right antigen to combat the infection."

"So . . . ," Brenna says, holding up her bandaged hand. "Amy didn't need to chop off my fingers?"

"We don't really know for sure," Rice says, looking from her to me and back again.

"Brenna, I was just trying to do anything to save you. Your fingers were shredded. I don't think you would have ever been able to use them again, and I thought it might stop the infection from spreading."

Brenna stares at her left hand, the space where her middle and ring fingers should be. "It's okay, Amy. I don't blame you. At least I'm alive . . . and I have my pointer finger," she tells me. "I can pull a trigger." She looks at me with a grin. "But I sure will miss the middle finger. Who knows? Maybe it did help the infection spread more slowly . . . letting that anti-thingy kick in."

"It's amazing that both Brenna and Baby carry this antigen. Maybe we would have even known right away if they had been in the same test group."

"There were multiple test groups?" I ask. "How many children did Dr. Reynolds test?"

His head snaps up. "Amy, it was harmless. This was before the outbreak, and the bacterium itself was tested on soldiers who volunteered. We just needed to see if the vaccine had side effects. We weren't going to infect the children."

"How many groups?" I ask again.

He sighs. "We used foster-care facilities as a cover and tested on only the children we knew wouldn't be adopted, older children and, in Baby's case, children with relatives under Dr. Reynolds's control. There were five initial groups we used to test the vaccine . . . Brenna's in Texas, one in New York City, two in California, and one in Kansas . . . right outside of New Hope, when it was a university. That's where Hannah started out."

"Then how did she make it to Chicago?" I ask. "She was alone when I found her."

"I don't know, not exactly. When the infection broke out, we didn't know if the university would be safe. We hadn't set up the emitters yet. We didn't have a plan. Dr. Reynolds had the children evacuated to a secure facility in Chicago, the one your mother stayed at before coming here. But there was some kind of accident. None of them made it there. . . . We didn't know Baby survived until you showed up in New Hope with her. We didn't know that we'd actually evacuate the Chicago facility to here after a few months. If we'd known then how quickly the infection would spread, we could have just brought the children here, but then it wasn't safe."

"It's not safe now," I say, horrified. "And the other children?"

"None made it, as far as we know. The ones who went to

Fort Black, we didn't reach them in time to evacuate before they were lost."

"Lost?"

"Dead . . . or like Brenna, simply surviving under our radar. Baby and Brenna are the only ones we've found . . . and that's because they didn't turn when they were bitten."

"Could others have a natural immunity?" Kay asks quietly.

"Who knows? Maybe . . . But I think it was the combination of the vaccine and the antigen that saved them. An antigen can be an outside agent, but in Brenna and Baby's case, it's produced by their bodies. Usually, naturally occurring antigens are ignored by the human immune system and don't do any harm or good. But this particular antigen can bind with an antibody and attack the weakened form of Florae bacteria found in the vaccine, neutralizing it. This would allow the body to fight off the full infection of a Florae bite. This antigen is rare, but if it can be synthesized . . . I'm telling you, Ken may have found something here. I . . . have to get to a lab and analyze this."

"That might be a little hard right now," I say. I don't like the fevered look that's come over him. It's too familiar.

Rice nods and takes a deep breath as though reeling himself in. "You're right, of course. I just think Ken didn't know what he had. He was too close to it. With a few modifications, this might actually work."

"A vaccine?" Kay whispers from the cot. "You think Ken actually did it? He discovered a vaccine?"

"I can't be sure until I run some tests, but yes." His ear-to-ear grin seems almost to split his face, but then fades just as quickly. "I wish I could have talked to Ken about this. If he'd only consulted me."

Kay tilts her head, listening.

"What?" I ask.

"That was Marcus on a call to all the Guardians. They've been dispatched to deal with the Florae breach."

"Well, that's good. Gareth would have gotten the call. He can help us. . . ." I stop. "Marcus and his cronies are going to be prowling the labs too?"

Kay nods. "And they've been told to eliminate you."

"Fan," I say, then laugh, despite myself. Even to my own ears the sound is hysterical, and Brenna looks at me with concern.

"I'm fine," I assure her. I look over at Kay, not knowing what to do. She stares back, a strange look in her eyes.

"Okay, I'm ready," she announces, standing. "Let's go get Baby."

CHAPTER FORTY-THREE

We leave the lab with a new sense of purpose. I'm worried about Kay, but she seems to have buried her pain and is ready to help me retrieve Baby. We also have Brenna, who is eager to remind us that we'll have her newly heightened hearing at our disposal.

Miraculously, we encounter neither ravenous Floraes nor murderous Guardians between Ken's office and Baby's dorm, and I'm relieved to see that the door is still closed and locked.

So she might be safe, but how do we get inside? Rice swipes a key card and punches in a code, then presses his finger to the door. No surprise when it doesn't open.

"What now?" I ask testily, scanning the hall behind us for threats.

Rice looks around, thinking. "There may have been researchers stuck inside this area when the alarms sounded. If they got caught in the lockdown, they wouldn't have left a secure area."

He fiddles with the panel and presses a button. For a long moment, nothing. Then a tentative voice on the other side says, "Hello?"

"This is Assistant Director Richard Kiernan. I've been locked out of the lab. Can you open the door?"

After a long pause, the voice responds. "It's against protocol."

"Yes, I realize this." Rice sounds commanding. "But there is currently a Florae breach and I am trapped on the wrong side of this door. If you do not break protocol, you could be responsible for not only the death of the assistant director, but of the future of New Hope."

Brenna looks at Rice, eyebrows raised. "Wow," she says.

Rice shrugs sheepishly as the door opens and a scared researcher pops his head out, his eyes darting over us and down the hallway. "Have any of you been bitten?"

"Yeah," Brenna blurts out before I can say no, "but it was forever ago and I'm doing just fine."

The researcher moves to slam the door, but I jam my foot in it, and Kay and I push our way in past him. Brenna and Rice follow, securing the door behind them.

"I'm going to get Baby," I call back to Rice as I hurry away down the corridor. Maybe this time I can convince her not to scream. She just needs to be reminded of the dangers, to remember how she used to avoid Them every day.

The door to Baby's room is already open. I rush inside and find her sitting at her table across the room, coloring, completely oblivious. But she is not alone.

Dr. Reynolds looks up at me from his seat next to her and smiles. "Hello, Amy," he says, the loose flesh under his jaw jiggling as he speaks. "How nice to see you again." His hand rests on the table, gripping a gun. Before I can think of moving, he stands, sweeps up Baby in his free arm, and presses the gun to her temple. She doesn't even look frightened; she just blinks blankly a few times, her eyes unfocused.

"No," I say, stepping forward. "I'll do whatever you want. Don't hurt her."

"He won't," Rice says, appearing at my side. "He has twenty

different researchers analyzing her blood. He won't kill her. She's too important."

"Are you certain of that?" he asks, staring me down. "You have managed to be quite the disruption. You've rendered your mother useless to me. You've turned her against me, her and I don't know how many Guardians." He looks past us and cocks his head. "Kay, is that you? Why don't you put your weapons on the floor? All of them." He digs the gun deeper into Baby's skin, and Kay begrudgingly throws her gun and knives onto the floor. His gaze falls back on me. "You too, Amy."

I nod and slowly place my weapons at my feet.

"Good girl," Dr. Reynolds tells me.

Unable to contain the fury welling up inside, I take another step forward—only to stop myself. He holds Baby's life in his hands.

"It's amazing that one emotionally disturbed girl could cause so much trouble." Dr. Reynolds shakes his bald head. "And you," he spits at Rice. "You've been completely useless. I should have left you in that orphanage, alone and unwanted. I should never have taken you into my care. You've become such a disappointment."

Rice looks as though he's been slapped, his face blazing red. "'Taken me into your care'? Is that what you call it?" I realize he isn't ashamed, he's livid. "You think I don't know about my parents' car crash? You think I don't know you had them killed so you could use me? What a sick, sad lunatic you are. You had to have been cooking up your crazy plans long before then, raising your stable of super-geniuses to do your bidding. What a gift the Florae infection must've been for you."

My heart breaks for Rice. How hard it must have been for Rice to work with Reynolds, filled with hate and bitterness.

But far from being taken aback by Rice's words, Dr. Reynolds's grin has been widening all along, and now he laughs out loud.

"A 'gift'? Are you serious? For a 'super-genius,' you're terribly slow on the uptake, boy. You think the Florae outbreak was an *accident*? You insult me. When I saw what this mopey young girl's mother had created, I alone realized its full potential. I saw it as a way to correct all the mistakes humanity had made. Everything could be undone, and the very building blocks of society could be reconstructed. New Hope is my Eden!"

No one in the room moves. No one can believe what we're hearing.

Dr. Reynolds created the After, *on purpose.*

My mother may have given him the weapon, but Dr. Reynolds is the one who pulled the trigger. It hits me like a gunshot. He killed everyone—my father, my friends, my neighbors. Everyone. Dr. Reynolds ended the world.

Rice keeps talking. If he's as stunned by this as I am, he gives no sign. "So," he says, "in that formulation, you would be . . . who? *God?*"

"And why not?" Dr. Reynolds says, beaming. "As if things were working so well before? At least now humanity can be controlled. I decide who lives, who breeds. I alone decide the future."

My attention is brought back to Baby as Dr. Reynolds shifts her weight in his arms. I'm so in shock, only now do I see that Kay has been creeping closer to Dr. Reynolds as Rice talked, keeping his attention on him. In an instant, Kay rushes him, dropping low and driving at him. Without thinking, I join in.

Seeing our charge at the last second, Dr. Reynolds swings the gun wildly and knocks Kay against the wall. He aims wide, the pistol discharging. The bullet flies harmlessly past me as Baby drops to the floor. I'm on him, driving my fist into his neck before he can begin to turn back, ripping the gun away from him. Brenna is at my side. She's grabbed one of the guns from the floor and now has it trained on him.

"Wow, what an asshole," she says.

Kay joins us. "Kid, you have no idea."

Kay hands me some cinch ties to bind Reynolds's hands and feet, and I turn to check on Baby, who sits in a ball, arms wrapped around herself, staring across the room. I crawl to her to check her for any injury. She's clear, though she may be badly bruised later on.

"Baby, are you okay?"

She doesn't answer but looks past me, over my shoulder. I follow her gaze to Rice, slumped against the wall.

Blood seeps through his lab coat.

CHAPTER FORTY-FOUR

"Rice?"

I pat his cheek to wake him. I've already stanched the bleeding by bandaging his upper arm with ripped sheets from Baby's bed. He opens his bright blue eyes, then squints, confused.

"I think I hit my head . . . on the wall," he says. He lifts his arm and winces. "What happened?"

"Dr. Reynolds shot you," Brenna calls from across the room. "You're lucky he has sucky aim."

"Where is he now?"

"We tied him up and stuck him in a broom closet," I say. "I took away his earpiece, so he's neutralized. I think now we should get back to my mother, and make sure she's safe, ask her what we should do next." We never got the research, but with Dr. Reynolds contained, we should be able to accomplish more. He can't give orders from a broom closet.

"Can you stand?" I ask Rice. He tries, and I have to help him get to his feet. He's still a bit wobbly.

"I'm going to scout the hall, make sure it's clear."

"It is," Brenna tells us. "I can tell."

"Brenna, can you help Rice while I carry Baby?" I ask.

Brenna takes Rice's good arm, propping him up. I go to Baby where she sits, staring blankly at the wall, and I pick her up.

I cradle Baby close and whisper in her ear, "I know that you're Hannah now. That this is your home. But you used to have a life with me. You used to be very good at keeping quiet, at avoiding the monsters. Do you remember?"

She doesn't respond, but when I carry her to the door, she doesn't scream, either. Maybe she can be Hannah, but still be Baby as well.

Despite Brenna's assurances, Kay goes ahead to check that

the hall is clear, then we make our way to my mother's office. There are no other Floraes in sight–if the Guardians haven't gotten them all, they've at least severely cut their number. Now, if we can just stay out of the way of those same Guardians, who'll still be on the hunt for us in the absence of any orders to the contrary, we might be okay.

To my relief, my mother is safe in her office. She hugs me and Baby close before turning to her examination of Rice's arm.

I sit in a chair with Baby in my lap, stroking her thinning hair. When I ask her if she's okay, I get no response. I continue to pet her head, hoping at least the contact is comforting to her. Kay watches us for a while, but then stares at the floor, lost in her own grief.

"We didn't get the research," Rice tells my mother as she properly bandages his arm. "But Dr. Reynolds is detained for now, and we can probably break into the safe or pry the combination from him." He pauses. "He admitted to us that he orchestrated the original outbreak. It wasn't an accident."

My mother gives him a long look, shaking her head, then sighs. "I'd begun to suspect as much. Everything awful began to feel possible over this past few weeks." She rubs at her eyes then seems to gather herself. "I don't know how many Floraes are left roaming the labs. I don't know how many researchers died. But I do know I've finally chosen to do the right thing. We'll get all the research and make it public. I know that New Hope will survive. There's a lot here worth saving."

Rice tells her about getting Ken's notes before he died. "We have to look into it," he says, "but I think he may have finally found it. A vaccine."

My mother just nods, smiling tightly. "That would be wonderful. But when I think of the cost . . ." She shakes her head.

"It wasn't your fault," I say softly. I blamed her before, and the truth is that she *is* still partially to blame. She engineered the bacterium. But she had no idea that Dr. Reynolds would release it into the world.

She comes to me, hugs me and Baby. "I'm so sorry for everything you had to go through. We'll get Baby some real help."

Just then my mother's office door flies open and a heavily muscled figure in a synth-suit fills the doorway, holding a gun. There's no doubt who it is, and there's nothing any of us can do. The guns sit uselessly on my mother's desk. There is nothing for me to do but hand Baby to my mother and stand.

My mother moves closer to me and, clutching Baby to her, puts on her director's voice. "What do you think you're doing?"

Marcus pulls off his hood and stares her down. "Following my orders," he says, "and they don't come from you."

"They certainly do," she says. "Dr. Reynolds has gone entirely mad–"

"Shut up," he says, pointing the gun directly at Baby, "and take a seat." My mother does what she's told, and Marcus swings the muzzle toward me.

I don't have it in me to feel the fear I should. I don't beg or plead. At least Baby is safe. At least my mother will take care of her.

Marcus raises his gun. "Sorry, kid," he says, though he's grinning as he says it. "Orders are orders."

And then his head snaps to one side hard enough to slam against the doorframe, and he slumps to the floor.

Brenna walks to the doorway and peers out into the hall and gives a little wave to whoever she sees there. Then she steps aside, shaking her head. "I'll never get used to the silent-gun thing."

Another figure appears in the door beside Brenna, reaching up to pull off his hood. It's Gareth, wearing a sad smile. "Glad to see you made it, honey." He looks down at Marcus. "'Orders are orders,' huh? Bastard."

"I'm Brenna," Brenna says, sticking out her hand, "and that

was awesome. Seriously. The way his head hit the door. Gruesome."

Gareth considers her, then takes her hand and shakes it. "I'm Gareth, and we've met . . . but you were a bit unconscious."

"Oh yeah . . . my abduction from Fort Black. I guess I shouldn't complain. From what I heard, that place was going to shit. Still, I would have liked to have a choice about being a lab rat."

I feel a twinge of guilt at being willing to sell Brenna out to save Baby. . . . But it's hard to feel bad now that I know Baby is safe. I look over at her, her blank stare and dead eyes. She could have permanent damage to her body as well as her mind. She may still not be saved.

"And what about Dr. Reynolds?" Gareth asks.

"We have him tied up in a broom closet," Kay tells him. "Good to see you."

He winks at her. "You too, Kay."

"You can torture him if you like," Brenna chimes in.

"We won't be doing that," my mother says, handing Baby to me, "but we're going to make sure everyone knows all the things he's done. I may have created the Floraes, but he released them into the world."

She puts her hand to her ear. "This is the director speaking.

I need to make an announcement to all of New Hope." She waits a moment and then begins. "Due to unforeseen, tragic circumstances, we have lost our new leader of the Guardians. Marcus will be missed, but I am reinstating Kay. As of now, she has complete control and my full support. Dr. Reynolds has also had to step down from his position, and I will be addressing everyone later tonight on the exact details. Please gather in Memorial Hall at eight p.m. or tune in to the news. Everything will be explained." She pushes the button on her earpiece again, ending the transmission. "Dr. Reynolds is done."

"That's something, at least," Kay says, stepping to the side and putting her own hand to her ear. She gives instructions to the Guardians, calling off the order to kill me. After a while, she steps over and looks at me, confused.

"Amy, there's someone on the radio for you."

"For me?" I look around. Anyone who would want to speak to me is in this room.

Kay nods. "They're definitely asking for you . . . and they say they're from Fort Black."

CHAPTER FORTY- FIVE

"Hello? Anybody there?"

It's a voice I never thought I'd hear again.

"Jacks?" I can't believe he's alive. Neither can Brenna, who's standing beside me, jumping up and down at the news. "How . . . ?" I ask. "What happened?"

Jacks explains that while the infection spread through the Yard and Cellblock A, the people inside the corridor within the wall and those in blocks B and C were fine. It took a while before anyone could leave the cellblocks, but they finally managed to kill all the Floraes. Fort Black is once again secure.

"It took some convincing, but my uncle gave me the communicator. I pushed the button and asked for you, and like magic, here you are."

"Jacks . . . I . . ." I look around, wishing I had some privacy to speak with him. How do I explain how much I missed him and how often I thought about him? "I'm so glad you're okay. I was scared you didn't make it."

"I had to keep myself safe. I knew it was my only chance of seeing you again."

My face goes red. Everyone in the room is staring at me, listening. Brenna's still bouncing up and down, asking to talk to him. "Jacks," I say, "Brenna's dying to talk to you. Hold on."

I take the earpiece out of my ear to hand it to her, but my mother takes it from my hand and plugs a wire from her computer into it. "Speaker," she explains. "Go ahead."

"Jacks," I say loudly, "Brenna is here too."

"Jacks!" she shouts. "I'm really happy you didn't die."

"Me too." He laughs. "I don't know how things are there for you, but there are a lot of people here who are scared. We don't have any food, and people are afraid to leave the walls." He's quiet for a second, then he asks, "Are you coming back, Amy?"

There's a hint of desperation in his voice.

"Jacks . . . I can't." I look at Baby, twirling her hair around her finger. She doesn't tug it out, though. I can't go anywhere. She needs me. "But you can come here. You can all come here."

"Amy," my mother begins, "I don't know if we can accommodate–"

"We can make room," Rice says.

My mother's shaking her head. "But all at once? And who knows what kind of people they are. And the diseases–we'll have to test each one to make sure they're healthy. I don't know if this is the right time."

Brenna has turned on my mother, her expression darkening. "Whoa, whoa, whoa: 'Who knows what kind of *people* they are'? What kind of people are *you*, lady?"

"Mom," I say, stepping between them. But I feel as angry as Brenna sounds. "Are you hearing yourself? What, you're worried they won't live up to New Hope's standards?" I give my head a sharp shake. "Yes, there are hard cases in Fort Black. Criminals, when it comes down to it. That useless vaccine that Doc was distributing didn't help either; it made people more violent. But if they don't have to fight to survive, they may not want to fight at all. If there are troublemakers, we can ID them, work with them. Jacks can help us with that. But I can tell you, there are a lot of good people in Fort Black. Maybe they're hardened, but they had to be to survive."

"I have to think about what's right for New Hope," she says, but softly, as if she's talking to herself. I can see she's hearing me, at least. Thinking.

"Of course you do," Rice says quietly. "But we can agree that New Hope needs to change, can't we?" When my mother nods, he says, "I think we need to open up to people, starting tonight. Now. Starting with this question, about bringing the Fort Black people in, helping them. Give people the whole picture, tell them what we think is the right thing to do." He shrugs. "I think we can trust them to want to do it."

"That's asking a lot of them, isn't it?"

She's been insulated in her lab for so long, she has no idea what regular people are like, how they feel, what they're capable of. I have to make her understand.

"Mom," I say, "believe me, the people in Fort Black have dealt with a lot worse. And they still are. There are sick, frightened people there. We can't turn our backs on them."

For a long moment, my mother and I look at each other, *into* each other. And then she nods, just perceptibly. "We can downsize the Ward," she says, "move people who need medical attention there. Start with them." She nods again. "We can make this work."

"The Guardians can run supplies out to Fort Black," Kay says. "Any medical staff who wants to treat them. Then we can start shuttling people here."

"How does that sound?" I ask Jacks. "Do you think people would want to come here? Do you want to come here?"

"I don't know, Amy. . . . I haven't left Fort Black in a long time. I . . . don't know if I can."

"Even to be with me?" I ask, uncertain. Rice gives me a sharp look, but I don't care anymore who else hears. "I have to take care of my sister. You know that. But I want to be with you. If you want to be with me, it has to be here," I tell Jacks.

There is a long pause. Then, quietly, Jacks replies, "Okay. I'll come. But what about everyone else in Fort Black? What if they don't want to move?"

"We won't make them leave, but it's safer here." I look at my mother. "Or it will be. Won't it?"

"We're going to try."

"No." Rice stands, still a little shaky from his wound. "We're going to do more than try."

"Jacks," I say, "we're sending some supplies for now. My

mother's going to be talking to the citizens here, and we're going to figure out how to fit you all in. Let everyone know they're welcome here. Let them know they'll be safe."

"All right, Amy," Jacks says. "Thanks. I . . . I can't wait to see you."

There's a silence in the room. Rice gives me another look, and I feel my face go hot.

"I . . . can't wait to see you too, Jacks. I'll check in with you soon."

We click off. I still ignore Rice's questioning gaze. Rice has done so much for me. He was the first boy I ever had feelings for, but he was too consumed by his work. Like my mother, he had all of humanity to worry about. How could I compete with that? Jacks was different. He understood what was important. He understood I needed to protect Baby at any cost.

I kneel next to Baby. "You may not know what's happened to you, or why," I say to her, "but I promise that you're going to get better."

When I squeeze her hand, it twitches in mine—and then her fingers begin to work into my palm.

Thank you, Amy, she signs.

I look into her eyes and see a spark of comprehension. *You know who I am?* I ask, signing into her hand.

She nods slowly. "You're my sister," she says aloud, her voice uncertain. I'm still not used to hearing her speak, having spent so much of our time together in silence.

"Yes," I say firmly. *"We're sisters."*

She smiles her sad little smile, her face looking much older than her six years.

"Amy"—my mother puts her hand on my shoulder—"let's go home."

I gather Baby in my arms and walk her out the door and down the hall.

Finally, going home.

Acknowledgments

I'd like to thank so many people for making *In the End* possible. Karen Chaplin is the best editor anyone could hope for. Thank you, Karen, for always making me dig deeper and for your much needed guidance and encouragement.

I'd also like to thank everyone at Harper Teen who made *In the End* possible, including my amazing editorial director, Rosemary Brosnan, and my fantastic production editor, Jon Howard. In addition, I'd like to thank my marketing director, Kimberly VandeWater, and my publicist, Olivia deLeon, and everyone else at Harper Teen whose tireless efforts have made *In the End* what it is today. I'm so lucky to have such an amazing team, I couldn't have written this book without them. And thank you to David Downing and Katie Crouch for additional editorial advice.

Thank you to everyone who picked up *In the After* and took a chance on a debut author, and who wanted to follow Amy as she concluded her journey in *In the End*. I am so grateful to all of my readers.

Thank you to my husband, whose time serving in Iraq gave

him a base of knowledge to answer all of my weapons/combat questions. I couldn't have written this book without his unwavering support and his uncanny knack for bringing me coffee exactly when I needed it the most.

And last but not least, thank you to my super agent, Katherine Boyle. She is, simply, made of awesome.

Turn the page to see how it all began. . . .

THEY DESTROYED BEFORE.
NOW WE LIVE . . .

IN THE AFTER

DEMITRIA LUNETTA

CHAPTER ONE

I only go out at night.

I walk along the empty street and pause, my muscles tense and ready. The breeze rustles the overgrown grass and I tilt my head slightly. I'm listening for Them.

All the warnings I remember from horror movies are wrong. Monsters do not rule the night, waiting patiently to spring from the shadows. They hunt during the day, when the light is good and their vision is at its best. At night, if you don't make a noise, they can shuffle past you within an inch of your nose and never know you are there.

It's so very quiet, but that doesn't mean that They are not near. I walk again, slowly at first, but then I pick up my pace. My bare feet pad noiselessly on the cracked sidewalk. Home is only a few blocks away. Not far if I remain silent, but it may as well be miles if They spot me.

I've learned to live in a soundless world. I haven't spoken in three years. Not to comment on the weather, not to shout a warning, not even to whisper my own name: Amy. I know it's been three years because I've counted the seasons since it happened. In the summer before the After when I'd just turned fourteen.

A branch snaps in the distance and I stop immediately, my body tense. I shift my bag slowly, carefully adjusting the weight so the cans inside don't clank together. Every little noise screams at me that something is wrong, but it could be nothing.

Clouds shift and moonlight suddenly brightens the street. I glance around, searching, studying an abandoned, rusted car for any signs of the creatures. When I don't spot Them, I almost continue on, but at the last second I decide to play it safe. Stepping into an abandoned yard, I disappear into the shrubbery. I'll wait until a cloud passes in front of the moon and darkness reclaims the night.

I can't take any chances, not with Baby waiting for me. My bag holds the food we need to survive. We only have each other. I found Baby shortly after the world failed, when I still believed things would return to normal. I no longer hold that hope. Nothing this broken can ever be fixed.

CHAPTER TWO

This is how I think of time: the past is Before, and the present is the After. Before was reality; the After, a nightmare.

Before I was happy. I had friends and sleepovers. I wanted to learn how to drive, to get a jump start on my learner's permit. The worst thing in my life was math homework and not being allowed to date. I thought my parents were so clueless; my dad with all his "green" concerns (I told my friends he was an eco-douche), and my mom, who was never home except for Sunday-night family dinner. I was kinder to my mom, though, and only called her a workaholic. Her job was with the government, her work very hush-hush.

I always thought of myself as smart, and I was definitely a smart-ass to my parents. I loved seeing them squirm, letting them know that I didn't buy into their "because I said so" crap. I was good in school. I could always guess the endings of movies and books. Now there is no school, there are no more movies, no new books, no more friends.

The creatures arrived on a Saturday. I know it was a Saturday because if it were a weekday I would have been at school and I would be dead. Sundays I went with my father to visit his parents at Sunny Pine, and if They had come on a Sunday I would also be dead.

I remember that the electricity flickered and I was annoyed because I was watching TV. I had wondered if my father was on the roof screwing around with the solar panels. They didn't require much maintenance, but he liked to hose them off twice a year, which always messed with all our electronics. I checked the garage. His electric car was gone. He was at the farmers' market, probably overpaying for organic carrots.

I microwaved some pizza bagels (the ones my mom hid from my dad at the back of the freezer) and sat back in front of the TV, flipping through the channels mindlessly.

I'd wished my parents would listen to me and upgrade to the premium cable package. I thought life was so unfair. My mother had bought my father a brand-new electric car for more money than I would probably need for college, but she wouldn't spend fifty bucks extra a month to get some decent television.

I checked my cell phone but there were no calls from Sabrina or Tim. I was supposed to go to a movie with them later. Tim had been madly in love with Sabrina forever but her parents would only let her go out with him if I tagged along. I joked with Sabrina about being the old spinster in a nineteenth-century novel. "No secret love child for you two," I'd tell her with a wink. "Not while Matron Amy is on duty."

I didn't really mind being their chaperone; they never made me feel awkward or like a third wheel. Sabrina hadn't even decided if she was all that into Tim. I'd been friends with her since fifth grade, when I was the weirdo who skipped a grade and she was the nice girl who didn't treat me like I had the plague. Pretty soon we were friends and stayed besties through middle school and into high school.

I tossed my phone on the coffee table and kicked up my feet, giving my full attention to the TV screen for the first time. But I noticed that even when I changed the channel, the picture stayed the same. I paused, curious. The president was making a speech. Boring. I ate my snack, only half listening.

"It has come to our attention," the president droned, "that we are not isolated in this attack."

I sat up, my bite half chewed. Attack? I was too young to remember the string of terrorist attacks at the beginning of the century, but my mother worked for the government and was constantly talking about our "lack of counterterrorist mechanisms."

I turned up the volume. The president looked exhausted, bags under his eyes, makeup caked on for the cameras. "The structure landed in Central Park early this morning," he said into twenty microphones. "As of now, the fate of anyone residing in New York City and the surrounding suburbs is unknown. We are working to find the cause of this interruption in communication as soon as–" He was cut short. The breaking news logo flashed across the screen.

I took a swig of soda. It was strange that the network had interrupted the president. I didn't understand what they were talking about, didn't know what it all meant yet. I glanced at the screen and what I saw nearly made me choke on my soda. They had footage of the "structure" in the park. Something emerged, turned toward the camera, stared. Still coughing, I pressed PAUSE on the DVR remote and stood.

That was the first time I saw an alien.

CHAPTER THREE

After They came, I did not leave my house for three weeks. The broadcasts stopped after the first few days, but they were not helpful anyway. They kept repeating the same things. Aliens had landed, they were not friendly, half of the planet was dead.

They were horrifyingly fast, traveling across the globe at an alarming pace. They didn't destroy buildings or attack our resources, like in so many crappy Hollywood movies. They wanted us. They hungered for us.

That first day, I was slow to understand what was happening.

My hands shook as I desperately tried to call my friends and family. My father didn't carry a cell phone. He didn't believe in them, said they gave people brain cancer. My mom had one of those fancy touch-screen phones that her job paid for, but she never answered, and her office line went straight to voice mail. Sabrina's phone just rang and rang. So did Tim's. I tried my cousin in Virginia and my mom's parents in Miami. No one answered. I went through the phone book on my cell, furiously calling one number after another. Eventually I could no longer dial out. I kept getting a recorded message. "All circuits are busy. Please hang up and try your call again at a later time." Soon I couldn't even get service. I stared at the screen for a minute, then, frustrated, threw the phone against the wall.

I curled into a ball on the couch and tried not to cry, but I couldn't hold back the tears for long. When my father didn't come back after a few hours, I had to admit to myself that he was dead. He had camping skills, but I could not imagine him holding his own against an alien attack. My mother might be okay, her government offices were high security, surrounded by soldiers. But I had no idea how to reach her, and could soldiers really protect her from those repulsive creatures? I had to face the reality that my parents could both be gone.

I stayed on the sofa and cried until I had no tears left and not enough energy to sob. I eventually crawled to the fridge and grabbed my dad's Ben and Jerry's from the freezer. It was the one junk food he allowed himself. He said life wasn't worth living without Cherry Garcia. I gorged myself on ice cream and ended up vomiting purple-pink onto the floor. I fell asleep there, exhausted and miserable.

When I woke several hours later, I couldn't figure out why I was on the kitchen floor. I opened my eyes and saw the mess I had made, instantly remembering everything. I wanted to stay there, but the smell finally got to me. I sat up and rubbed my deadened arms. Sobbing hysterically wouldn't help my dad or my friends. It wouldn't help me. Something inside me shifted or maybe just broke. I had to take care of myself.

I stood carefully, my legs still shaky, and went to retrieve the cleaning supplies from under the sink. When I was done cleaning the mess, I numbly grabbed a book from the shelf and hid in my room, unable to face my own thoughts. I needed to escape, if just for a short while, into a story from long ago.

My first night alone, I still assumed things would settle down. I stayed glued to the TV, watching the news report the same thing over and over. People were dying, and I was sick with grief, but I knew that we would overcome the invaders or whatever they were. We were the strongest nation on earth.

The second day passed and the TV was out, but there were still people on the radio. I was comforted by their voices, even though they spoke of mass chaos. People tried to run away, but They were everywhere. People tried to hide, but They found them.

Then on the third day, the radio went silent. I stayed in my room and obsessively read one book after another, to keep my mind on anything other than what was happening. I'd always escaped into books, but now reading had become something more. It allowed me to be somewhere else, to feel something else, not just the numbness that overtook my body and made me wonder if I was still alive.

My father loved Shakespeare; he would read passages with me and discuss all the intricacies. I reread *Romeo and Juliet* and cried my eyes out over their loss. Before I'd always argued with my father that the star-crossed lovers were idiots who should have coordinated their plans better, but this time they got to me. I completely broke down and crawled into my parents' bed. Draping their covers over my body, I sobbed myself to sleep. I was like that back then; my mood would swing between an almost hysterical sense of loss and having no feelings at all.

On the fourth day, I made myself eat and then tidied the house, trying to do the normal things that people do. I put out all the pictures I had of my friends and parents, gluing a collage to my bedroom door. I ransacked every photo album, placing each picture with great care, keeping my mind occupied. It was so much easier than facing reality. Sometimes I found it hard to concentrate, what with the world ending and all. I wanted so badly to leave the house, to see if anyone else was around, but I was scared of Them.

I finally decided to go out on our rooftop deck, and watch Them chase people down the street. They were faster than I'd thought possible, a blur of green, the color of pea soup. Glowing yellow eyes sometimes caught the light and flashed gold. The creatures pounced, not bothering to kill their prey before feeding. They ripped skin and flesh from their victims, who screeched in agony. The cries always brought more of Them, eager for their next meal. Those first few days were full of screams. It was terrible, but the real terror came when there were no more shrieks, when the world went quiet. I thought I was the only one left on the planet. There was only me and Them.

The fourth night, I turned on all the lights in the house. My block was dark, except for our home, my home. No one else had electricity, but I still did. I silently thanked my father who wanted to live footprint-free by installing solar panels and insisting we always put more into the grid than what we took out. We were as close to self-sustaining as current technology allowed.

I didn't know then that They were drawn to the lights, like moths to a flame. I didn't know that they couldn't see very well. They were attracted to anything bright, especially once they realized that where there was light in the darkness, there were humans, which for Them meant food.

The electric fence saved me, and that was my mother's doing. Even though we lived in an excellent, safe neighborhood in Chicago, she needed to protect the work she brought home. She had the fence installed behind our beautiful iron gate, the one They ripped up and destroyed in just a few minutes. She needed to make our house a "secure area." My mother and father were so different I wondered sometimes how they managed to stand each other at all. Still, they were so in love. Their public displays of affection were always embarrassing and I used to make gagging noises to try and get them to stop. Now I regret the way I acted toward them. I regret a lot of things that happened Before.

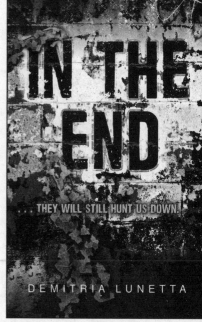